ENTER THE

As she neared the clinic, Beth heard a thump against the inside wall of the lab. There was a scream. A man's scream, she was sure of that. Her stomach tightened. She burst into the clinic office, put her hand on the doorknob to the lab, and hesitated. It took all her will to turn and push.

Her eyes swept the scene even as the stench of the beast and the muggy fog of hot blood smell hit her in the face. Empty cage. Door open. Blood splatters.

Three screams pierced the heavy air of the lab. Beth's at the sight of the man sitting against the wall drenched in blood. The man's as the beast whipped its head around, jerking a yard of bowel from the man's abdomen.

Finally, the shriek of the beast as it whirled to attack. . . .

BEASTMAKER

JAMES V. SMITH, JR.

A DELL BOOK

Published by
Dell Publishing Co.
a division of
The Bantam, Doubleday, Dell Group, Inc.
1 Dag Hammarskjold Plaza
New York, New York 10017

Jeremy Rifkin—you may be right.

Portions of this book first appeared in *Allison's Baby*.

Dell ® TM 681510, Dell Publishing Co., Inc.

ISBN: 0-440-20042-3

Printed in the United States of America

March 1988

10 9 8 7 6 5 4 3 2 1

KRI

BEASTMAKER

ACKNOWLEDGMENTS

Thanks. To Bob Mecoy, for taking on and polishing the book. To Lori Perkins, for taking on and polishing the writer. To my friend Herb Blanks, Army Lt. Col. and pilot extraordinaire, for technical advice about Hueys and shared recollections about Fort Hood. To Patrick McKeand, for his penetrating insights about the writing—and for his friendship. To Sue, for harboring a beast in her basement for all those months. And to any friend who doesn't disavow me after reading the book.

PROLOGUE

DECEMBER 1981

The Labrador bitch scrambled to her feet, startled by the impatient roiling in her belly. It was as if an angry sleeper had stirred inside her, resentful of being squashed against the floor of the cage. It was the dog's first pregnancy. Confused, she began whimpering.

The Lab's whine greeted the lab assistant as he stepped into the room and signed the log.

"Hey, Bitch, how's my baby today?" Babe was her name, but he called her Bitch when the research chief wasn't around. In fact, he called her lots of things—some better, some worse. But the Labrador never objected. If he kept a smile on his face he could call her anything and she would smile an adoring Labrador smile right back.

But when he looked at her for the first time that day, he saw that Babe was not smiling.

She stood on quaking legs, with her back hunched, gut sucked in, tail drooped, and her tawny eyes rolled up into her low-slung head. As he watched in disbe-

lief, Babe toppled like a vandalized statue, her legs
stiff and quivering.

He saw her belly undulating.

He dashed for the wall phone and tapped out the
emergency number for Research Chief Warren
Howell, called Dr. Clean for his meticulous dress and
fastidious hygiene.

"The Lab's in labor," he shouted into the phone.
"Halfway through her term."

Calmly as he could, Howell gave instructions to the
grad student. But when he hung up, he felt like collapsing on the sofa. It was over. Again. Maybe he
could sleep it off; find it had just been a nightmare.
Maybe he could just walk away.

No, that wouldn't work. He couldn't leave it to
that stupid kid.

Brad Spellers hung up and clasped his hands to
control the shaking.

What the hell's going on? he thought. Howell's instructions were crazy. Don't open the cage? Use the
drugs hidden in the first-aid kit? For what?

The Lab snarled. Her tongue hung out the side of
her clenched jaws, sluicing blood into the tray beneath the wire pen.

He watched dumbly as she attacked her belly, biting savagely at the undulations. The writhing fought
back, and she yelped.

The dog's shriek broke his trance. He tore the first-
aid kit from the wall. He found a vial and syringe
and, hands still shaking, he drew ten cc's and shot a

stream of two of them toward the ceiling. Shit. Eight cc's of Lobaxin would kill her.

The bitch ripped into her gut again, tearing a triangle of hide from the wound she had opened before as Spellers opened the handling access doors, large enough for only his arms. He rippled a thumb over her ribs and plunged the needle where her heart would be. He injected the Lobaxin as fast as it would squirt.

In seconds she was quiet, the savagery dissolved from her face. He shared her relief.

The undulations continued in her belly.

Maybe he could save her puppies.

He reached deeper through the cage's access holes and slung her body around. He lifted up the tail.

He hesitated. Howell had told him not to handle her.

Academic. She was gone, but he might save her litter. The heart might not have had time to pump the trank to the puppies. If he could get them out in time to keep them from suffocating . . .

He slid two fingers into her vagina and felt a jerk of life recoiling from the touch.

Spellers smiled and reached deeper inside. He heard the lab door open and saw Howell. "We can still save the puppies," Spellers said.

"Get your hand out of there," Howell commanded. He drew his own hand from his jacket pocket.

"I . . ." Spellers saw a pistol emerge from Howell's Harris tweed coat.

* * *

Howell roared at Spellers, but his shout was lost in the lab assistant's screams. Spellers convulsed, shrieking as fastidious Dr. Howell fired six shots into the dog's heaving abdomen. Spellers gazed stupidly at the spurting stumps where the first two fingers of his right hand had been, not yet aware of the rivers of blood and urine coursing down his legs from the two bullet holes low in his belly.

A steel slab adorned with oak paneling swung out, and a hulk of a man filled the opening. He hesitated, then shoved the three-hundred-pound hatch shut and padded across twenty feet of forest-green carpet.

The hulk's pockmarked, granite face wore a permanent scowl below piercing gray eyes. He fell into an overstuffed chair and flicked the scrap of paper clutched in his paw.

Across a half-acre walnut desk, a silver-haired aristocrat waited, wrinkling his straight, delicate nose as the scent of stale cigar smoke and sweat stung his nostrils.

The hulk flicked the paper again. "From Winston," he said. "In Texas. The Michigan thing.

"Howell fucked up another one. One of his creations went batshit. He shot the dick off his lab assistant. A&M's already fired him today. Probably blacklist him."

"Is the kid okay?"

The answer was a smirk that said, "Who cares?" He shifted his bulk, squeaking the leather upholstery. "He'll live."

"Where is he?"

The hulk seemed almost amused. "Nut ward. Monsters and magnums were too much for the boy. Probably spend some time inside the padded walls trying to stitch his joystick back together. Guess Freud was right."

The aristocrat raised his eyebrows.

The hulk snarled, "Nobody likes to have his dick shot off."

The aristocrat's face showed his disgust. "Think Howell will give up his research?"

The hulk sat up straight and smiled, showing stubby, cigar-stained teeth. "No way. The little bastard's too greedy."

"Tell Winston to keep a long-distance eye on him." The silver-headed man nodded at the door.

The hulk rose and retraced his steps on the dark carpet. When the door had chunked shut, the aristocrat pulled the Michigan file from his drawer and began reading the case he already knew by heart.

He finished an hour later. His deputy was right. This was a setback, but Howell wouldn't quit. To date, only a handful of men in the world knew of Michigan. But only he knew its significance. When it came time to break the story of this new weapon, *he* would do it.

The glory would belong to him alone.

"And the beast was like unto a leopard, and his feet were as the feet of a bear, and his mouth as the mouth of a lion; and the dragon gave him his power . . . and I beheld another beast coming up out of the earth; and he had two horns like a lamb . . . and he spake as a dragon. . . ."
—Revelation, Chapter 13.

BOOK I

THE BEGINNING

July 1984

1

West Fort Hood stands apart. It curls beneath the sprawling mainland of Fort Hood, the largest military installation in the free world and home of two armored divisions, an air cavalry brigade, and all the support necessary to sustain them.

West Fort was once Gray Air Force Base, a tiny garrison of five hundred blue-suiters and a ten-thousand-foot runway.

The air force gave West Fort Hood up gladly to the army, which took it over just as gladly. The corps commander put his support aviation units there, freeing up space for combat aviation units at crowded Hood Field. The army renamed the airstrip Robert Gray Army Airfield.

At Gray, the air force, with all its experience in noise abatement, had put its housing area two miles away from the field and well away from the takeoff and landing routes. Likewise, its bad experiences with drinking pilots led those same planners to put the officers' club within walking distance of the squat ranch-style duplexes that were the military's version of projects.

The West Fort Officers' Club was a *real* pilot's club.

As such, it mainly stocked beer, bourbon, and tequila, with music too loud to be intelligible and drinkers— many, crude and boisterous.

Everywhere, except in the darkest, most aromatic corners of the bar, small knots of pilots re-created the day's escapades, using zooming hands.

At one table, two captains were refighting the Vietnam War.

The captain, with his patent-leatherlike hair and sweat-slickened face, hunched over his beer. The name tag on his flight suit read Poole. He snarled at his companion, Payne, who then snarled back.

Their argument was lost in the din.

Thirty-three-year-old Captain Mark Payne had the rugged good looks of a cigarette-ad cowboy, but too many cigarettes and too many nights at the officers' club, too much squinting from cockpits and too little attention to health, had carved extra years on his face. He stood up and shouted, "Who gives a shit?" And no one seemed to notice.

Other pilots had come to expect indifference from Vietnam vets, seasoned platoon leaders, and instructor pilots. Payne was all three. His shouted question was also his favorite expression. And not as much a question as a pronouncement of that indifference.

For a moment Poole was silent, then he too stood up, and the two men stormed out of the club.

Nobody noticed their departure.

At the flight line, Payne stood outside the operations quonset waiting for Poole, hoping the guard would show himself and end this escapade. The guard did not appear.

Poole, the company operations officer, staggered from the quonset, aircraft logbook and keys in one hand, flight helmet bag in the other. "I found the Huey you're scheduled to fly tomorrow," he slurred. "We'll take it."

"Hey, you win, Ken."

"Win what?"

"The bet, the dare, the argument—whatever. You win—scout pilots are better than gunnies. Okay?"

Poole blinked. "Don't patronage me, asshole." He narrowed his eyes, glaring as if at an enemy. Daring.

"Patro*nize*, stupid."

"See? *See?* I din't think you could resist patronizing me."

"No, listen. I'm . . . getting cold feet. Honest, I want to call this thing off before it gets us both in trouble." He knew it would do no good. He knew the script.

"Good," said Poole. "I'll go by myself." He pushed Payne aside and tacked toward the flight line.

Payne leaned against the front fender of his Camaro, pulsating red in the light of the security lamp, and watched Poole stop at each UH-1H helicopter, splashing a tiny penlight beam on the vertical fin, reading tail numbers until he found the right one. He untied the blades and swung the main rotor perpendicular to the fuselage. His keys jingled as he unlocked the cockpit. He sneered back toward the Camaro as he slid open both cabin doors.

Payne searched for the guard to end the standoff.

Poole climbed into the left seat.

A stream of obscenities poured from the cockpit, followed by Poole, who stumbled over the collective lever at the left of the seat and almost tumbled out on his head. For a moment Payne thought the night and the macho confrontation were over.

But Poole righted himself and lurched to the nose of the Huey. Two snaps and the radio compartment door flew up. The battery. When Poole connected it, the cockpit lights came on.

And Payne knew his buddy didn't have sense or sobriety enough to end this stupidity. So he heaved himself off the red fender and caught Poole as he stepped up on the toe of the left skid to climb into the cockpit.

"Ken, let's call it a night."

"I'm going flying, asshole."

"Look, I'm sorry for insulting you. I'm sorry for putting you down. I'm sorry for saying anything bad about the scouts. I'm sorry for living, for chrissake."

Poole grabbed him by the chest pockets. "See? What'd I say, you bastard? You can't get a goddamn sentence out without being sarcastic."

"I'm sorry. I said I'm sorry. What the hell do you want?"

"I want things to be like the old days. I wanna go flying." Poole shoved Payne and turned toward the cockpit.

"Okay. Let's tie this thing down. We'll go flying tomorrow."

Payne never saw the roundhouse coming, never thought a drunk could move so fast, never suspected

it. When the punch smashed into his ear, his knees
buckled. Before he could fall, Poole heaved a shoulder
into his midsection. Payne watched a dazzling display
of fireworks inside his head; felt the air rushing out of
him accompanied by a wave of nausea. The fireworks
display climaxed into white, then red, then black. He
knew he would throw up. Then he knew nothing.

Private First Class Willis Tealer knew he was dead
the instant he heard the ticking whine of a Huey's
turbine firing to life. He grabbed his shotgun and
used it like a cane to help him stand.

"Damn." His leg had fallen asleep. As had the rest
of his body and mind. Now everything but the leg
came awake in terror. He started jogging, limping,
jogging north on the ramp, cursing his screw-up.

The turbine wrapped up to operating RPM.

He broke into a limping run.

The blades started chopping into the air. He'd
never make it. He was dead for sure.

A hundred yards away, the Huey lifted unsteadily
into the air. It wobbled and touched down, then
weaved up and hovered toward the runway. The rancid breath of the helicopter's exhaust reached him.

"Holy shit," he whined. "Somebody's stealing one
of our birds."

The night breeze washed him down, and Payne
came to his senses, knowing he was in flight and un-
derstanding the aircraft was not flying in trim. Otherwise there would be no crosswind in the cabin of

the UH-1H. For a moment, he wondered what rookie was flying. His eyes snapped open as he remembered.

The control tower flashed by close enough for him to see the greenish interior, close enough to see terror on two faces as the men backed away to the far side of the booth. From the cockpit, he heard Poole howling.

Payne struggled to all fours. His eyes danced in time to the helicopter's vibrations. His head pounded.

Payne realized his face was wet. The pool of vomited beer between his hands told him why. He reached for his handkerchief, sat back on his heels, and wiped his face. He threw the hanky into the night wind and it blew back inside.

The helicopter lurched down and to the right, throwing Payne up and to the left. Suddenly he was wide awake, jolted by an injection of his own adrenaline. Suddenly the lights below waltzed into view. No longer was the floor of the craft between him and the lights. He sailed toward the door opening, his knees and boots sliding in his own vomit, and he knew the life he had spent so much time diligently screwing up was over. What a relief. And what a way to go out. Drunk. Flying. Sailing toward Earth. *Who gives a shit*, he thought. He screamed as a blast of night air slapped his face into reality. "*Aiyeee* doooo-o-o-o-o."

2

Warren Howell didn't fit Texas definitions. He seemed taller than his six feet. "A clean-cut fella," they called him when he was around. "A wimp" they said when he wasn't. His stiff posture and slim build exaggerated his height. Howell emphasized the illusion by seeking to physically dominate any conversation—standing on a step to diminish someone, leaning over a shorter person, or intruding on a person's private space.

He was clean. Meticulously so. A trait out of place in a working veterinary clinic in central Texas, birthplace of informality, geographical center of the universe for rednecks and shit-kickers.

"Never open the cage," Howell warned Albert Kiser. "Don't even touch the cage." He laid aside his research logbook and stood stiffly at Kiser's side. His fists were jammed into the pockets of his white lab coat, its starched crispness wilted in the humid hours after midnight. Outside, the sky rumbled with distant explosions from Fort Hood's ranges.

Kiser, the janitor, stared at the cage and worked his full lips. His watery eyes swam behind thick lenses, widening and narrowing like a matched pair of fish mouths.

"Never, Doctor Howell, never," he said in a hushed voice. "I'd never open this cage."

So this is it, he thought. *This is the reason I been asked to work late. This is the big secret locked away for a month behind the lab doors.* His eyes pored over the black lump of matted fur crouched four feet away in one corner of a battered dog pen. He looked for clues to the creature's identity, but for all he could see, it looked like nothing more than a wadded-up dirty fur jacket. The cage was strapped to a stainless steel lab table with two battered strands of baling wire.

"What is it, Doctor? It stinks like three hogs in a closet." He glanced around the lab. What he saw told him why Howell had revealed the big secret to him. Before Howell had locked everyone out of this lab in July, the room had been as crisp and clean as the doctor himself. But now scum, in varying thicknesses from film to paste, had dulled the sparkle. Splattered offal and bits of dog food lay everywhere within a radius of five feet of the cage. Clumsy attempts at sanitation were revealed in blackened streaks and shoe prints dried on white tiles.

"Take a month to clean this up," he said, blinking at the stench. He lifted his glasses and dabbed at welling tears with a red bandanna he pulled from his pocket. He stooped lower and stared at the pile of shaggy fur in the pen.

A pair of eyes stared back at him. They were black, flickering ebony bits rimmed in yellow.

Yeah, some secret. Dr. Clean will let Kiser in on the secret if he'll wipe up the shit.

"It's a badger?"

"I don't think so, Albert. It's a . . . freak of nature that Mack Dodson caught killing his goats. Mack nearly beat it to death with a piece of kindling. He brought it to me from Marlin Junction in a gunny-sack so I could tell him what it is."

"Wonder if it was the same thing that carried off our goat?"

"I don't know, Albert."

Inside the lump of matted fur, a fevered brain sorted through a bombardment of sensory stimuli. Alternately, the animal received signals of fear, discomfort, aggression, and affinity. In one instant the brain decided it would be all right to touch one of the docile creatures outside the cage. In the next instant the body coiled to leap and tear them apart. Immediately the urge to flee, bashing into the wire mesh, supplanted the previous impulses. No single stimulus would permit itself to be analyzed and acted upon before it was contradicted.

So the affinity toward man, like a romance gone wrong, manifested itself as rage; made the animal want to attack. The urge to flee, thwarted by the wires of the pen, became yet another drive to lunge. The aggression simply urged the thing to attack for the hell of it, for pleasure. The thing wanted—needed —to rip and tear something, anything. Anyone.

So, pulled in every direction yet no direction, the animal lay immobilized, a seething caldron of an-

gered panic, a ferocious volcano of energized flesh
and bones poised to erupt, to break out of the cage,
the only habitat it had ever known.

Always looking to attack, attack, attack.

Kiser's eyes narrowed. "Hey, are those horns?" He
stepped up to the cage and used the bandanna to
brush off a piece of muck blocking his view.

"Don't!"

Howell grabbed Kiser's overalls strap and jerked.
The matted ball sprang to life with a hiss.

As the creature lunged, the cage lurched away
from the hand. Metal screeched against metal as the
wire scratched a streak on the table's surface. The
two strands of baling wire went taut.

Kiser saw a flash of enormous fangs and recoiled in
the same instant Howell jerked on his overalls. The
bandanna snagged on the cage. Kiser felt his feet slip
as the animal hit the end of the pen. He reeled backward as the cage slammed forward with the impact of
the beast on the mesh nearest them. Kiser felt the
doctor tugging his overalls, saw the brightness of the
lab and the collection of claws and fangs swiping
through openings in the mesh, batting his hand away.
He was going down.

Screaming—the beast's and Kiser's—filled the lab.
The farthest anchor wire snapped. The cage tipped
up on end as Kiser hit the floor.

He landed flat on his back in the excrement below
the table. He dragged the doctor to his knees in the
slime. On the tabletop above them, the beast thrashed
around in fury, shredding the bandanna into a bliz-

zard of red lint. It threw itself against the wire netting, bashing it outward with its muzzle and pulling the wires inward with claws and teeth, rumpling the strands as if the pen were made of common window screen instead of heavy gauge wire. Alternately, it shrieked, barked, and snarled.

"Jesus. Goddamn, get me away." Kiser squirmed, trying to propel himself backward with his heels and elbows, but he could get no leverage in the scum.

Howell, still clutching the strap, dragged the janitor clear of the table, leaving red-tinged streaks in the filth. The sight of blood renewed Kiser's panic.

"Goddamn, Howell, goddammit. He got me."

The animal chimed in, pawing at them, strumming the cage wire with its claws. It backed off and sprang repeatedly at the two men below. Kiser saw that the yellow rims around the black eyes were bloodshot. He saw teeth, many teeth.

Each time the thing threw itself against the cage, the remaining piece of baling wire snapped taut and vibrated like a guitar string.

It wanted him, Kiser sensed. Something told him the beast hated him. It was as though it were seeking revenge for some past transgression. This thing knew about his touching that girl in Killeen. This thing would kill him for it.

"Calm down, Kiser," growled Howell through his teeth. "You're safe, for God's sake. Don't get him any more excited. I don't know how long that other baling wire will hold."

"Excited?" Kiser shrieked. "*Excited?*" His glasses

were gone, lost in the fall. There was panic apparent in the watery eyes, the blubbering lips.

The creature stopped its thrashing to glare at the two men. Its lips were drawn back. Blood flowed from cuts on its muzzle and stained the daggers of its teeth. Shreds of red cloth hung from them, fluttering in and out from the beast's rapid panting, thereby exaggerating the effect of dripping blood.

Kiser went limp, panting in time with the creature.

"Let me see your hands," Howell said with forced calmness, trying to distract Kiser from the creature's bloody features.

Kiser held up his hands, waving the fingers feebly. They were all accounted for, but the flesh of his forefinger lay open, slit neatly from middle knuckle to the nail. Blood oozed across the back of his hand onto his denim shirtsleeve.

"It doesn't hurt. It's nothing. I'm okay. Let me up. Please, help me find my glasses." He looked pasty and sheepish.

The animal, with its hairy, human paws, hung on the wire panting, clamped there by the grip of its curved inch-long black claws and its teeth that clenched and unclenched the mesh.

The lab was quiet except for the panting of the trio.

Kiser wiped his lenses on a shirttail and fitted the frames into the dents on his temples and nose.

Through his streaked glasses he could see the beast in greater detail as it clung spread-eagle on the wire. It was about the size of a German shepherd. But this was no dog—it was a monster, he decided, a beast. It

had the torso of an ape. Its long snout was scaly, as
long as a shepherd's but flat and round with the nostrils on the top. It displayed six sets of slender fangs,
less like a dog's canine teeth than the tusks of a razor-
back hog. Slaver ran over the flat ranges of its rear
teeth and flowed out the corners of its mouth and
down its scaly belly.

Kiser stood as straight as he ever got and wiped his
hands on his overalls, leaving a smear of blood on his
thigh.

"God, it ate my hanky," he whispered.

Howell's stomach turned at the thought.

Kiser began circling the outside of the cage. The
beast followed him with its eyes; teeth still clamped
to the wire.

Howell wrung his hands dry on the hem of his lab
coat and grimaced at the stains on his clothes.

Kiser pointed with his torn finger. "Doctor, he's
got goat feet—hooves. Paws in front and hooves in
back."

"I know, Kiser." Howell studied the man studying
the creature . . . studying the man.

One cloven hoof beat a warning tattoo against the
cage. The other hoof braced the beast, a strand of
wire in the split. The fangs released the wire and the
massive head swiveled, tracking the man.

Kiser characterized the beast in terms of animals he
knew. Hind quarters of a goat with a young goat's
spikes on its head. The lump of fur beneath each horn
was an ear.

"That ain't no badger."

"No, probably not. But I can't say for sure whether

it doesn't have some badger in it. It seems to be part goat. The rest is . . . I don't know . . . freakish."

"What are you going to do with it?"

"I'm studying it, Albert. I'm not sure what I should do. One thing for sure . . . I need your help to build a stronger cage."

The janitor stiffened. "I ain't going near that somebitch anymore, Doctor. And don't you worry about me opening the cage, because I ain't getting this close . . ."

He threw his arms apart, and the beast flung itself across the cage at him. Kiser stumbled backward and nearly fell down again. The cage rocked as the thing went into another tantrum.

"No sudden movements, Kiser."

"No shit." Kiser whispered.

The animal skulked to a corner of the pen, drawing itself back into a ball of matted fur, yellow-rimmed eyes peering out.

"Look, Kiser, I just need help building a cage. Beth and I will do all the feeding and cleanup. After you help me build the cage—if you do; it's your choice— you'll never even have to come into the lab anymore. And I might be able to squeeze out a bonus, too."

As he spoke, Howell jammed his fists into his lab coat pockets, feeling for the pistol in his belt beneath. Muscle knots rippled across his temples, pulling his shiny scalp tight under the thinning fine hair.

Controlled again, he sighed and said, "I want to study it."

"Then what?"

"Then I euthanize . . . put it to sleep . . . overdose of barbiturates . . . a tranquilizer . . . drugs."

"Okay."

"Okay what?" Howell held his breath.

"I'll help with the cage . . . and nothing else. Absolutely nothing else."

3

As he slid into the blast of the night, Payne grabbed blindly for something to save him from a five-hundred-foot swan dive. His left hand came up empty. His right found the inertia reel cable to the copilot's shoulder harness.

His feet flew into the one-hundred-knot airstream. The edge of the hinged doorpost panel hit his shoulder, and the cable bit into his palm. But his grip held. He grabbed the doorpost with his left hand and dragged himself into the cabin.

Poole's helmet lolled back against the armored seat; his arm pulling on the cyclic control stick.

"Ken, lower the goddamned nose," he shouted. But Poole was out, pinned in his seat by the locked shoulder harness.

Payne got to his feet and slapped Poole's helmet. "Wake up, goddamn you, before you kill us."

The blow spun the head to the left, jerking Poole's right hand off the cyclic.

The climb was finished. At zero airspeed and an indicated three thousand feet the cyclic tipped forward, the nose dipped, and the descent began.

The negative Gs, as in a roller coaster whipping

over the top, lifted Payne and held him back. But he gripped the wings of the armored seats and launched himself forward, climbing onto the pedestal panel. Switches and dials crunched like twigs under his soles as he walked on the face of radio control heads. No matter now. No time to be delicate.

He slid into the right seat as he pulled power with his left hand and raised the nose with the right, trimming the craft against the pressure of Poole's motionless feet on the copilot's pedals. The landing light swept over the West Fort Officers' Club as it flew by below at one hundred twenty knots. Poole's black Nissan was the only car left in the lot. Still the Huey descended. Payne pulled it left to avoid overflying the housing area adjacent to the club. Still, he was close enough to make out individual chain links on a backyard swing set as the landing light swept by. He knew the whopping blades of the UH-1H must have awakened a lot of families.

Not as much as a crash, he thought, realizing he had sobered up.

At eleven hundred feet indicated, less than a hundred feet from the ground, the instruments finally showed a climb. Payne sighed and banked the craft south toward the runway and . . . and what?

He turned off the landing lights, the rotating red beacon, and all the navigation lights. For a second, he considered trying to sneak directly back to the flight line. Then he remembered the terrorized tower operators. Fat chance.

To confirm the implausibility, a helicopter swept

off the end of the runway, its landing light and searchlight raking the ground.

Lifesaver. The fort's medical evacuation and crash bird, a peacetime monument to *Dustoff* crews who ferried the wounded in Vietnam.

He groped through his mind for a way out. Of Poole's mess. While Poole was sleeping through it.

Every idea he had was crazy. But the craziest of all was surrender.

So after leveling off at fifteen hundred feet, he steepened the banking turn, veering away from the runway and *Lifesaver,* now less than a mile away and closing. He straightened out on a northeast heading and dropped the helicopter's nose to pick up airspeed.

He snapped on all the lights. The landing light and searchlight beams stabbed into the darkness, inviting *Lifesaver* to follow. To guarantee it, he turned on the transponder, automatically identifying the Huey to the electronic query of radar. He wished he had a helmet so he could eavesdrop on the standard emergency frequencies.

He continued to trim the aircraft, milking nearly one hundred thirty knots from it. The Huey protested being driven ten knots past its limits. It tried to toss its nose up and right. It bounced heavily, like a horse trotting. Payne clenched his teeth and held the cyclic forward, forcing the nose to stay down, like a jockey urging a Thoroughbred to the wire, demanding everything his mount could give. To his right were the lights of Killeen and Fort Hood. At their boundaries lay the black void of the artillery impact area.

He aimed for the heart of darkness.

Three controllers huddled over the radar scope.

"Who is that?" muttered the first.

The second backed away, his gaze lingering on the scope. Then he ran for a phone.

The third jumped back as if the scope would blow up in his face. "Range Control. Get Range Control to shut down the fucking artillery. For chrissake, he's flying into the middle of a gun-target line . . . get Range Con—"

The man on the phone screamed, "What the hell you think I'm doing here? . . . Range Control . . . No, I'm not shouting at you . . . Get those artillery ranges shut down . . . All of them . . . We've got a goddamned runaway helo flying right into the middle of the firing."

Payne crossed the last lights bordering the sea of ink. He tried to imagine the pandemonium on the radios. No. No time for speculation. He concentrated on matters before him. Foremost were the orange bursts on the ground, the unspectacular showers of fading metal cinders in the distance. He wondered about the g-t line—*what the hell*—*if a single 155 mm round hurtling through the air was meant to occupy the same coordinate in space as a helicopter flown by a drunk on a dare, then the fucking round must have his name engraved in gold on it. Let it fly right up his ass.* It'd be way less complicated than what he had in mind.

He saw the terrain drop away toward Cowhouse Creek. The craft's searchlight poked into the valley, bouncing off floating mists.

"See what you got me into?" he shouted at his unconscious buddy. "See . . . aw, shit . . ."

He twisted the transponder's master control switch to EMER, sending a UHF emergency signal to every radar interrogation system within line of sight. He wished he had a helmet so he could scream a couple Maydays.

He dropped the collective and rolled the throttle off. The Huey sank at twenty-six hundred feet a minute in autorotation. He flicked off all the exterior lights and then the transponder. He thought about praying.

"Fuck it."

The second controller plastered a phone to his head with one hand and worked the mike button with the other. Into his boom mike he said, "*Lifesaver*, this is Gray Approach. Turn right to one-two-zero immediately, turn right. . . ." Into his phone he said, "Range Control, is that artillery off yet?"

The third controller said, "Never mind, *Lifesaver*'s already turning. . . ."

A double-image emergency blip showed up on the scope.

"Shit," said the first. "The runaway's crashing."

"Artillery's off," said the second, taking the phone from his ear.

The double blip disappeared.

"Too late," murmured the third. "He's augured it in. Send in *Lifesaver* to pick up the pieces."

When he saw the rim of the valley sweeping its ragged, black edge up the gun-metal blue of the night sky, Payne rolled the throttle on full, pulling power and hauling the nose back.

A partial moon bounced up at him from the water of the creek. He leveled off and banked toward the west, keeping below the line of sight to radar, navigating up the creek and out of the impact area.

Three miles west of where he had dropped down into the valley, he brought the Huey to a standstill barely above the hardwoods lining the creek. His heart thumped in time to the Huey's vertical vibrations. He turned the craft so he could look back to measure his success.

The sight made him giddy. It was a light show. Three helicopters, their searchlights dancing, circled the spot where he had left the illusion of a crash. From the south, two more aircraft approached. A sixth bird came across the impact area from the direction of Hood Field. Before long, he knew, the airspace above the Cowhouse would be certifiably dangerous. Pilots. Flocking to a crash. Moths to a bonfire. Endangering themselves in the name of search and rescue.

Payne again turned the Huey around the mast until it pointed west, upstream. He nudged the cyclic forward and added a touch of power with the collective. His mount eased along in the heavy air, picking its way through the treetops, responding obediently to every delicate control touch, behaving like a plow mare stepping through a stony field. He ransacked his memory for the placement of power lines in this section of the maneuver area and, for a second time, even thought of praying.

He remembered flying in Vietnam. Wartime flying meant something. It usually meant something to do with life and death. That in contrast to peacetime flying, which meant endless hours of make-believe wars and bullshit rules that spoiled even the best make-believe.

Tonight—although it might mean a court martial and the end of his career unless he could continue to pull things outrageously miraculous out of his ass— tonight, he was flying with a purpose for the first time he could remember since Vietnam.

4

Captain Kenneth Seth Poole, twenty-nine, awoke screaming; his cries drowned out by a flight of three Hueys turning final in formation to land north at Gray Army Airfield. After they had passed and the fumes of spent jet fuel wafted over him, he came to his senses—burning eyes, throbbing head, aching limbs, raspy tongue of bitter Brillo.

He found himself lying belly up. The sky was the color of stainless steel. His digital showed 6:32:17, counting off the seconds in slow motion as his eyeballs fluttered, trying to focus. He rubbed his face, his hands coming away greasy, and sat up to survey his situation.

He seemed hardly surprised to find himself atop Manere Mountain, the two-hundred-foot flat-topped pinnacle south of the airfield. On the parking ramp a mile and a half away, he saw three helicopters taxiing and several others with rotor blades coasting to a stop. An indistinct knot of men in green clustered around his buddy's red Camaro.

He got to his feet and, half stumbling, half sliding, started down the steep slope of Manere Mountain as

if this were any ordinary day and any ordinary way
to go to work.

Payne hardly had time to wonder how he could
have slept—had he passed out?—or had he blacked
out again? He bit into his lower lip and inhaled as
deeply as he could, knowing he'd need all the hot air
he could muster to carry off one of the biggest lies of
his life. Thus fortified, he burst out the door of his
platoon quonset shack and demanded of the men loi-
tering around his Camaro, "What the fuck is going on
here?"

By midmorning, the crowd of men in the battalion
commander's office had dwindled to four. Three of
them stood stiffly at attention. Lieutenant Colonel
Andrew Forman hunched over his desk, coiled as if
about to spring into Private First Class Willis
Tealer's face. Major Joseph DePree, the company
commander, stood beside the desk, his eyes darting
from Forman to Tealer to the rigid Payne, whose
gaze stared beyond Forman to a spot somewhere on
the south ramp.

Forman was trying valiantly to scream at Tealer,
but hours of raving had reduced his voice to a
squawk. "Tealer, I'm only going to ask you one more
time," he rasped. "Were you sleeping on guard? Did
you see the captain here take off in that helicopter?
Did you see anybody bring a helicopter back? Did
you see anybody—any-goddamn-body—on that flight
line?"

"Sir, like I told you, I was at the south end of the

ramp. I heard the bird cranking; before I could stop it—"

"Bullshit."

Forman flopped back into his chair. He rasped at DePree, "Get him out of here."

Tealer saluted and tripped out of the office as if on stilts.

Forman launched himself to his feet again. His red-rimmed blue eyes glittered. As he spoke, his upper lip twitched, lifting into a sneer.

"Okay, Payne, you bastard . . ."

Payne's lips parted.

"Don't say it, you lying bastard," Forman squawked. "Maybe I *can't* court-martial you, *can't* send you to jail. Maybe I can't even prove it was one of our birds that buzzed the tower and went into the restricted area." He sat down and sighed. "Maybe, maybe, maybe. Maybe I don't want to prove it. Maybe your story will stick. Maybe the general won't find out." His voice rose in pitch as he recited his litany. "Maybe we didn't have sense enough to count aircraft until we rounded you up. Maybe we didn't inventory keys and logbooks right away." He glared at DePree. "Maybe you didn't sneak that chopper back in during all the confusion of the search and rescue. Maybe you did spend the night sleeping in your platoon shack. Maybe, just maybe, we can keep the entire seamy episode under our hats and save a few careers."

Payne stared at the spot he had picked on the south ramp.

"Look at me, Payne."

Mark obeyed. He saw the blue eyes brighten.

"Whatever happens, Payne, your career is up for grabs."

Payne guessed he wouldn't be court-martialed— not when the helicopter couldn't be absolutely identified, certainly not as long as nobody with stars was screaming for heads. It would become a case of a phantom helicopter, a chimera, a fairy tale. Among pilots, it would be a legend. He had already heard pilots calling it the UFO, Unidentified Fuck-Off. *As for my career,* he thought, *Colonel, you've got me confused with somebody who gives a shit.*

The blue eyes twinkled sadistically. "So, Captain, I'm left with only administrative measures. We could put you on admin leave and appoint an investigating officer under AR fifteen dash six."

Forman sat down and lounged in his chair. He looked at the ceiling.

Payne remained impassive. *Who really gives a shit.*

"Or we could let your efficiency report reflect the character of your continual drinking and carousing with that . . . animal, Poole. It wouldn't have to be a negative report that you could appeal—just a lukewarm one. Faint praise. Know what I mean, Captain?"

"Yes, sir." Payne's mask remained the same.

"Or we could just take you out of that platoon command and run you up here as an assistant to the intelligence officer or the adjutant's helper. You know, I'm sure we could find *something* on staff."

Payne's eyes flinched, but he quickly restored his best deadpan.

Too late. Forman had seen it.

"What's this? We've hit a nerve?"

"Sir—"

"Well, well, well, Mr. Hardass."

"Sir, if I could—"

"Shut up, Payne. Well, I'll be . . . You need a staff assignment if you ever hope to progress in this man's army, Captain."

Payne grimaced. The game was up.

"Sir, I know I can best contribute to the battalion in a platoon."

DePree chipped in. "That's true, Colonel, he—"

"Shut up, Major." A sardonic smile darkened his face. "We finally got the tough guy by the balls." He stood up and walked around his desk, his forehead coming within an inch of Payne's ski-jump nose. "You bet your ass, you bastard. By the balls." He backed off and began strutting around the office with his hands clasped behind him. "Let's us see here. We have us a guy who wants to be a platoon leader more than anything else in the whole world. Why, he might even start coming to social events, might even talk to my wife—Christ, he might even buss her on the cheek like an officer and a gentleman if I let him keep his platoon. Am I correct?"

"Yes."

"Don't you mean 'yes, sir,' Payne?"

"Yes, sir." Payne stared at his spot on the south ramp.

"Okay, Payne, let's deal. You just meet one condition."

Payne's eyes locked with Forman's.

"I can't let the men think you got away clean. You stole that chopper, and no use trying to convince me otherwise. Either you pay or I'll lose the men's respect. You need your slap on the dick."

Payne raised his chin and waited.

"You got to take the alcohol rehab program in Marble Falls."

"Colonel, you think I'm a drunk?"

"I didn't say that, did I? Fact is, I do. But that's not important. What's important is you take your medicine for three-four weeks so the slate is clean when you come back—to your platoon, if you stay sober."

Mark gulped involuntarily.

"Well? Marble Falls or assistant monitor in the enlisted swine's latrine?"

"Marble Falls." He choked on the words.

"You must volunteer for it," croaked Forman.

Mark nodded.

"In writing."

Defeated, he nodded again.

Beth drove to Marble Falls the day after Mark called to tell her he'd been admitted. An orderly led her across the manicured grounds and left her beside him. They sat on a bench beneath a mushrooming pecan.

They were distant relatives, small talking about the inferno of August and the memory of long-forgotten aunts at home in Montana. It took about a minute and a half. Then they sat and stared.

Ten minutes into the silence, she patted him on the

thigh. "Well, I have to get back to my flocks. Have you had any more of those . . . spells?"

"Nope." *Not counting the other night after shutting the helicopter down, sneaking the logbook and keys back into operations, and slipping into his platoon quonset,* he thought.

"You should tell your doctor about those things."

He didn't answer. Instead, his gaze intensified, locking onto a spot across the grounds. *Was it the booze causing the blackouts? Am I really a drunk?*

"How long have you had them anyway?"

No response.

She followed his gaze with her own, seeing nothing but nature and the marble buildings, beacons of white in the afternoon sun. She kissed him on the cheek and excused herself, leaving him to his trance.

His head came up abruptly as if he'd just remembered something.

"Since basic training," he replied.

But she was gone.

He remembered the two painful weeks of hospitalization at Fort Ord that had begun his career. He had regained consciousness and nearly his full strength. They assigned him to another training company.

He had reacted abnormally to a new meningitis serum, they said, catching a mild case of the disease rather than becoming immune to it. But he would survive. Unluckily, six others in another group had contracted the deadly contagious sickness and died.

"Fucking shame," said his new drill instructor, compassionate as a DI ever gets.

5

Kiser had taken on building the cage for two purposes. First, the doctor was incompetent as a mechanic. Second, he could ensure the beast would never escape from a cage he put together.

The men reversed roles. Kiser became boss. Howell let himself be bossed for the two weeks required to build the cage. He rented an arc welder and bought iron bars. He lugged the bars into the lab and took directions from the janitor in laying them out while Kiser did the welding.

Kiser's plan was simplicity. He built two iron boxes, six-feet cubes with crossed bars four inches apart, a steel-hinged door on each box.

The men heaved the cages into position in the lab until they were four inches apart, with the doors at opposite ends. The janitor welded the boxes together, using spacers to keep the four-inch gap. Then he cut an access hole between the cages. A drop gate slid up and down the gap in metal channels. To the drop gate, he bolted a sheet of three-eighths-inch Plexiglas. Finally, he rigged a steel bar to slide over the drop gate to lock it down and bought heavy padlocks to hold it in place.

Howell balked at the extra expense of building a double-cell cage. Kiser insisted, knowing that no matter what the doctor said, he would be the one to clean the cage and feed the animal. And that would be impossible with a raging beast confined to a single compartment. The truth, though, was that he knew the beast wanted him. Why else was he dreaming about it. The double cage was his defense.

The beast's blood boiled in a mad, driving anger that never subsided. It had no mind or memory as such, only the desire to destroy the men creatures. It knew it could kill them, shred them, eat parts of them, and scatter the rest. If only the wires would part and set him free long enough.

It hated other things too, things it knew but had never seen. The beast wanted to destroy other creatures in other places in other cages. It needed to kill other animals that were like men. It wanted to attack river creatures and living things from the forest, though it had never seen a forest or a river. It only knew it must ravage and destroy them.

Sometimes when it threw itself around or clawed or bit steel, it hurt itself. Unlike normal animals that find pain a brake to wild behavior, a signal to back off, this beast was spurred by the pain, driven to further excesses.

The beast did not know evil or hate. It simply *was* evil, the essence of hatred and nothing less. It had never known satisfaction or comfort or any good feeling, not even the contentment of a full stomach. It attacked its food, eating only enough to stem the hunger pains and to survive and hate awhile longer.

It never wanted to rest or sleep. It simply tired itself after incessant wariness and frequent rages and then slipped into a restless sleep that sometimes erupted into another outburst if startled. At other times, it would stare out through slit eyelids, waiting for the opportunity to spring at the men. It needed no excuse for its rage.

It could not slip into unconsciousness in the presence of the men, no matter how exhausted it had become. It knew that the men could harm it. It knew it might get the fat man who stank of fear.

The fat one would be the first one to kill.

The animal grew rapidly during the two weeks the men were lugging, cutting, and welding the iron bars. Howell worried that the dog cage would not bear many more rages, so he loaded up his tranquilizer dart and shot it into the beast's haunches every morning before they went to work.

Still the beast did not sleep. It lay helpless, unable to move even its eyes. But it could see. It could hate. It could wait for the fatal slip.

At night, when the drowsiness had worn off, the beast worked savagely on the cage, butting it, ripping it with tooth and claw until it had fatigued one of the wires. One night it snapped the strand and pawed at the hole like a dog burrowing after a gopher.

During the day it crouched against the hole, hiding it, waiting for the man in the white coat to shoot it with the dart. It wasn't any special intelligence, just instinct, the jungle cat guarding its kill.

And when it had been shot with the trank, the beast lay in hate of the men, suffering the most intense of all rages—in its head where there was no physical outlet for the explosions of fury, anticipating the chance to ambush its prey but knowing it was incapacitated. Hating, hating.

Early in the second week of building, as Kiser stood gawking at the doped beast, he found the hole in the pen and several fatigued wires. It sent a chill down his spine, and he felt cold long after the doctor had mended the damage with half a dozen strands of baling wire woven into the mesh.

The next day Kiser brought in six feet of chain-link storm fence and insisted they drape it over the cage and wire it down even tighter, just for good measure. Howell didn't protest. So they wrapped the dog pen in a wire cocoon and redoubled their efforts on the iron cage.

Howell tried to reassure the janitor that the beast wasn't intelligent enough to be sneaky—to work on the cage at night and lie over the hole during the day.

Kiser remained unconvinced. He had a festering sore on his hand, memories of too many bad dreams, and a feeling that the animal's eyes never left him— here in the lab or even at home. He became more sullen than usual. The dreams wouldn't leave him alone at night. During the day, its eyes were always on him. Then the eyes became bolder in his home, showing up in the bathroom and the closet, locking

on his own eyes when he tried to catch them. It was
worse than when they flickered away.

Eva began asking why he'd taken to leaving lights
on at night.

He grumbled at her about burglars.

What burglars? she asked him.

He told her to shut the fuck up.

The weather added to everybody's misery. It was a
brutal August even for Texas—savagely hot outdoors,
shriveling the sparse grass, drying up stock ponds,
multiplying the number of dry streambeds, killing
many livestock and not a few old people.

Indoors was worse. The lab's atmosphere never
cooled, despite the laboring air conditioner. The humidity and welding smoke nullified any benefit of the
struggling machine. And the stench of the monster
would not be diluted. So the air gripped their lungs;
stung their eyes.

The men opened the lab's small windows, letting
in the drum beat of artillery, mortar, and tank fire
from the fort, permitting dust and pollen to mingle
with the acrid welding smoke.

Kiser could hardly wait until the cage was finished.
Then he knew he'd be excited, maybe even happy
again.

But the day they dumped the drugged, stinking,
one-hundred-seventy-five-pound monster unceremoniously onto the floor of one of the cage's cells and
slammed the padlock shut, he was not at all excited.
Let alone happy.

6

It was September, more than two weeks after the cage was finished, when Beth visited Mark again. They were much more comfortable with each other. Their conversation was still small talk, but warm small talk.

When it was time for her to go, they hugged for a long time. Finally, he whispered in her ear and she pushed away.

"This afternoon? You're getting out this afternoon?"

He smiled. "Parole."

"Oh, you . . . do you have your car? Want me to pick you up and take you to our house for dinner?"

"Naw. Ken Poole is picking me up in my car. It'll be too late for you to get dinner tonight. Let's do it tomorrow."

"You promise you won't stand me up?"

"Promise."

They hugged again, and she skipped across the grass to her old pickup. He watched her drive off, the Ford bouncing on worn shocks.

A voice behind him asked, "You feel good enough to go now?" It was Junkers, his shrink.

"Yeah."

"Take care of yourself. Exercise. Balanced diet. You, being a compulsive type, will probably go back to eating junk foods and coffee and cigarettes."

"I'll lay off the liquor, though."

"In moderation, it wouldn't hurt you."

"But I'm a drunk." His raised eyebrows added, aren't I?

"No, you're not. Oh, you've had your episodes, but those are problematic, not any worse than anybody who overcelebrates the new year."

"But what about the blackouts?"

"They don't seem to be related to drinking—at least they're not confined to drinking episodes. More likely, they're a stress reaction. You go see the physician I recommended and he'll solve that mystery. Meantime, you should take yourself off flying status."

"Sure. Uh, one question. If I'm not a drunk, why did you let me stay in that group and call myself a juicer for three and a half weeks?"

"What else were you going to do?"

Mark threw his handbag through the T-top into the backseat of his Camaro and jumped into the passenger seat. "Hey."

"Hey." Poole shook out a Kool and offered it.

"No thanks. I've quit. Hey, thanks for taking care of Shep."

"No sweat. What's the verdict? They cure you?"

"Yeah. Like a Virginia ham. Doc says I'm not a drunk."

"Well if you ain't, I ain't. Want to go get a . . . Coke?"

"Nope."

"Visit your sister?"

"Nope, bad enough I have to go there tomorrow. My brother-in-law's such an asshole."

"So . . . what do you want to do?"

"Let's go get drunk."

Poole reached under the seat and fished out a bottle. "Hot damn. I brought Mr. Walker along just in case the cure didn't really take." Suddenly he looked very serious. "But you can't drink too much."

"Why so? I tell you, I'm not a drunk. I'm allowed."

"Naw, that's not it. You gotta fly a newby tomorrow. Thought you'd want to be right back in the saddle after watching me pass out at the controls. Bet it scared the shit out of you."

Payne stared off across the grass as Poole touched the key, sparking the Camaro to life. "Not as much as it did after I sobered up."

Poole shoved the clutch down and hesitated. "Thanks for dropping me off on Manere that night."

"Don't mention it."

Poole didn't. He dropped the clutch and aimed the squealing Camaro down the road.

The sun had long since dropped into its greasy slot on the horizon west of Radar Hill. The two captains sat overlooking the flight line, watching night-training helicopters come and go.

Mark took a shallow swig and passed the bottle. "No matter what, I ain't going flying tonight."

"No shit." Poole gave the bottle a deep, squeaky kiss.

Hunkered down, heels braced in gravelly Paleozoic shell beds, they looked like two more of the wild juniper shrubs squatting on the hillside.

"You sure you don't want to get laid, Lone Ranger?"

"Another night. I got a lot on my mind."

"Like what?"

"Like turning over a new leaf."

"More like a new tree."

Poole proffered a Kool. This time Mark took it. He leaned into the light from Poole's cupped hands and coughed on the menthol. Instantly, he was dizzy. He reclined against the rough hillside. "Funny," he said.

"What's funny?"

"I miss my ex."

"Oh, that's fucking hysterical."

"Haven't thought of her in years. And my kids."

"You're a laugh a minute, you morbid bastard. I'll be in stitches any second. You'll be in tears if I don't do something to cheer you up."

"So cheer me up."

"Let's go for a ride."

Mark sat up. "No helicopters."

"No, tomorrow will be soon enough for that."

"In what, then?"

"*Shitbird.*"

Poole opened the double doors to his office on the back of the quonset and dropped two planks. Mark stood aside. An angry whine came from the office.

The sound was followed by a nonissue jeep. Mark threw the planks in beside Poole's desk. He dropped into the passenger seat as Poole dropped the clutch, throwing gravel on the quonset.

Shitbird was the Vietnam era label given anybody who didn't cooperate or perform up to expectations. The company dud was a shitbird. Anybody from another unit was a shitbird. Even a mother who didn't write often enough was one.

Shitbird had been a standard M151A1 vehicle, utility, general purpose (GP). Jeep for short. But that was a long time ago.

Its body had been bent, straightened and rebent, cracked and rusted beneath many blistering paint jobs—some sprayed, some brushed. The colors were camouflaged shades applied in tiny patches and puddles like a Jackson Pollack dripping. *Shitbird*'s name was painted in Day-Glo orange on the passenger side by a hand with the DTs. Vultures, the nickname of the 162nd Aviation Company, looked like Yultures. Oversized snow tires gave it the look of a poor man's dune buggy.

Dust and bugs kept pinging off Mark's face. Once off the flight line, Ken sped into the scrub woods beneath Radar Hill, so they had to duck from stinging nettles of juniper and the stabbing from pin oaks. Payne was relieved when Poole drove back onto the asphalt, although *Shitbird*'s yellowed headlight beams reached only half as far as needed.

Grinning wildly, Poole screamed over the whining engine and rush of air in their ears, "Cheered up yet?"

Mark smiled weakly. The boundary of the fort appeared. He expected Poole to turn around.

The snow tires rattled across a cattle guard. "Hey," he shouted at Poole. "You'll land us in jail for driving this thing with no license."

"License? What license? Hell, I got this thing by midnight requisition. Why do you think I park it inside my office?"

"Great. Stolen. This time I'll get life."

"You worried about the cops seeing us? Never happen, GI." To reassure him, Poole turned off the headlights and passed the bottle.

They were racing through the dark alongside Seven Mile Mountain, the ridge that runs on the western edge of West Fort Hood, separating Copperas Cove from the flight line. The road snaked like a ribbon of blue in front of *Shitbird*—what Mark could see of it through watering eyes. He took the bottle from Poole and sucked deeply on it. He knew the wild-eyed Poole was beyond control now. Nothing to do but ride it out. He wished he hadn't taken that drink, the smoke, the ride. It was almost as if he were . . . too old for this kind of stuff anymore. And just when he'd begun thinking he cared about things.

Four miles up the asphalt, Poole spun the wheel to the right. They were on a dirt road, a white strip floating in the darkness. Payne looked back. A white fog of dust billowed up behind them.

"I suppose you know that Seven Mile Mountain is dead ahead."

"Yep," said Poole.

"And this is a dead-end road."

"Yep."

Poole fumbled with the switches and turned on the headlights. Ahead, scrubby woods edged down to the gravel.

The road hooked left and opened onto a circular gravel plateau about a hundred feet in diameter. It was a mere turnaround, littered with beer cans. Poole skidded to a stop.

Mark relaxed.

Poole threw a lever to engage the front differential and gunned *Shitbird*, throwing gravel from all four wheels.

Shitbird, surefooted and deliberate as a burro, picked its way upslope.

In thirty seconds, they were deep into the brush. Minutes later *Shitbird* heaved itself over the rim, the headlights no longer trying to illuminate the sky. Poole grinned at his partner. "Gimme that bottle."

The Walker bottle was below half empty when they crossed the flat top of the hill, only two hundred yards wide at that point, and dropped down the east side toward West Fort.

Mark felt odd. It wasn't just that he was drunk for the first time in weeks, or that he had to brace his feet against the dash to keep from being tossed forward over the hood, or that juniper branches kept swiping at him, leaving his face scratched and stinging. For the first time in weeks, he felt like howling into the night as his insane chauffeur was howling. He felt as if he didn't care what happened to him. At Marble Falls he'd begun thinking about his career, his sister; the present, the future. He'd begun caring about those things, considering how he might put his relationships in order. Especially the relationship with himself.

Now he was bounding recklessly down the slope, throwing his head back to an impossible angle to drink, drenching his face and neck.

"Hey, you're spilling the goddamned whiskey," shouted Poole.

"Who gives a shit?"

7

The morning dew turned the dusting of caliche clay on the Camaro into a coat of mud. The Z28 sat behind the operations quonset, where it had been parked since yesterday's sundown. The double doors to Poole's office closed only as far as the ramp boards allowed.

Two pilots approached the doors cautiously, as if finding a burglary crime scene. Inside, *Shitbird* rested over its drip pan. Poole lay snoring, sprawled on his back across the hood, his head resting upside down on a fender, a stream drooling from his mouth into his hairline below.

A pair of bare feet dangled from the back of the jeep.

"Are you in early or working overtime, Captain?"

Poole swallowed hard several times against the force of gravity, smacking his lips. "Zat choo, Anzola?"

"Yeah, Captain. You promised to get Larson here a checkride early this morning. It's early."

"How?"

"Little after six."

"Who?"

"Warrant Officer Larson. P. J. Larson."

"Oh, yeah, the newby."

He sat up with effort. His oily hair stayed erect. "Hey, you got a new perfume, Anzola."

"Oh? How can you tell?"

"No dogs jumping you."

"Funny, asshole."

"Asshole *sir*, Anzola."

"Asshole *sir*. It's Larson's perfume."

"Fuck me . . . My head is constipated. . . . Hey, Payne, wake up. Your newby is here. I scheduled you for a checkride, remember?"

His feet slid down into the back of the jeep. "Why'd you do that?" he slurred.

"I told you. You need to get back on the job flying. Besides, the newby is assigned to your platoon. Get your ass up and moving."

He tried to open his glued eyelids. "Tell him to come back later."

"Smell that perfume? It ain't a him."

Payne sniffed deeply. Finally his eyes opened and beheld a green-eyed blond woman dressed in the rumpled Nomex of her flight suit. He jumped from *Shitbird* and ran out the door, one hand on his mouth, the other across his belly. From the side of the quonset came the sounds of retching.

Poole winked at the newby. "Guess he don't appreciate the subtlety of your fragrance."

"Welcome to the Vultures," said Warrant Officer Two Maggie Anzola.

* * *

The beast, agitated by squabbling, prowled inside the near cell of its cage. Beth and the two men watched from a distance.

"Albert, what about the common decency of two weeks' notice?"

"Doctor, I can't stay two weeks more. I'm going nuts as it is. I can't sleep. I'm losing weight."

"Look, I'm going into town today—to the bank. I'll get you the bonus I promised."

"I 'preciate that, Doctor, but you'll just have to send it to my house."

"If you stay, I'll double the bonus."

The beast was howling now. Kiser stood erect and snapped, "Look at that, Doctor. Listen to that. All day I put up with that. Then at night . . . No, Doctor, today is my last day."

Howell set himself to lunge at the janitor. But then he relaxed. "Moron," he muttered. He snatched his research log off a table and stomped out of the lab.

Beth hollered after him, "Don't forget Mark is coming tonight."

"Another imbecilic macho moron son of a—" The slamming of the lab door cut off the rest.

"Hot as hell," Payne said anonymously.

On the south ramp of Robert Gray Army Airfield, a UH-1H helicopter beat its blades—actually, its rotating wings—against the air, sending pulsations down the skids to quake against the concrete parking pad and rebound back up into the airframe. The cockpit pointed into the early-morning sun. The temperature on the asphalt ramp was ninety-five.

But the helicopter's free air-temp gauge, its probe sticking through the windshield, showed forty-three Celsius—one hundred ten degrees Fahrenheit. Inside was even hotter.

Sweat collected in little vibrating beads on Payne's face. He tried to act indifferently to the heat, though he was anything but indifferent.

"Hot enough to fry," he grumbled aloud—loud enough to be heard half the flight line away if the roars, whines, rattles, and whistles of the Huey hadn't drowned him out. As it was, even he couldn't hear his own voice through the soundproofing of his flight helmet and ear cups.

Preoccupied with the tenacious pounding in his head and the tenuous condition of his stomach, he listened absently to the intercom conversation between the crew chief, Sergeant Stambrough, and the pilot undergoing evaluation, Warrant Officer Larson.

Stambrough sat hunched over the checklist in the jumpseat behind the pilots, reading off the item to be checked. "Inverter switch . . ."

Larson, at the right-side controls, replied with the proper response and performed the action required. "Inverter switch to spare position."

"Engine and transmission oil pressures . . ."

"Check."

"Radios . . ."

"All on."

Payne sat, staring straight ahead, watching Larson's every move in his peripheral vision. A droplet of sweat clung to the end of his nose. He swatted it away. The veneer of indifference wore a little thin on a sweltering day with last night's alcohol percolating through his pores, smelling up the cockpit with the disgusting odor of a hangover. He needed a smoke, something to stifle his sense of smell. He needed to get off the ground, to get his mind off his gut, more so off his throbbing head. So much for drying out at Marble Falls.

Larson struggled with the hydraulic system check. Moving the cyclic without hydraulic assistance was like driving a Lincoln Continental with failed power steering. The feedback through the controls bounced her shoulders as if she were a rag doll.

Mark pressed the boom mike to his lips and mashed the floor intercom button under his boot. This time so he could be heard.

"C'mon PJ, move your ass," he said through a forced grin.

"About ready, sir."

Warrant Officer First Class Pamela Jane Larson caught the flash of even teeth and was not reassured by it. The cold, gray eyes unnerved her. She'd seen the superior look before, in flight school. She thought she'd left it behind after graduation a month ago.

"AC voltmeter . . ." Stambrough said.

She spun the overhead rotating switch to check the spare inverter. "Hundred fifteen volts plus or minus three in each position—Damn," she muttered to herself when a nail snapped inside the Nomex glove.

Stambrough pressed ahead. "Inverter switch . . ."

"Switch off. Check caution light on . . ."

* * *

Damn you, Payne.

Maggie Anzola had warned her he'd be difficult. "Poole is a prick. So is Payne, but you'll get to like him later on."

A lot later, no doubt.

She kept calling back the checklist.

Payne bothered her. He didn't seem to notice her ability or even her presence. Didn't seem to care who was flying this bird or whether it was flying. It was hard enough being a woman pilot without having a stonefaced turd for an IP.

She had the technique, the control touch—that she had proved in flight school. She had the book knowledge, too. Ordinarily, none of that would be a problem for her in flying under the stern gaze of anybody but this guy Payne.

This was one of the flying organizations where women were allowed to serve—the 162nd Aviation Company, The Vultures, a relic of Vietnam, a unit out of the combat training mainstream, an outfit relegated to combat support. The 162nd was a glorified truck company of the air, whose pilots flew Hueys, more relics of the Vietnam era. Real combat units were flying the sleek new Blackhawks. The Blackhawks would out-fly, out-transport, out-gun, out-anything three Hueys.

And she had to land an assignment with these Vultures.

Payne watched her fumble with the remaining electrical checks overhead, exposing a darkening

Nomex armpit. He felt savage satisfaction at the wet-ness—a sign of her discomfort. He could smell her dampness, a perfumed fragrance musked by natural woman scents. He felt a stirring under his lap belt. Indifference became yet a shade harder to maintain.

A loose strand of blond hair fluttered from under her flight helmet. Untidy stuff—thick, wavy bundles of golden filaments. Beautifully untidy. And eyes. Eyes too large to be real, green eyes begging to be stared into, penetrating eyes too often catching his own staring at her, always forcing his gaze to flit away to the realm of indifference, a place he did not especially care for today.

She called out: "Low RPM audio switch to Audio." The alarm *boing-boing-boinged* into the intercom system, warning the crew the engine RPM was below sixty-two hundred. A frightening sound in flight.

"Governor increase-decrease switch to full increase." She tweaked up the button on the collective lever. "Low RPM audio goes off at sixty-two hundred, plus or minus a hundred." Mercifully. "Sixty-seven hundred max RPM, plus or minus fifty." The button was called inker-dinker for the INCR-DECR abbreviation on the console label. During power changes, the inker-dinker would maintain a constant flight RPM.

Her full lips were chapped. He thought he saw the redness that might mark the onset of a cold sore.

"RPM sixty-six hundred."

He saw a couple of angry pimples incubating on the point of her chin. Probably starting her period. . . .

Christ, why are you looking for fault? he asked himself.

An IP's nature, he answered. *Bullshit,* he countered. *Objection. Sustained. Who really gives a shit? Forget it.*

If you can.

She lifted the collective pitch lever. The rotor blades began catching air and washing it down over the craft. A blast of freshness swept through the cabin as the toes of the skids lifted. The moving air chilled their bodies as sweat evaporated; hers sweet, his stale. The Huey wobbled, scraping the heel of the left skid against the concrete. With a final tug on the collective, she broke the bonds of gravity and sent the craft four feet into a hover in the air. She moved the cyclic control stick in slow, small circles between her knees, balancing the rotor system atop an invisible cushion of air.

She hovered the Huey forward, following the yellow line that led to the takeoff spot. Tower cleared the Huey for a south departure.

The Huey shuddered as the rotor began screwing into undisturbed air. PJ climbed out at five hundred feet a minute and seventy knots. Her palms were cold and wet. Her whole body chilled at the cooler altitude and at the thrill of nailing down the takeoff perfectly. Beautiful start. Army aviation was beautiful. The dark-green juniper-covered earth, brilliantly highlighted by the arc-light of the sun, spread itself as far as she could see until it merged with the misty horizon. Texas was jade-beautiful. God, she loved it.

She turned, smiling to confirm her feelings with the captain.

"You forgot the HIT test."

The engine health indicator test. Her smile vanished.

Stuck it to her. Inwardly, he grinned savagely.

He watched Manere Mountain slide by as it had hundreds of times before. He wondered how he could have landed blackout on it weeks ago and missed the pole up there. Texans called it a mountain. In Montana, a piss ant mound like that wouldn't even rate a name other than Piss Ant Hill. Texas was full of piss ants. Ditto army aviation. God, this was boring.

He shook his head, waving off the nausea. He stole a glance at her. *Nice—no, pretty—come on, she's beautiful —Who's kidding who? Or was it whom?*

What was wrong lately?

His left hand played over the collective lever, toying with the inker-dinker. His mind took a walk outside where the fresh air let him think better.

When he looked again, she was flying nude, utterly buck-ass naked. For a second, it occurred to him that flying without the fire-retardant Nomex suit and gloves could be dangerous or at least against safety regs. But then her dangerous green eyes bored into his own, asking a question. She raised her eyebrows. He knew the question being asked. Yes, he said with his own eyes. Yes, let's join the Mile-High Club.

He threw off his seatbelt and shoulder straps and clambered over the radio console to the rear. Stambrough was gone—where, he didn't care. He grabbed a blanket—it was handy, right there in the cargo area —and spread it on the deck. Then, hands shaking, he broke the safety wires on the quick release handles and tilted her seat back.

Shit, there was even a bottle of wine, iced and stuck into an empty slot in the pedestal panel. Did Stambrough think of that before he left? Damned considerate of him. Her nipples were hard, sort of miniature Manere Mountains telling him it was not time for wine but for other, more urgent matters. Maybe later, he decided.

She closed her eyes. He kissed her eyelids, then her cheekbones. She reached for him. He pulled her from the seat and laid her on the blanket, her eyes still closed, their faces together so he could inhale her intoxicating breath. He started to unzip his flight suit with one hand—how she'd gotten undressed without his noticing, he didn't know—but she pulled him close so he couldn't work the zipper. For a moment, he was self-conscious about his rancid body and hangover breath.

That concern vanished as the warmth of her body penetrated his uniform. She slid a knee between his legs and shot her tongue between his lips. Instantly he knew he'd never last until he got out of his clothes. Goddammit, he was going to shoot his load. A hair trigger. Wet pants.

If this got out, he'd never live it down.

He struggled to pull away—so at least she wouldn't feel his member convulsing against her leg. But she held him fast. He was reaching the point where he wouldn't even fight it when it occurred to him that nobody was flying the helicopter.

He jerked his head away from hers. God, this was a replay of that night with Poole.

The helicopter's nose began tipping high and right.

He lurched, going for the controls.

She held him fast. "I need you." Her eyes pleaded.

His orgasm was coming.

"Let me go," he said, torn between the instinctive will to live and the desperate need to have an orgasm. "We're going to die. We're—"

He saw the engine and rotor RPM begin to unwind.

She began writhing against him.

The *boing-boing-boinnnng* of the low RPM audio told him they were going to fall from the sky and die. Hell with it. Hell with dinner at Beth's tonight—he didn't like his brother-in-law, Howell, anyway. Who gives a shit? he said—and meant it.

He let the orgasm come.

"How'd I do?" she asked.

"Great," he murmured.

"Captain?"

He opened his eyes, expecting to see the earth rushing up to meet him. Instead, he found himself looking into her emerald eyes. She was fully dressed, sitting in the pilot's seat where she belonged. And he sat where he belonged, a wet spot growing cold against his leg.

"How'd I do?" she asked again.

"Huh?"

"The forced landing. How'd I do?"

"Uh, fine. Certainly satisfactory," he said to her.

Great, he said to himself.

Great for a degenerate. A goddamned degenerate. He almost wished they'd crashed.

He lit a Kool and pulled desperately hard, filling his lungs with choking hot-cold smoke, an after-sex treat he couldn't deny himself.

Fucking degenerate.

Later, she went through the shutdown on the parking pad. As the exhaust temperature stabilized, she recorded flight time and fuel in the aircraft logbook. He scribbled on a kneeboard, recording the evaluation results. She saw Poole zipping out in *Shitbird*, weaving among rows of parked helicopters toward them. He locked the brakes, skidding to a stop beneath the whipping rotors of UH-1H 96257. He stepped up onto the toe of the helicopter's skid to shout something at Payne, who peeled away the ear cup of his helmet in order to hear. Payne shouted something back. Poole stepped onto the jeep's seat and dropped down to sit.

Payne freed himself from the harness. Before breaking the connection on his helmet cord, he said, "Larson, we got a ship down south of here. I have to go out with Poole and talk to the crew. What do you say we debrief your ride when I get back? It'll be a short debriefing—you were nearly perfect anyhow. Can you meet me at the club around five?"

"Yes, sir. . . ."

He broke the connection and leapt onto *Shitbird*'s rear seat. Poole took off before he could sit and nearly sent him reeling over the back. PJ grasped the cyclic to level the rotor plane. Although the blade tip cut its path nearly thirteen feet above the ground, she knew it could dip as low as seven feet nine inches. Low enough to take the head off a man standing in the back of a jeep.

" 'Nearly perfect . . . Meet me around five,' " she said aloud to herself, trying out his words. It was impossible for her to suppress a smile. She'd beaten his best shot—dropping engine RPM with the inker-dinker. And she had done it perfectly. She could hardly wait to talk to Maggie Anzola.

The two women pilots sat inside the dank West Fort Officers' Club, PJ talking excitedly about her checkride.

Maggie interrupted, "There's more to this than a checkride, PJ. You got the hots for Payne. It's written all over your face. When you talk about him you start banging your knees together."

PJ reddened. "Come on," she whispered. "He's too crude."

"And too much your platoon leader, which makes it illegal to jump into the sack with him."

"Yes."

"So why you got the hots for him?"

PJ gave her an exasperated look. "Let's get a drink."

"Let's get laid."

"My God, you're as bad as Payne and his pals."

"And I suppose you're a virgin." PJ's redness deepened. "Sorry. I'll buy the first round. And don't order a goddamn Grasshopper or something."

"Why not?"

"They wouldn't know how to make it. Besides"—
her eyes reflected the twinkle of a Lone Star neon
clock—"nobody wants to lay a woman with Grass-
hoppers on her breath."

8

Howell's Pinto had barely rattled out of earshot before Kiser started his final chores with the beast. He planned to do no more than the minimum—hose the bastard down, throw in fresh food, lift the drop gate so it could pass into the clean cell.

Kiser stood behind a barrier of smeared acrylic, hosing the empty cell longer than necessary. He was screwing up his courage.

The beast sulked in a corner of the dirty cell of the cage, not even protesting the water spray. It just sat. Watching. If his luck held, Kiser knew he might finish without having to suffer another tantrum. Finally, he shut the nozzle off, unlocked the padlock, entered the clean cell, and poured dry dog food into the pan.

From behind him came a thunderous crash and snap, launching Kiser toward the hinged cell door. He didn't even glance over his shoulder. Outside, he slipped on the wet lab floor but caught himself and slammed the door shut, threw the hasp over its loop and dropped the padlock into the steel loop. His heart pounded in his chest; his injured finger stung.

In the other cell the beast was swinging from the

cage roof. It drew back its hooves and sent them
smashing into the Plexiglas bolted to the drop gate.
The panel snapped again and fell into the cell that
Kiser had just vacated.

No harm. Just another scare. Kiser thanked heaven
that he was quitting today. No more scares. No more
nightmares. *Hell with this.* He decided he wouldn't
even wait for Howell to come back from town. He'd
just finish up here and walk away.

The beast shrieked in triumph. It hung by one paw
from the cage roof and put its free paw beneath its
rump.

Kiser had seen the move before. He dived away
from the cage door to the Plexiglas barrier just as the
beast's filth plastered the acrylic wall in front of his
face. Its scream ended in a series of yelps.

Kiser's blood gelled. He wondered what all this
fear must be doing to his heart. He edged around the
barrier to the middle of the cage, never taking his
eyes from the beast. He unlocked the sliding bar that
kept the drop gate down.

The animal returned his stare.

The janitor drew the bar out. The beast dropped to
the cage floor, crouching, anticipating the raising of
the drop gate and passage to the clean cell.

It's stupid to be doing this, he told himself. Nobody
would blame him if he just walked away and left the
bastard hungry.

When the bar was out, he edged back around the
wall and took a deep breath. The worst was over. For
the final time, all he had to do was raise the drop gate,
let the beast through to the clean side of the cage,

drop the gate, replace the slide bar, and walk out of the lab. It made him giddy to think of it. The last damned time.

He walked to the far wall. He took a rope end from a hook on the wall and began pulling hand over hand. The rope wormed its way through block and tackle, and the drop gate crawled up its channel. The beast, its eyes on the gate, flattened, ready to leap through the hole.

It was the first time Kiser ever remembered the beast not staring at him.

A simple mental error—that was all it was. A little slip.

The first instruction was: Never, never leave either cage door open. Not for a minute, even if the cell was empty. And Kiser never did. He had closed the door. But . . . he had just dashed away from the flying excrement . . . he shot a glance at the far cell door where . . . the open padlock hung on the closed hasp.

His reaction took only an instant. He dropped the rope and ran along the Plexiglas wall. The drop gate fell, rasping through the channels of metal, the rope sluicing through the pulleys. A hundred and twenty pounds of iron would clang against iron. Kiser had heard it dozens of times. He prayed for the sound. Just one more time.

The beast sprang as Kiser released the rope.

There was the sound of one hundred twenty pounds of metal against fur, flesh, and bones. The beast squealed so horribly that Kiser was electrified.

He glanced back at the drop gate. It had fallen on

its goat legs. Kiser giggled at the animal's pain. Great. Now he could make it to the lock in time.

But, just as in his nightmares, time seemed to slow down. The beast clawed at the cage bottom, pulling itself through.

The monster howled as the bottom edge of the gate drew its blood. Kiser saw that the thing was actually skinning itself, tearing the hide off the backs of its legs under the angular edge of the drop gate. A scream rose in Kiser's throat.

Just as in the dream.

He wanted to wake up screaming in bed. "Eva," he screamed. He felt hot tears filling his eyes, blinding him.

Eva had not awakened him by the time he reached the end of the acrylic wall. As he turned, he slipped on the filth. On all fours, he looked up. The gate still held the beast's hooves. Bloody fur and flesh lay stripped off the backs of its legs like socks around its ankles.

Tears blocked Kiser's vision as he lunged for the lock.

The shrieks turned to a roar.

Iron clanked against iron.

His hand closed on the padlock. All that was needed was a twist and a push. Then dive away. A twist and a push—that was all. Why didn't Eva awaken him?

A twist and a—

—set of daggers closed on Kiser's hand, crushing it, piercing it through the back and out the palm. He felt bones snap. His screams went up in unison with a triumphant screech from the beast. He tried to wrench free. The animal threw the hand back at him, hitting him in the face with the sodden mess of flesh and bones. Kiser looked down in thankful, dazed disbelief. The animal had not torn the hand off. It was still connected to his arm. He was alive. Oh, there was blood pouring down the wrist. And the ring finger dangled by a thread of sinew, but it could be reattached, and the flattened oval could be made into a spherical wedding band again. The important thing was that he had not been killed.

A spear of translucent white bone stuck out of his palm. Funny thing—it didn't hurt, even though the web between his thumb and hand was split to the wrist and the thumb lay back along his sleeve. It would mend.

At least he was alive.

He tried the fingers. They wouldn't work. The bloody padlock was imbedded in the torn palm of his hand. That was the reason he couldn't work the fingers. That . . .

He looked up. The hasp was open.

The beast backed away from the door and stood erect on its goat legs, horns knocking on the cage roof.

Kiser struggled to his feet and threw himself against the door.

The beast crow-hopped forward, toppling headfirst toward him.

Kiser dug at the padlock with his good hand. It

came free of his palm, and he went for the metal loop of the hasp.

"God help me," he cried.

God didn't.

Kiser wasn't even close with the lock. The beast hit the door squarely with its horns, two hundred fifty pounds driven by the pistons of its rear legs. The door blasted open.

Kiser flew across the lab like a stuffed doll and landed sitting against the wall. His glasses had flown off, but he saw a dark form coming, heard the tap-dance of hooves, the clatter of reptile claws on the tile. Just as in the nightmare.

The sphincters in Kiser's bladder and anus let go as he screamed till his voice broke, then he began to cry.

The beast cuffed the helpless form, raking the lower ribs clean and pink, opening flaps of belly flesh and the peritoneumlike tent doors, exposing shiny coils of mottled intestines.

For a moment—just one—the beast felt something like contentment. But that passed and its hunger for harm returned, like a flame leaping up from banked embers.

9

Beth Howell, standing at the farthest stock pen from the clinic, heard the beast shrieking. She glanced at her watch. Five o'clock. Feeding time. Silently, she thanked Kiser for taking care of the beast.

Were there two screams there? No.

She turned her attention to the Shetland mare.

The Shetland muzzled her belly through wooden slats, lipping the tail of her blouse. Beth let it tickle her; felt the hot breath. She wondered how the shaggy mare could endure the heat. It was her mare. Her special friend, the only one she had who always listened and never talked back. The perfect companion.

"Want me to wet you down?" she asked the animal.

The mare tossed her head and danced in a circle. She whinnied in her throat, a shrill hiss.

Beth turned and walked back toward the lab, her pink skirt flying. As she strode past the goat pens, the animals stampeded in short rushes from one side of their enclosure to the other. It was the time of day for all the animals to be keyed up. The thing in the lab. It was time to get rid of it. What if some of the customers, the farmers and ranchers, came during one of these rages?

As she neared the clinic, she heard a thump against the inside wall of the lab. There was a scream. A man's scream, she was sure of that. She broke into a run and burst through a side door to the garage, where dogs, cats, and rabbits in the back shop were dashing around in their cages in a dozen separate frenzies. There was a din of barking and whining. Their panic infected her.

Her stomach tightened. She felt ill. No telling what Kiser had done. Another wound? Maybe he had lost an arm this time.

She burst from the back shop into the clinic office, once an entry and family room. On the left was the customer entrance. To the right at the end of a counter was the laboratory door. She couldn't hear anything except the racket. Beth put her hand on the doorknob to the lab and hesitated. It took all her will to turn and push.

Her eyes swept the scene even as the stench of the beast and the muggy fog of a hot, bloody smell hit her in the face. Empty cage. Door open. Blood spatters. Shaggy hide, bloody flaps of skin hanging from goat legs.

Three sounds pierced the heavy air of the lab. Beth's scream, at the sight of Kiser leaning against the wall, drenched in blood. Next came a hiss from Kiser's body as the beast whipped its head around, jerking a yard of bowel from the man's abdomen. Finally, the shriek of the beast as it whirled to attack.

She slammed the door and shot the bolt.

Clattering hooves slipped on the tiles.

She went for the safe against the wall at the end of the counter. She fumbled with the dial, and opened the door.

The creature bashed into the wooden exit.

A glance over her shoulder. The door held, but a horn pierced it about eighteen inches from the floor. Claws and hooves battered the door, and the horn disappeared into the lab, taking a slat of wood.

She found the trank gun.

Heavy hammering: Beast at the door; her heart against her ribs.

CO_2 cartridge slammed home.

Another hole in the door, horns twisting and pulling.

Syringe.

A chunk of the door ripped away.

Twice the needed dose to put a horse down. She kept pulling. Twice again the dose. Kill it once and for all.

Claws and fangs ripping away at the hole. The head nearly through; the stench pouring out of the lab.

"Damn," she said as she dropped the dart. Damn, damn, dammit.

The head and horns out. A blizzard of splinters and dust. One shoulder nearly through.

Fumbling. The gun loaded. Aimed at the hole.

The empty hole.

* * *

Nothing remained but the ragged hole in the door and her own ragged breath. There was silence except for her heart pounding. No, the racket of the small animals was still there. The mare's whinny from the back of the yard drifted up to the clinic. Had they been making that much noise all along? Had she been deaf to it? Or was the beast outside in the back, stirring up the livestock?

No, it must be in the lab. She would have heard it breaking out a window. Wouldn't she? No, the windows were too small. Weren't they?

She shouldn't have gone for the trank gun. She should have run for the trailer to get the shotgun. The tranquilizer would take several seconds to work even if she hit the beast in the chest.

In the back shop, the animals flew into another outburst. God, maybe the beast was coming through there. She had to make a run for it. Out the front door. To the Ford.

She crouched and gathered her strength, gathered her courage for a leap past the hole in the door.

Inside the lab, the rage continued, but quietly, inside the beast. It crouched, waiting, excited by its freedom, aroused by its kill, barely feeling the hurt of its skinned legs.

It heard the animals raising their alarm outside. It would destroy them. After the woman. The beast could smell her scent mixed with fear, could hear her ragged breathing.

There was the squeak of a rubber sole on the tile.

The beast coiled its sinews.

It sprang at a shadow that darkened the hole in the door.

As Beth leaped to the end of the counter, trank gun held high, she heard that rattling on the tile. It was in there.

She reversed herself.

The beast tore the hole wider as he squirted through. Beth saw a paw slashing at her canvas sandal. Her foot was slung aside and she fell awkwardly to the floor. A sharp pain shot through her knee. Blood welled out of a slice in the canvas. She swung the trank gun.

The beast scrabbled its claws on the tile, dragging its hind quarters through the hole.

The muzzle came around as it gathered its bloodied legs under it. It leaped.

She fired. A heavy paw swept the gun barrel aside.

She saw the dart sticking in the horned crown of its forehead, flopping loosely. Uselessly.

An instant before their heads met, she smelled its hot, wretched breath. There was a fragmentary memory of her once cutting open a bloated cow and vomiting as the putrid gases hit her.

This time, she passed out before she had time to vomit.

Suddenly Mark awakened as if from a daydream. But this was no dream. He was staring into the maw of an agitated tiger baring its fangs at him.

"Ole Sambo don't like to be disturbed."

Mark spun to face the voice. He nearly fell.

The owner of the voice was a wiry little man with

a tough, crooked smile. He looked stringy, his leathery skin barely hiding fibrous muscle.

"Son," said the man, pointing to a hand-painted sign, "the zoo is closed." The sign identified this as Mack Dodson's Roadside Zoo Attraction and Wild Animal Kingdom. Admission $1.

"How'd I get here?" His dry throat squeaked on the words.

"I din't lock the gate yet, son. You can stay awhile if you like."

"No, I . . ." Payne fumbled in his pocket and withdrew a dollar.

"On the house, son."

"No, I . . . never mind . . . I was on the way to . . . the Howell's vet clinic when I got . . . side-tracked."

"Just across the road there a ways you head north."

"I know how to get there. I just . . ."

"Well, y'all come back anytime. Mack Dodson's my name."

"Mark Payne," he muttered.

Mark let Dodson shake his hand. He walked past the double-wide trailer and found his Z28 parked in the gravel lot next to State Road 36. But how did his Camaro get there? There had been plenty of mornings he'd driven in a daze and arrived at work without remembering the journey. And there'd been far too many instances of closing the officers' club and awakening to the alarm next morning without remembering getting home.

But this was different: From the Cove to Beth's was a thirty-mile drive around the north side of the fort and anything but routine; and two beers did not a drunken stupor make. This was ridiculous.

He mentally backtracked, trying to recount events since leaving the club—he glanced at the dashboard digital—nearly an hour and a half ago. Christ, what had he done?

You stalked out of the club, he told himself. *You must have showered and changed because you don't stink anymore and the clothes are civilian. You . . . woke up at a two-bit zoo a mile from Flat, Texas. . . .*

Nothing in between. Not a damned thing. No memory of feeding Shep—He flicked on the dome light and spotted a couple of silver-tipped black hairs on his thighs. He must have fed the dog and wrestled it around the backyard, but—nothing.

He backtracked to the club, to slugging down that second beer, to . . . nothing. He couldn't trick himself past that spot.

He backtracked further—maybe if he had a running start. To the perverted checkride, the erection. Next thing you know it was a wet dream. *God, daydreaming an orgasm.* He went through events after landing. Okay there—he remembered it all. Going to the club. Okay there—he remembered his anticipation at meeting the woman of his daydream. There was the disappointment of walking in and finding her surrounded by other pilots. That made him mad.

Then downing that beer. Then . . .

Nothing until the tiger staring him in the face.

God, two spells in one day.

Then he arrived at his sister's.

The crunch of gravel under oversized tires in the

rural Texas driveway announced his coming. A set of
furry ears perked at the snapping rocks; sounds carrying half a mile through the humid air. A massive
head swiveled, trailing strings of pink spit across the
blackening junipers, and zeroed in on the noise. A
pair of eyes, black beads rimmed in yellow, peered
into the deepening shadows. Unable to see even a
hundred yards into the scrub and mesquite, the eyes
—guided by the ears and driven by an instinctive hatred—began homing in the direction of the sounds.

Mark had arrived late. Too late for dinner. Too late
for swigging sun tea out back. Too late to watch the
Texas sundown, murky as a Tequila Sunrise.

He opened the door and threw his feet out of his
Z28. The evening air mugged him with its ninety-
three degrees and seventy percent humidity. And
with its deathly strong stench.

Something was wrong here.

It was twilight, yet there were no lights on. Beth's
clinic and her husband's lab were both dark. Even the
mobile home a few yards away from the building was
dark.

By itself, that was no big deal, but Payne was late
and bossy baby sister, Beth, had not run out to meet
him as she had always done. It was her ritual. She'd
always met him with a hug and some wisecrack. But
not today. So he began to worry, concern seeping
through his veneer of indifference.

The capper, though, was the stench—The Stench.
It was like what he'd experienced in Vietnam, when
he solved the case of Dak Lo's missing orphans by
sticking his head down the well of the village's or-

phanage. Since then, his olfactory memory would not forget the fragrance of death. And this was it.

Suddenly he cared a lot. He started running toward the mobile home just as a pair of headlights stabbed him in the back.

Howell had wheeled the rusted-out Pinto southward, at its top speed of sixty, through the gathering mist toward home. The car, oxidized from baby blue to white, growled its disapproval through a holey muffler.

The banker—*arrogant prick*—had merely snuffed at Howell and his Pinto. "Yes, sir, Mr. Howell, I don't doubt that it's completely paid for. But it can't secure much of a loan."

"Yes, but if you add it in with the clinic and the trailer . . ."

"Yes, sir, but the equity is still too small because you refinanced so recently. Surely, you understand we can't go as high as you want."

"Ten thousand isn't so high for the Gatesville Bank, is it?"

"No, sir, it ain't so high for the bank." Emphasis on bank.

Howell had spent the rest of the afternoon phoning from a coin drop in a dank bar. Already sickened by Gates and the sweet smell of three-quarters of a century's spilt beer, he grew sicker every time somebody failed to answer the numbers dialed from a special section of his journal. Even sicker when somebody would answer and fail to remember his name. Especially sicker when even fewer somebodies did remember Warren Howell and still left him hanging . . .

* * *

Yes, Howell, I remember you. . . . Click.
You got a load of nerve calling me, Warren. . . . Click.
Leave me alone you poor, sick bastard. . . . Click.

. . . before he could even degrade himself by begging for money.

The Pinto bounded into the driveway. In his headlights, Howell saw first the red Camaro and then his brother-in-law. For a moment he considered hitting up Payne for some money. Then it occurred to him that something must be wrong. There were no lights on but the backyard floods.

There could be a million simple explanations. Beth could have been called out to mend a calf. . . . Kiser might have left before dark. . . . If that shit-for-brains moron had screwed up . . .

Instinctively, he reached under the seat to touch the hard cover of his worn journal.

Mark Payne wheeled to face the Pinto's cross-eyed headlights—left beam pointing down and in, the right aiming high. He felt a little sheepish for worrying. Beth had probably been on a call.

The four-banger engine shuddered and went silent. The lights stayed on. A metal hinge groaned and a door slammed shut.

"Hey, Beth, I must have the wrong night for dinner, eh?"

"It's me."

"Oh. Warren. Beth's not with you?" His neck hairs tingled.

"No. She's . . . supposed to be here. You check inside the trailer?"

Howell's slender figure passed in front of the headlights. His gaze was fixed on the clinic door.

"No, I just got here myself. You suppose the electricity is out?"

"No, the floods are on out back."

"God, what's that smell?"

Howell, eyes riveted on the clinic, said, "You got a gun, Mark?"

"Not on me, Warren. I don't usually pack a gun to dinner, for chrissake. Why would I need a gun?" The skin on his neck percolated into goose flesh. "What the hell is going on, Howell?"

"I've got a twelve-gauge in the trailer. C'mon," he said, his voice shaky.

He stepped out with Howell toward the trailer.

Mark yanked him back by a bony shoulder. "Where's Beth, you sonofabitch?"

"Goddamn it, Payne, I don't know," he muttered. "She was here when I left this morning. She was fine. Took the afternoon off to cook for you. Now suppose we stop playing twenty questions and find her."

The yellowing Pinto's lights threw the men's shadows ahead. As they approached the trailer, their shadows slithered over the hood of the Ford pickup and crept up the warped aluminum walls near the doorway. The open doorway.

And once at the steps, Mark saw that the door,

built to swing out, had been bashed—frame and all—into the room.

"What the hell?" he whispered.

They leaned up against the wall and peered into the darkness inside. A rancid, gassy, eye-tearing odor —different from the smell of death yet mingled with it—hit them.

"Dear God," Howell said. He reached inside for a light switch. *He seems to know what he'll find*, thought Mark.

Howell knew indeed what he would find. The knot in the pit of his stomach told him something had gone wrong. Yet again. Somebody had been hurt. Again. Just as with that damned dog three years ago. That goddamned fucking black dog.

Pausing less than a quarter mile away from the clinic, the yellow-rimmed eyes strained to catch a glimpse of the men whose scents now reached the dilating nostrils in wisps. They were scents it would not forget. Its eyes saw no farther than before. But the ears could hear voices muffled by the brush. Prodded by a seething rage, the dark bulk adjusted its course and pressed on directly toward the sounds, growing even further enraged as the acrid man-smell strengthened. Its course was straight as it moved on all fours. It was not a stealthy approach. The thing mindlessly pushed through the strands of juniper, snapping off dead branches as thick as ax handles, ignoring the nettles. Occasionally it would rise erect to its seven-foot height to regain its bearings or to crash over the largest bushes. It knew no fear, had no natural enemies—though every living thing was its enemy. It knew of nothing it could not kill.

Mark shoved Howell aside and stepped into the trailer's living room—what had been the living room. There was utter destruction: the wall opposite the door bashed out as if the implement driven through the opening had been unable to stop; furniture slashed, its padding scattered, one wooden chair splintered, another thrown against the wall so hard that a leg had penetrated the paneling. It hung there like an art-deco sculpture. The carpet had been wadded into ripples. And everything was spotted with black slime.

Wordlessly, Howell slipped past him toward the back rooms, climbing over the toppled refrigerator. The kitchen was trashed—cupboards bashed and splintered, glass shards everywhere; appliances thrown about; phone receiver missing, mount hanging by one thread of wire from the wall; paneling torn away to expose insulation, cheap studs and wiring. The remnants of a meal—Tex-Mex, by the paprika-red looks of it—splattered everything. Water squirted somewhere beneath the sink, askew in its setting. Mark smelled natural gas. He looked behind the range, wrenched from its slot in the counter, and saw the flex hose torn from its fitting ahead of the shutoff valve. If the open door had not ventilated the trailer, he reasoned, the invisible spark from contacts inside the light switch might have set off an explosion.

Howell picked his way back through the rubble in

the hallway. He carried a double-barreled shotgun in one hand and half a dozen loose green cartridges in the other.

"She's not back there," he said, fumbling to break open the gun, dropping several shells.

"Not under a bed or in a closet?"

"No." Howell snapped the gun open.

"The clinic?" Mark saw a pained expression flash across his brother-in-law's face. Howell jammed two shells into the breech, the rest into a pants pocket.

Howell swallowed hard. "Yes. Must be in the clinic."

Mark saw Howell soften for a moment. He was about to tell him what he knew. But the expression hardened again.

"I'll check the clinic," Howell said. "You check the animals out back. Maybe she's feeding."

"Bullshit. She wouldn't be feeding out back while a . . . tornado was destroying the trailer." He swept his arm at the kitchen. "What the hell are you thinking? I'm going with you."

"Suit yourself."

"You got another gun?"

"No."

"Never mind. Let's move. Where's a wrench and where's the gas meter? I've got to shut off the leak in here."

Howell snapped the shotgun closed. "In the Ford."

Outside, Mark retrieved an adjustable wrench from a chest in the bed of the pickup. He noticed his brother-in-law's hands shaking.

He didn't scorn Howell's fright. His own chest had

tightened. All his senses tingled as adrenaline trickled into his bloodstream.

Howell motioned for Mark to follow. He led the way to a stand of short junipers beside the garage. Kiser's dilapidated Volkswagen blocked the darkened garage entrance. Howell pointed past the van to the bushes.

Mark saw the meter squatting in the darkness. He wished he had a flashlight. Bending over, he groped for the shutoff valve with his left hand and found it. As he was bringing the wrench and the valve together, Braille fashion, it occurred to him that the animals inside weren't raising hell as they did every other time he'd approached the garage.

Why no yapping dogs? he was about to ask.

There was a sudden crunch of gravel. Of somebody lunging. The flash and heat and explosion of the shotgun. A massive injection of adrenaline to make him recoil. Not quick enough to spare him a crushing blow behind the left ear. Flash of lights inside the head. Or was it another shotgun blast? Enough adrenaline to keep him semiconscious. Or was he dreaming?

He collapsed in a heap, was aware of juniper prickles stinging his face, couldn't move, could only hear—and feel the contents of his stomach rising.

Goddamned Howell. *He's done something to Beth*, Mark thought. *And now he's shot me in the head. Dead for certain.* He marveled at how little pain he felt, at how he didn't fear death. So this was the out-of-body experience he'd read about. He had hoped for better than this.

* * *

Mark swam from dream to dream. He couldn't be sure of reality. He thought he heard a hoarse whisper, a command.

Somebody tried to choke him. The mind told the body to fight back, but it would not answer the command. Goddammit.

But he was not choking, after all. He was being dragged by the collar. Over one of those damned prickly junipers. Through the garage. He tried to open his eyes to see exactly where he was. Either they wouldn't open or it was too dark to see anything. The smell of death hit him again.

He knew he was being dragged into the clinic. The death-smell grew even stronger than it had been in the trailer. His stomach convulsed, and he gagged on his vomit. Then he smelled gasoline, remarkably refreshing by comparison. He heard footsteps; the sounds of grunting, wheezing. He wished he could get his hands on Howell one last time, not just to save himself from being murdered but to avenge his sister —he knew with certainty that Howell had killed her. No doubt for the insurance money.

From far off, he heard the irregular blasts of tanks and artillery firing on the ranges of Fort Hood. Then a car spit gravel as it roared away.

Seconds later—or was it hours?—a flash of light blinded him through his eyelids, which filtered it red. A blast shook the clinic, breaking glass somewhere, blowing a gale of air hot and dry enough to mean only one thing—fire.

Mark saw himself burning to death, his flesh splitting like an overgrilled frankfurter. The vision shot a jolt of adrenaline into him. He jackknifed up to a sitting position and saw the reality of the fire. He grasped his head to arrest its spinning.

He took inventory. He was in the reception area of the clinic. The door to the garage was open. The wet floor reflected the burning trailer's skeleton, a blown-apart silhouette against a background of orange. The very ground was afire; a trail of fire snaking across the driveway toward the clinic.

The smell of gasoline shot him to his feet. He weaved to the counter to steady himself. He felt his head behind the ear, half expecting his hand to find a bloody crater. But there was only a knot, hard and tender—a golf ball implant. Goddamned Howell. The shotgun must have gone off when he smacked him with the barrel. Somewhere nearby a smoke detector rang incessantly. Or was the ringing inside his head? He chewed his tongue, working up moisture to spit out the bitterness.

The burning trail reached the wet garage floor and went up, exploding into a lake of fire, knocking him to his knees. He climbed to his feet, groped his way across the reception area and tried the front door. Locked. He fumbled with the deadbolt; felt above the doorjamb for the key but didn't find it.

Smoke poured into the room, hovered at the ceiling, and began working its way down. He dropped to his knees to find breathable air. He remembered a ring of keys kept behind the counter. He crawled that way. The flickering illumination showed the lab door with a hole bashed through the bottom panel. And—

he could feel and smell it—an invisible torrent of natural gas poured through the hole. He was groping around inside a bomb.

Behind the counter, something detonated inside him, an implosion of breath and pain, an involuntary gasp drawing smoke and gas into his lungs.

A woman in a patterned skirt. No, a pink skirt drenched in blood, half torn from her body. It couldn't be, but it was.

Beth. She lay on her back, legs splayed out, the sides of her feet lying unnaturally flat on the floor, one foot bloodied. Her head was turned, resting in a blackening pool that had spread from her hair, her matted hair, hair glued to the floor. He turned her chin and saw the face had been smashed. Blood oozed from the nose and squirted from her mouth when his fingers closed on the cheeks. Two trickles of watery blood, like pink tears, ran from her eyes. Beth's forehead was that of Cro-Magnon—flattened, even concave. Her eyebrows crowded down over her puffed eyes.

Forgetting where he was, he stood up to leave, to vomit again.

The cloud from the ceiling had descended to the counter top. It seared his face. In moments he knew he'd be out from the gases. Minutes later, he thought his clothes might burst into flames about the same time as the curtains. Then he'd fry, just as he dreamed.

Beyond Beth he saw the open office safe. No money, Beth had said, just a good place to secure drugs. He sidestepped Beth and hugged the safe.

Bending low, feeling the pull on his back, he tried to step back over her. His weighted heel crunched a hand, and he let out a sob.

He choked back his pain—no time to worry about broken fingers. Crouching, partly in, partly out of the cloud, he ran at the front door with the safe. Steel smashed into the oak. He felt it give a little on the second bash. Again and again he hit it. He felt the fingers of his right hand go numb. Still he ran at the door.

Finally the door frame separated from the house. Just a slit, a splinter of space, opened with the squeal of framing nails. One more blow.

He dropped the safe and crawled through the cloud to Beth. He grasped an ankle and saw the little finger on his right hand had grown to double its size. Funny, it didn't hurt. As he pulled her out, the shreds of her dress separated from her body. He was ashamed for her. Her belly and chest were ripped and bleeding. He began to cry.

He dragged her clear by the ankle, cradled her to his chest and literally threw their combined weight at the door. With a final screech, the nails gave way and the door crashed outward. They lay flat on the front porch as oxygen rushed into the reception area. A minor explosion blew the pair off the porch. An instant later the gas-filled lab went up in a major blast.

The first explosion blinded the yellow-rimmed eyes. The burst of fire dropped the black form in its tracks. A minute later, eyes readjusted, the beast saw a pair of humans drop onto the front porch.

It moved in to tear them apart.

The clinic erupted.

The ball of fire billowed into the sky, bathing all of the Leon River valley below King Mountain in a momentary orange glow. The blast set the beast's hair to smoking and scorched its eyes as it blew it off its hooves. It stood up and roared, defying the fire. The fire roared back. The thing had finally discovered something to fear; found something it could not kill. It felt the threat of fire. The beast turned and melted into the blackness, stumbling and crashing among the junipers, half blinded by the light, the heat, and its rage.

Moving southwest, it was scrambling up the foot of the escarpment, King Mountain, by the time the first curious pilots swooped their helicopter over the burning clinic and trailer to investigate.

Mark landed on Beth next to the Z28. The second explosion set a patch of Beth's exposed hair smoking. Mark slapped the fire out, then put his hand on the car bumper to steady himself, scorching his palm. He stood up bewildered. He spun around drunkenly on his feet, looking for the apparition he thought he had seen just before the explosion.

There was nothing. The intense heat took his breath away.

He picked up Beth and carried her to the end of the driveway. Behind him he heard roaring and growling. He turned but saw only the fire.

Beth uttered a little moan.

His skin felt tight.

When the night air seemed freezing by comparison to the fire, he put Beth gently beneath a majestic pecan tree, a golden torch, its leaves reflecting the glowing fires.

He started back toward the house to try to reconstruct the apparition, the nightmare, the . . . whatever it was. But a wave of dizziness hit him.

He blacked out, crumpling in a heap not far from his sister.

> "... the beast that ascendeth out of the bottomless pit shall make war against them and shall overcome them, and kill them ...."
>
> —Revelation 11:7

BOOK II

THE BEGINNING ENDS

1

Two men labored in the harsh metallic glow of a mercury vapor bulb near the double-wide trailer. Both were tall—one thin and graceful enough to pass for a college basketball player; the other big-gutted enough to look like he was smuggling basketballs.

The animals picked up the men's agitation, prowling and growling, reacting to the scent of gasoline spiked with acrid traces of smoke. A lioness coughed as she paced behind bars. An adult male tiger, bounded from side to side, hissing and rumbling. Not-So-Gentle Ben snuffed and grunted more like a pig than a silvertip grizzly bear.

The "basketball player" slipped from cage to cage, picking locks one by one until the animals became too restive. The "basketball smuggler," eschewing stealth, then finished up by inserting the tip of a pointed crowbar into each padlock's loop and lowering his two hundred sixty-five pounds. The locks were strong, but the cast-iron hasp loops snapped easily.

Either Dodson or his wife might have heard the disturbance among the animals if they hadn't been lying in bed engrossed in their own sex video. Hav-

ing just enacted and taped an absurd plot, they were
watching the production, becoming aroused again. So
they didn't hear anything suspicious until all the animals were out of their cages.

The fat man's Cadillac roared out of the driveway,
spitting gravel, horn honking as Dodson burst from
his mobile home. Twenty feet down the path he came
face to muzzle with Not-So-Gentle Ben, named more
to attract tourists than for his ferocity.

The bear stood to eight feet, casting his shadow
over the man.

Dodson whirled, snagging his robe on the mailbox.
The robe jerked him up short. He bellowed, fearing
that the bear had him. The bear bellowed a reply.
Dodson literally ran out of his robe and into his naked wife waiting at the door.

She stared at him as he shivered. "Mack, what the
hell's wrong?"

He slammed the door and, unable to find words,
screamed in her face.

The animals scattered in all directions. Ben saun-
tered west, lumbering along across the impact area,
the heart of Fort Hood.

An escaped wolf, an old female, headed southeast
toward Belton Reservoir, guarded by steep banks like
a Scandinavian fjord.

The lioness went east to the Leon River. After
drinking, she turned to the northwest, toward North
Fort Hood. She ran into an encampment of national
guardsmen on summer training. Actually, they were
not so much training as sitting around a campfire

drinking beer and swapping stories. And she did not find them so much as a full-bladdered private from Lufkin found her. She terrified him with a roar—shutting off his stream and completely disproving his later story that she scared the piss out of him—and he answered with his own scream. His shrieking pronouncement of a "fuckin Aferkin line," coupled with her roar of confirmation, sent everybody scrambling helter-skelter, running for the civilian pistols smuggled to camp so guardsmen could defend their country from copperheads, rattlers, and that most reviled species of snake—other guardsmen who would steal an ice chest full of beer.

The lioness went west, trailed by guardsmen in tanks, jeeps, trucks, helicopters, civilian cars, and one brave—or stupid, or drunk—soul on a Kawasaki. One bunch tracked her for a couple of miles. But darkness gave her all the advantages. She turned south between the hills called Dalton Mountains and headed, confused and edgy, on a meandering line that would take her the six miles to tiny Hubbard Lake.

2

"We've been watching Warren Howell's genetic research for nearly a decade." The aristocrat nodded at the file on his desk. "It's all in there." His face showed the strain of a night without sleep, a night not yet ended.

The hulk shifted his weight in the leather chair and smacked his lips around the remnants of a cigar, log-rolling it with his tongue from one downcast corner of his mouth to the other. He'd heard it all before.

The recipient of the briefing was a nondescript man in his late thirties, medium build, medium height, brown hair, dressed in pinstripes like any one of Washington's thousands of lawyers, accountants, and mid-level bureaucrats. He was an ordinary man with ordinary features. Except for his eyes.

"In the last three years, it's been casual," said the aristocrat. "Two weeks ago it got serious—twenty-four-hour surveillance. And last night—tonight—the lid was blown off the whole affair. Now it's a Yankee priority."

The nondescript man spoke in an ordinary voice. "What's the importance of this genetic research?"

The eyes, too dark to be brown, darted from man to man. They were like snake eyes: hard, angry, alert.

"This research may lead to genetic engineering as a national security effort, perhaps even a decisive new weapon."

The hulk smirked, then sobered as snake eyes flicked at him.

"Is it our research?"

"Not . . . exactly. We've watched Howell develop it. We didn't want to claim it. Can you imagine what Congress and the press would do if they thought the U.S. was siccing *monsters* on our enemies? Anyway, Howell wasn't trying to make weapons. He wanted to create a subhuman race of slaves he could sell like robots. He simply wanted to make a few bucks."

"Where do these . . . monsters come from?"

"It's a process called recombinant DNA—rearranging the building blocks of life, transplanting chromosomes from one cell to another. It's even possible between cells of different species. For instance, the growth genes of humans have been transplanted into mice."

"And?"

"Giant mice. Howell didn't exactly break new ground—he simply was ready to gamble more than most researchers are. His real breakthrough was an improved method of transplanting multiple chromosomes, a chemosurgical process using a combination of microsurgery under chemically-induced stable conditions. Lately, he was able to transplant reproductive chromosomes to mingle the species."

The head nodded almost imperceptibly. The snake eyes remained fixed, unblinking.

The aristocrat continued. "His latest creation combined three species—we're not sure which, but he may even have used his own genes. We need to see his research notes to be sure. Previously, isolated effects could be observed in simple bacteria. Howell went beyond that. The results were spectacular—random but spectacular."

"What do you mean by random?"

"Usually the cells of one species will reject cells from another. But drugs can delay such rejections and if the rejection can be delayed long enough, cells can combine and take on their own identity so they don't even recognize differences between the original ingredients. But Howell had no way to predict or control which gene of one species would select and weld itself to the gene from the other species. He couldn't know how the resulting mutant cell would react or how the new total creature would grow or behave. He could only put the chromosomes together and wait for the results."

"And?"

"He got monsters. Apparently, every time the early experiments were performed, even with every step controlled, even with the identical . . . ingredients, the result was a different creature. The only consistent features were that the things incubated in half the normal gestation period or less, and the creatures grew to maturity remarkably fast. But they were always violent. Furiously violent and unpredictable."

"Any clues as to precisely how he did it?"

"Nothing but guesses. Howell's research journal is missing."

"And Howell?"

"Dead."

The hulk jumped in. "Drugs. Our three stooges down in Looneytunes, Texas, picked him up after the monster broke out and gave him drugs to cool him out. Fucking killed him. If we want the recipe for these . . . monsters, we've got to find the journal."

"Tell him about the zoo," the aristocrat said.

"Our dipshits burned down Howell's place, then released a bunch of tigers and the like to cover any destruction the monster might cause. Central Texas is about to wake up and go apeshit."

"And what do you want me to do?"

"Get that research log."

"And?"

"Keep a close eye on 'Larry, Moe, and Curly Joe.' I think Winston is soft—they all are. They've never been under fire till now. If they screw up any more. . . ."

"And?"

The hulk said, "Howell's wife and brother-in-law. The ones who were supposed to die in the fire. If they get in the way again, you may have to kill them—"

"Discontinue them," interjected the aristocrat.

"Discontinue them," muttered the hulk. "They're in hospitals. The woman is critical in Gatesville. The brother-in-law is comatose in an army hospital—he's a captain. From what I know of army doctors, he may never get out alive anyways."

"And?"

The aristocrat sighed. "That monster will have to be killed or captured."

The hulk frowned.

The snake eyes caught their every nuance of expression in voice, posture, and facial insinuation.

"And?"

"That's all."

3

Every year by September, the Texas sun has burned whatever grass has not been overgrazed by livestock to brittle residue. So the cattle, and especially the goats, begin to browse on the lower branches and leaves of trees, giving the scrub a manicured look. The cattle spend the entire day, from before light to after, scouring the barren ground for crackling spears of grass, unable to afford more than two trips a day to the evaporating waterholes. And those journeys are made in the dark because no daylight can be wasted.

One calf, this year's heifer, knew the route and the routine. She led the way through the darkness along a rut toward the stock pond, a dammed ravine half a mile from the collection of dwellings known as Flat, Texas. The rut was a one-lane path deepened by hundreds of hooves tramping for years to and from the dam.

Behind the heifer a string of cattle plodded along methodically, a slight breeze blowing at their switches. The herd needed water. Then they needed to strike out to distant reaches of the pasture to begin the day's grazing. That was simply all there was to their existence.

When the heifer reached the drop-off from the dam to the water, she hesitated, peering toward the darkness below, looking for a safe place to step. She dropped her nose to the ground, the better to see into the blackness. An acrid, powerful stench hit the snuffing nostrils, and the calf would have bolted backward if its impatient mother had not butted her from behind.

The calf would have bleated if the beast's jaws had not clamped down on its muzzle, choking off its breath, crushing its forehead.

The beast tossed its head, throwing the stiff-legged, quivering heifer down the hill. Then it lunged at the wide-eyed cow wheeling away from the dam. The string of cattle had bunched up. They blocked her retreat until a triumphant roar scattered the herd.

The beast rammed its target full in the side, lifting the bulk clear off the ground, shattering two ribs with a sound like muffled shots. Before the bellowing cow hit the ground, it had been raked from brisket to flank. It tried to raise its rear quarters but was battered down and thrashed again and again. Finally, mercifully, a spear from one of its ribs impaled the racing heart and ended the agony.

The beast found the heifer in the crusted mud at the pond's edge. It disemboweled its victim, going for the liver and heart.

After a brief, savage meal, it hunkered down in the ooze to drink of the warm slime. So awful was the alkaline taste and so painful was the stinging in the open wounds of its legs, the beast flew into a rage, thrashing at the pond until it was spent.

Exhaustion came shortly. The beast had lost blood. And it had been on a nearly constant rampage since breaking free of the cage. After climbing King Mountain, it had chased a couple of cows, quickly learning that they would not stand still as it advanced roaring and shrieking. Cursed by its mutant immobility, it didn't travel efficiently, either on all fours or walking erect.

So, full of cactus spines, slivers, cuts, and bruises— things that further aggravated its unstable disposition —and laden with a blood-rich meal, the beast limped away from the pond, looking for a lair.

The tiger had turned away from the river, skulking due west until it crossed a scent even worse than man's. It turned south to follow the stench. About dawn, the scent led the tiger to a pond and the carcasses of a cow and its calf. So the big cat settled down to a meal.

The sky lightened and a blue pickup approached.

A fusillade of rifle bullets drove the cat westward. Toward Hubbard Lake.

The trio met in the steamy morning at a Burger Bar in Temple.

Nolan Parish arrived at 6:30, ten minutes after Winston, and slid into the booth beside him. "Too bad about the Yankee," he said.

"I can see your heart is bleeding all over your three-piece."

Parish smiled wryly, thin lips drawn taut, dimples pocking his cheeks. Trustworthy brown eyes, dark and sensual, glittered . . . happily? Or was it sarcastically? Paul Winston could not tell.

"I don't mind a little excitement now and then, Paul. You probably still have a yearning for action now and then yourself."

Bloody lawyers, Winston thought.

"A Yankee alert is more than a little excitement, Nolan." The color rose to Winston's full, shiny cheeks. "A Yankee may give you a hard-on, but it's still a sign of failure to me. Failure to keep the low profile, a loss of options. Once we put out the fire, we have to turn the case over to somebody else. Then it's transfers all the way around." He sniffed at his own reference to fire. Bloody ironic after last night.

Parish ignored the harshness of the speech. A transfer wouldn't bother him. He didn't screw this one up. A transfer might mean a promotion if he could salvage something out of the assignment. "This involves Payne, doesn't it?"

Winston nodded.

"Do we discontinue him?"

Winston swallowed hard. Parish immediately catalogued the reaction as a sign of weakness. "We tried to invent an accident last night to . . . discontinue him. It didn't quite take. We're under orders to create . . . favorable circumstances for another accident."

"Who's our third man?"

"Buchanan. Ellis Buchanan. That's him at the counter now. Keep your pants dry. I'll give you the rundown soon enough."

A glance at Buchanan gave Parish enough data for an opening chapter in Buchanan's dossier. He would tip the scales at two hundred sixty easily, overweight by forty pounds for his seventy-four inches of height. Age forty-one. Probably had fifteen years on the job. Last bought a new suit thirty pounds ago. Hadn't had this suit cleaned in a month, and the sheen on his ass indicated he'd spent more time sitting on his butt than walking in the scuffed wingtips.

The telltale pistol lump under the left armpit would not have showed if he hadn't been overweight. Buchanan looked like a polyester detective off some midwestern city force. Parish grimaced in distaste.

Because of the Yankee he, too, carried a piece, the standard 9mm, two-inch silencer stowed in a holster beneath the barrel. His own tailored suit hid the bulge.

Buchanan lumbered up and hunkered in beside Winston. Parish saw that the hair on the backs of his hands had been singed off, leaving sandy brown stubble peeking out of dirty pores. The scent of rancid, smoky grease hit Parish's nose. Christ, the man hadn't even showered today.

Winston introduced them, and they shook perfunctorily. He sighed and gulped a huge mouthful of lukewarm coffee.

"Let me tell you why last night's fiasco forced me to call a Yankee. Take only mental notes. Be prepared to brief each other on the pertinent details of your respective case files. Be prepared to lay these cases to rest as early as possible. And, because ours is the only domestic Yankee now working, be prepared for some-body to be looking in on us."

He felt both men staring at him. "That's right," he said. "This thing might go Spec-one unless we can put it to rest right away—unless something bigger comes along to distract the big guys."

4

P.J. drove a silver 1984 Ford Tempo GL with five-speed—a modest, practical, determined car. Like its owner. She set her jaw on the way to the flight line, determined to be cured of yesterday's ephemeral crush on her platoon leader. From now on, she would be Warrant Officer Larson to the captain and to every one of those vultures in the 162nd. From now on, she would be strictly business.

When she arrived at the flight line, a grim-faced Maggie Anzola stepped from the platoon quonset into the south ramp's perpetual dust cloud.

"What?" PJ said cautiously.

"Payne . . . the captain. He was out at his sister's . . ."

"And what?"

"Well, the place caught on fire. Some people killed, his sister tore up pretty bad in the explosion . . ."

"Is he . . . one of the . . . is he . . . ?" She found she couldn't say the word.

"No, he's alive. In Darnall. Coma or something. We're going out. You want to come along? After he stood you up and walked out of the club, maybe you don't. You didn't know him so well . . ."

PJ had already started walking away, stunned. Just when she was all ready to be the most determined, hard-nosed—

"Hey, Larson, you coming with us?"

She kept walking so Maggie wouldn't see her fighting back tears.

Mark Payne lay unconscious, a captive of his own mind.

The smells were antiseptic, as if alcohol fumes were piped in—nasal Muzak—vapors of heady ether, stoic hospital food, and fragrant nurses.

Hushed came the sounds—whispers, distant chimes, muffled tinkling of glass.

Bitter alcohol coated his tongue like filmy grease on a windshield. Sometimes cold hands fingered his pulse, sometimes a wet cloth whisked over his body, cooling his stretched skin, soothing the hot muscles. As good as the cold felt at first, it quickly turned to the exquisite agony of fevered chills. His body remembered too well the alternating hot flashes and chills. In this sensation in particular, he could not discern the dream from reality, the past from the present.

His eyes saw nothing but a red haze that sometimes faded to black. His mind saw visions of himself. Yesterday morning. Lying in an ice bath. Last night. A blinding-hot explosion. The drill sergeant. Beth painted in the floral pattern of her own blood. The face of a monster. No—his father. His father a monster? No, his father dying. Gasping for breath until there were no more gasps left in that hearty chest. Blood. Breath. Fire. Ice.

He lay in the mystery ward. Three other beds were occupied by soldiers who should have been dead: one, a frail skeleton tucked into a fetal position—yet to come awake from a vasectomy a month old; two, a motorcycle accident victim—a scab with tubes in the middle; three, a face dented by the breech of a cannon.

Number four was Payne. A knock on the head, glancing blow from the looks of it, and a bruised pinky on the right hand. That was all. The mystery was that he hadn't come to yet, considering the minor nature of his injuries.

The doctor completed a cursory inspection of Payne. He had started down the hall when he saw the mob drifting his way. The mob weaved from side to side, seven pairs of eyes reading door numbers as it went, seven sets of lips moving as the mob read. The doctor, a captain, folded his arms and stood in the center of the hallway. He wasn't a particularly imposing youth. And the only clues to his occupation and status were the insignia of rank and medical branch. Otherwise, with his drooping sandy mustache, hair over his ears and collar, scuffed shoes and high-water trousers, he might easily have been mistaken for just another of the legions of used-car salesmen in Killeen.

"May I help you, gentlemen?" From the back of the mob a pair of emerald eyes locked onto his. "And lady?"

"Lay-*dees*," added Maggie Anzola. One of the warrants almost uttered a wisecrack, but she froze his face with an arctic glare.

Poole spoke up in his best imitation of a well-bred manner. "Yeah, asshole downstairs said we'd find our buddy in thirteen forty-three."

"I'm afraid room thirteen forty-three is off-limits. Is it the pilot . . . ?"

Poole looked down at his own flight suit. "No, the cocktail waitress, asshole. We wanna see Payne."

"He's not ready for visitors. The sheriff just left and even he couldn't speak to Mr. Payne. Even if he was awake, visiting hours aren't until . . . hey, how did you get up here anyway?"

"Elevator, dipshit. We'll ask Payne ourselves if he wants visitors." The mob stepped forward with Poole.

The captain uncrossed his arms and held out his palms. "You can't."

Poole looked around. Seven pilots, one doctor.

"I'll call security," said the doctor, his voice wavering.

Poole stepped up, placing his chest against the open palms. "Knock yourself out, dipshit." The mob began to edge past the doctor.

"Payne is unconscious. In thirteen forty-three . . . all the patients in thirteen forty-three are out of it. Please, let's be . . . uh . . . reasonable."

Poole's lips worked as his brain searched for reasonable.

The hands dropped. "I guess you could look through the door."

"One of us will go in and leave a card. He gonna be all right?"

"He seems fine. Minor injuries, sprained finger, light burns no worse than a weekend at the beach, contusions, a knot on the head."

"So what's wrong?"

"That's a . . . mystery, a medical mystery."

The pilots stared into thirteen forty-three for a few minutes. Then, one by one, they turned away, ashen. PJ let the mob pass by and went into the room. She circled the foot of the bed and dropped the platoon's get-well card on Mark's night stand. Then she too turned away, feeling faint. Why was he in a room with all those . . . corpses?

In the hallway, she found herself alone. She stopped to catch her balance, propping her back against the wall. She pressed her fingertips against her temples and breathed deeply, trying to clear the cobwebs.

The beast skulked three miles from its kill at the pond, crossing Route 36 when no traffic could be heard. Its wariness was born of pain and exhaustion rather than fear.

At the edge of Fort Hood's northwest boundary it found a tiny pond fed by seeping springs. It drank deeply from the fresh water and searched the brush for a shady place to lie, for already the rising sun had begun its scourge of the land. From a steep-sided deep ravine above the springs came a warning growl. The beast found a coyote blocking a cave entrance, eyes slit, ears flattened, head lowered, slim fangs exhibited. But when the beast bunched for a lunge, the coyote abandoned its exhibition of a defense, slinking off not just for the day but forever.

Mark smelled aviation fuel and sweaty pilots. Then there was the fragrance of a woman. Not just any woman. PJ Larson.

He was back in the air with her—no, in the back of the Huey—she was naked; he was on the verge of orgasm. . . . No. . . . He would not let himself relive that degenerate dream. He refused to degrade her and himself.

She insisted, throwing back the covers and climbing into the bed. Her perfume. Her hair, silken and cool, fell over her face and his. He brushed it back so he could look into those green eyes. . . .

. . . Instead, the eyes were ebony, the face was that of a monster with a muzzle full of fangs. He lurched away. A scream grabbed at his throat. He . . . was awake in a hospital bed, the other beds filled with cadavers. A dream. A dream so real he could almost smell her perfume hanging in the air.

He lay still for a moment, eyes closed, allowing his head to clear, inventorying his body. It all seemed to be there, and the only part that really hurt was the throbbing finger. But those dreams . . .

Early-morning sunshine blues. Sun climbing toward its zenith, mindless of beating down everything it touched on the way up. Mammals already hangdog, pummeled into submission, too whipped to hunt reptiles. Reptiles hiding, shielding their cold blood from the boiling point, too hot to hunt bugs. Even bugs in torpor, too stupored to eat gritty grass and leaves. Leaves sun-sick and wilted, too often vanquished in these days of the dry spell to even follow the sun across the sky. All things vegetable and animal waiting for either death by sun or reprieve of dusk, whichever mercifully comes first.

Nearly invisible heat waves rising. Also a cloud of dust.

Behind the pickup truck with the gold star on the door. Blasting across the range toward the Walker ranch, hurtling along like one of those Chevy-trucks-are-built-tough-to-stay-tough commercials.

The dirt road led the pickup into the front yard of a ranch house where two men stood in the drench of sun. The pickup stopped, making a total of three trucks in the yard. Already there was a four-by-four Bronco and a silver-over-maroon Dodge—each with the ubiquitous rifle rack visible inside. The Bronco held two rifles. The newly arrived pickup had three.

As the dust cloud caught up and enveloped the pickup, a troll of a man stepped to the ground and marched toward the pair in the yard, sending up tiny dust devils as he peppered the ground with his boot heels.

Coryell County Sheriff Jacob "Jake" Z. (for Zebulon) Beard. Immediately he accosted the Texas entrepreneur and proprietor of Dodson's Zoo and Roadside Attractions, Inc.

"Let me get this straight, Mack," he rasped through the dust and a cloud of cigarette smoke that clung to his head. The cigarette, unfiltered, half-smoked and damp, dropped ashes on his shirt front. "You're telling me that some kids busted into your zoo last night after dark and let out"—Beard stabbed his fingers out one at a time as he named the animals —"a lion"—stab—"a tiger"—stab—"a cougar"—

"Jake—" said the wiry Mack Dodson.

Stab—

"Wait"—stab. Beard's pitch rose after every stab. "A pair of bobcats"—

"Jake, let me tell you—"

Stab. Beard began to shout. "A goddamned timber wolf"—stab—"a bear, not a ordinary bear, mind you, but a grizzly bear"—he was almost out of fingers to stab—"and a partridge in a goddamned pear tree?" His voice broke at the rising pitch of the question.

"Jake—"

"Shut up, Mack." Beard lowered his voice to the raspy whisper. The wheeze in his lungs chimed in with the whistle of air through the space between his front teeth. He leaned forward, stabbing all his fingers at Dodson as though he might tear into the man's darting eyeballs and rip them from their sockets. "I'm dangerous, Mack, I really am," he whispered menacingly. "I been up all night, and I don't know what I might do if you start feeding me a line of shit. Now what we have here is Lion Country Safari on the loose ever since last night and you didn't even call me?" he gasped, at the very end of his lung capacity, diminished as it was by half a century of smoking.

"The phone lines were cut."

"Couldn'ta come in yourself?"

"I come in, doggone it, Jacob Beard. I come in and

nobody was there. . . . How the hell was I supposed to know you was out to the Howell's with the fire crew? You didn't even leave a dispatcher."

"Everybody in town was out to the fire, Mack. You couldn'ta waited till we got back?"

"Two hours I waited." Dodson stiffened. "I couldn't wait all night. I had to get back and tell the neighbors. And some of them animals might come back anyways, they get hungry enough."

Beard retracted his claws. He wheezed and looked to his deputy, who'd been sitting on the Dodge's tailgate out of the line of fire.

"One, probly two, barbecued bodies out to the Howell's. Two cooma-toes. One with a head bashed like a punkin. Halfa Aferka loose all over the county by now. My county. Why my county, Bob?"

Deputy Robert Britton shrugged. Even seated, he was as tall as Beard, standing to full height in his cowboy boots.

"What are we gonna do, Bob?"

"Mack, any of them animals come back this morning?" asked Britton.

"One of the bobcats."

"Great," rasped Beard, rolling his eyes skyward. "Grizzlies, lions, tigers. But what comes back? Damned fleabag wildcat. Why me, Lord?" he asked the god of sheriffs.

"Sheriff, why don't we send Mack back on out to his place to round up a couple ranchers to see what damage has been done by them excaped animals. It can't be too much because we'd have had a dozen calls by now."

Beard brightened. "That's a start. Then what?"

"Call the paper and the radio and tell them the story so people will be careful."

Beard grimaced and spat between his browning teeth.

"Have to, boss. Better call the Rangers and DPS. And the other law offices, at least in Bell and Lampasas counties."

Beard slumped against his pickup.

"They have to know, Jake."

"I'll be dipped in shit," he whined. "Every peace officer in Texas will be telling Jungle Jake jokes by dark."

"It's not your fault, boss."

Dodson chimed in. "Nobody's fault, Jake. Just some doggone vandals. Kids. Or drunks. Not your fault." He looked at Britton. "Not mine, either, y' know."

Britton said, "We'll have things under control in no time."

"Yeah, maybe I'll get lucky," Beard wheezed.

"Yeah," said Dodson.

"Maybe the tiger will give me a blowjob."

The sandy-haired doctor decided to take another walk through the mystery ward. Maybe he'd be surprised by some new development. Maybe somebody had died or something.

He found the pilot standing unsteadily, rummaging through the steel cabinet beside his bed, unmindful that his gown had come open in back.

"What on earth are you doing?" he demanded.

* * *

Mark suddenly realized why his butt was so cold. He spun, reaching behind him to close off the draft, and went reeling. The doctor caught him by the gown and propped him half on the bed.

"Good grief, Payne, how long have you been awake?"

"Couple minutes," he gasped. "My sister. How is she?" He shook his head to clear the black fuzz.

The doctor pressed his racing pulse. Payne's sprained finger throbbed, keeping time.

"Your sister went to Gatesville with head injuries, extent unknown. Their neurology department doesn't report to me. I don't know how she is."

"Find out."

"ASAP, General Patton."

"Sorry. Uh, maybe I ought to talk to the cops about last night."

"You already missed the sheriff. He came by while you were napping."

"Would you mind calling him? Tell him I'm awake."

"The sheriff suggested I do exactly that. He was very interested in your condition, or so he said in his unique manner of speaking."

"Minute that fuckin' Payne comes to, I'm going to kill his ass."

The pair of lawmen stood on the porch of Walker's untidy ranch house, faded gray from years of neglect. The sheriff dragged a quarter inch of new coal onto his cigarette, sucking hollows into his cheeks, bulging his close-set eyeballs, packing his pony-keg chest with smoke.

Britton grunted.

"Goddammit, Bob," he wheezed, gushing smoke, "where's Walker?"

The deputy pushed his John Deere baseball cap off his expansive forehead. "He should be here."

"Goddamned right he should be here. I expect he wouldn'ta even left if he really seen a tiger like he says. And why hasn't that two-bit army doctor called? I told him to call me the minute that french-fried pilot come out of his cooma."

"Maybe he hasn't come to."

"Hope the shithead does the right thing and dies. He probly done it anyways. Be easier to blame this shit on him if he don't come to."

Britton didn't answer.

It was early afternoon and ninety-eight degrees. Both their shirts had dampened in a girdle from darkening armpit to armpit.

"I'm tarred," said Beard. He sat down on Walker's step. His grilled forehead channeled sweat laterally to his temples.

Britton nodded and sat beside him.

"Jake, you reckon a fire could burn a skull plumb to ashes?"

"They cremate people, don't they? How else they get they heads in them little pots? What'd you find out to Howell's?"

"They're about ready to knock it off over there. They got a few piles of bones. Mostly rabbits and cats . . . maybe the larger ones are goats and dogs.

There's several tore-up carcasses outside in the stock pens. A dead pony. Soon as I told the firemen about the excaped tigers and such they decided they'd done enough searching around the property. They'll bag the bones from the fire and take them to the coroner. . . ."

Britton cocked his head, tilting his right ear toward the cluster of buildings called Flat. Then he stiffened and stood up. "Uh-oh."

Beard stood beside him. His full-crowned Western hat came to the deputy's bicep. The sheriff stepped up on the porch to see what had caught Britton's attention.

A plume of pulverized white caliche rose from the dusty trail between Walker's and Flat. The cloud climbed skyward, churned over and over by the string of pickups plying the road.

"It's a goddamn convoy," Beard said.

"Looks like old Luke been busy."

"Fuckin' A. Look like he been organizing himself a fuckin' safari."

Beard stood, hands on hips, cigarette on lip, squinting from Walker's porch, watching a string of eleven pickups pull into the yard.

A man jumped from his blue mini-pickup and scuttled up to the sheriff, his equal in height. He stroked his gray beard nervously.

"Sheriff."

"Luke. Goddamn you. First you call me up with a national emergency about tigers. Then you go off drinking."

"Jake, it wadn't like that. I went over to Bingo's to

get some hands. Case you need help with this bidness, y' know."

"Bullshit. You let 'em buy you drinks long as they would. Next thing you'll be on television trying to get some fleabag reporter to buy you drinks."

The darting eyes froze.

Beard pinned the glazed eyes with his own. "You didn't. Luke, you somebitch, tell me you didn't," he rasped as if it were his last breath.

No answer.

Beard whirled and pushed through the crowd. "Why don't you nice men go on back to tending chores?"

It was an eighth of a mile track from Walker's yard to the stock pond. Britton watched in the rear view of the Bronco as the convoy grew. He counted nearly two dozen vehicles as they approached the dam.

He turned on his AM radio. An excited woman blared a live "Red-Hot on the scene report" to her Temple-Belton-Killeen listeners. She confirmed that "Red-Hot reporter Karen Wilson" was on the scene "at the Richard L. Walker ranch northwest of Killeen in response to a red-hot tip that the escaped tiger has created havoc with the Walker livestock, threatening the ranching industry of the Centro-plex region."

In minutes Walker's stock pond began to look like an ant swarm; all manner of curious people tramping around the carcass of the dead cow.

A purple-faced Beard had had enough. He started for his pickup. But a powerfully perfumed woman grabbed his elbow.

"Sheriff, I'm Karen Wilson, Red-Hot radio 950, Temple."

"Leave me alone, dammit."

"Sheriff," she said, "is this the first report of tiger attacks?"

Beard whirled on her. "No." He looked as if he might cut loose and punch the reporter but then, as the crowd closed in again, his color improved to blotchy red. "No. Last night at the Howell place yonder." He lifted an arm to point feebly into the belly of a bystander. "Several, uh, livestock were tore up pretty bad."

"By what?"

"I—we don't know. Probably one of the excaped animals."

"And what kind of animals besides the tiger?"

Beard pulled off his hat and rubbed the red stripe the hatband had etched in his forehead. "Uh, only one tiger, lion, bobcat—two of those—wolf, grizzly bear, uh, that's all I can think of."

"And what is being done to recapture these wild beasts, Sheriff?"

"Why, we're—I mean, we're out here doing all we can. We been out to the zoo and to the Howell place—"

"When will you have the wild beasts rounded up?"

"Rounded up? You think rounding up tigers and shit is like herding cattle?"

"Will you form a posse from citizens out here today?"

"Posse!" a voice from the crowd shouted.

"No posse!" boomed Beard.

But the crowd heard only "posse" again—the word it wanted to hear.

Beard charged the crowd and broke out of the bedlam. The cluster followed him to his Ranger. He slammed the door and started up. The crowd wouldn't part to let him pull away. So he hit the strobes and flicked the siren only enough to make it growl. It was exactly the wrong move.

"The posse!" came a shout. "Follow the sheriff." The mob took up the chant. Clusters broke up, individuals ran to their rides. Another convoy had formed behind Beard. When he saw what he'd started, he slammed the brake and shut down the strobes. He locked the doors and sat in a pout, watching the hysteria run out of control.

A camera crew had backed Walker knee-deep in muck, putting the heifer in the foreground of the shot. Reporter Robert Ely—only ankle-deep—leaned out with the mike and asked Walker to repeat the story. "Leave out the bullshit about the feed and seed, okay, Mr. Walker?"

"Okay. I woulda got that tiger, too, but he was a quick 'un. Quickest tiger I ever seen."

Several tiger hunts were being organized by men and teenagers collecting around ice chests in pickup beds.

Britton shook his head. He walked past Beard's Ranger, saw the sheriff hunkered down, purple and sweating in the cab, a fresh cigarette dangling. He shrugged. Beard gave no acknowledgment.

The deputy drifted to his Bronco, climbed in, and

opened the doors. He watched the mob break up into small bands. Vehicles left in all directions, veering into each other; men shouted obscenities, threw beer cans, and urinated from the beds of moving pickups.

Wait it out, Britton told himself. *Nothing else to do.* So he sat and waited, puzzling over Payne, the locks at Dodson's, the missing skull, the fire, the huge goat hoofprint down by the pond—Walker didn't have goats.

5

Half an hour after dark the beast was awakened by the snapping of brush. It crept to the opening, filling the cave entrance. A dark shadow moved by. Then a second plodding, rangy black steer picked its way down the path toward water. The third shadow the beast tackled, breaking the stout back, disembowelling the animal in seconds.

It began devouring the heart of the crooning animal before the steamy, self-delivered meal could even stop beating.

Then, legs stiff, the beast defecated on the path and crawled back into its commandeered lair to sleep its uneasy sleep again.

Eleven P.M.

Beard and Britton sat in the Coryell County sheriff's office at Gatesville, heads cradled in their arms on desktops like two kids in dayschool at naptime.

"I'm tarred," Beard said.

"Me too."

Both men talked into the tops of their desks.

"Payne did it, Bob."

"Maybe not."

"Sure he did. Domestic disturbance. Howell takes to thumping on his wife. Payne don't like him roughing up his sister. Payne kills him. Tries to make it look like an accident by starting a fire. Screws up and blows everything up—himself, Kiser, Howell. *Blam!*" He rose up to simulate a mushroom explosion blossoming out of his arms. Then he collapsed on the desktop again.

"I can't understand only one set of bones with two men missing."

"They's plenty of bones to go around out there."

"Goats and dogs, I'll wager, Jake."

"Okay, 'nother plot. This time, Howell busts a bottle over Payne's noodle and *he* blows the place up."

"All the cars were left there. How did he run away? Why not take Payne's Camaro? He could be all the way to Mexico City before we'd check for that car."

"It's that fucking Kiser, then."

"Kiser's not the type."

"He's got him a record. You wouldn't let him babysit your kids."

"Child fondlers don't grow up to be arsonists and murderers."

"It was Payne. He did it or I'm dipped in shit."

"Why only one skull?"

"Bullshit. They'll find two. You've heard of these killers that chop off the heads of their victims? Besides, the other skull could've burned up, 'member? We already talked about cremation once today."

"I checked. Ordinary fire ain't hot enough, Jake."

Riley stepped meekly into the room. "Sheriff," he said, "coroner on line one."

Britton lifted his head as the sheriff talked. Beard hung up solemnly, tiredly. "You were right. One dead man. Kiser. Cause of death unknown—roof fell in on him so he had a lot of broken bones. Rest of the bones was animals. Just like you said."

Britton nodded.

"That leaves Howell," rasped Beard as he left. "I better see Eva."

Riley broke into Britton's concentration. "Bob?"

"Pat?"

"I got some nervous mothers telling me their teens ain't home yet. Probably out on beer-drinking safari. Got some complaints of people tromping fences down and shooting on their property. And ever' other call is from some paper or television or radio station. Houston. Dallas. Even got one from Chicago."

"It's only going to get worse."

Before morning, the beast had slept itself out, regaining some of its strength. Outside the cave in the dampness before dawn, it stretched and ripped unenthusiastically at the carcass of the steer. But it decided it was not so hungry, preferring a hot kill.

The beast began hobbling south. It had learned much in its short freedom. It had learned not to defeat itself crashing through deadfalls. It found stealth more effective. So it picked its way through the scrub.

Toward tiny Hubbard Lake.

* * *

Another dawn oozed between the edges of earth and sky as the lioness began her stalk a quarter mile away from Hubbard Lake. She had watched for half an hour as the doe and fawn approached the water, grazing as they went. The doe's head would drop for a nibble of sparse grass and jerk back up, swiveling from side to side to stare. The fawn jumped erratically, too young to sense danger on its own but springing on stiff legs as if electrified by its mother's fear. Finally, the doe went spraddle-legged at the edge of the pond.

The beast hulked down to watch the lioness.

The tiger caught the scent, hot and rancid—the same irksome smell it had first picked up yesterday near Walker's stock pond. It flattened its ears and began loping, tracking into the breeze.

The fawn's head dropped. The lioness rushed, streaking low and tawny. The doe sprang away on stiff knees. The fawn spun to follow but was smashed down into the mud. The lioness clamped onto the willowy neck, biting until bones gave way to meshing fangs. She dragged the dishrag carcass from the water, drinking of the warm flow pumping into her maw. Her attention was fully on her kill.

Until the awful scent hit her nostrils.

The beast, not at all stealthy, scrambled over the edge of the ravine. The lioness turned and snarled a warning. The beast advanced. The lioness answered with a rush of her own—head low, fangs bared, feinting in and darting out. Incapable of finesse, the beast simply clubbed her head as it came in once more, bashing it into the dust. Before the stunned lioness could come up, it was on her back, battering her.

The tiger sprinted across the last hundred yards of open ground. Only when the cat leapt did the beast glimpse the attack. It responded instantly by driving up like a catapult. The tiger had the weight advantage, three hundred fifty pounds to two hundred fifty pounds. But the beast caught the tiger in the open muzzle with its horns, driving it back like a determined linebacker spearing a diving tailback at the goal line. The tiger was a brawler. Standing erect, it raked the beast with its front paws, hooking into the shoulders, trying to drop down so its rear claws could slash the beast's belly. But the beast's claws were just as long and more effective as weapons. Its hairy paws worked like hands tipped with two-inch daggers. It stiffly clutched the throat of the tiger. Then it threw its own hooves into the underbelly of the tiger. The force drove the pair apart, peeling one from the other. The tiger's claws cut four slits down each leg, and the tiger's throat was torn out by the claws of the beast.

Once parted, each dropped into a crouch. The tiger found itself breathing scarlet foam through its spurting neck. It couldn't hold its head up for the severed tendons and muscles, the opened arteries, trachea, and esophagus. It fell on its side, drowning in its blood.

The beast, unmindful of the blood cascading down

its forearms, roared in triumph. It circled to get behind. The tiger's legs began to run horizontally, pinwheeling the body on the ground, blackening a circle of soil as its blood gushed out. The beast continued to circle until the gurgling tiger weakened. The beast's utterances were the animal equivalent of a shouting, cursing rage. Finally, the tiger couldn't move fast enough to face the beast any longer. Then it couldn't move at all as the beast's fangs punctured the vertebrae below the ears, severing the spinal cord.

It wasn't enough for the beast. It shredded the luxurious pelt, scattering tufts of bloodied fur for the breeze to pick up and deposit on the slimy pond. Then, its rage spent, the bloodied beast took the fawn into its stinking mouth and struck out eastward—away from the deserted impact area—toward the scattered farms and ranches of Bell and Coryell counties.

6

Ken and Mark ran across the hospital parking lot toward Poole's sport turbo. Mark had just discharged himself from Darnall, leaving a note on the bed. He felt like an escapee—thrilled to be free, yet afraid of the freedom after two days. He'd recovered fully, as far as he was concerned. The lump on his skull wasn't even tender unless he probed it. He felt strong. His appetite had come back, and all his senses seemed sharp. The worst of it was his constant worry about Beth. Even at that, he'd begun to feel better about himself—because he cared.

In the hospital lobby he had called the Coryell County sheriff's office. He left a message with Riley, the dispatcher, saying he'd be going to visit his sister at the Gatesville hospital. Then he'd be over to claim his Camaro and give a statement about what had happened the other night, since, as he put it, "Nobody seems to give a damn about attempted murder."

The dispatcher tried to tell him to wait for the sheriff, who was on the way to question him. Mark told him he couldn't wait.

Poole tapped on the accelerator, warming the engine. Then he tore out of the parking lot, sending the black bullet fishtailing toward Gatesville.

Angry bruises started at the top of the bald woman's head and ran like a black and yellow cloud down to her bright purple lips. She lay in terror—terror of the worst kind because she couldn't do anything about it. She couldn't do anything at all.

Once almost pretty, she now looked like the bride of Frankenstein's monster. They had brought her in with her skull dented like a deflated basketball. They shaved her head hurriedly, slit her scalp from temple to temple above the hairline—the slightest concession to the remote possibility she'd ever regain consciousness—and peeled it down over her nose like a mask. They lifted bone from her brain like shell fragments from an egg. They rebuilt her nose—functionally rather than cosmetically, so air could pass—and kept it from collapsing with tubes. Her eyes were swollen to weeping slits.

They did the best they could, or should, since even if she lived, she'd be useless, having suffered a partial lobotomy from the bone shards. A convex stainless steel plate held the forehead and scalp in place.

Had she been able to see herself, Beth would have been terrified at the vision. But her terror was not that she wouldn't ever again be smart or pretty. It simply was that her last waking moments played on the screen of her mind. She was powerless to fight or flee or even to change the action. All she could do was watch the monster attacking her—over and over.

* * *

If ever eyes were windows to the soul, this man standing in a doctor's smock was the proof. Probably they were once brown. Now they were seething charcoal peepholes to the hatred smoldering inside.

He had decided to put her out of her misery. He knew she'd suffer always, even if she recovered from the immediate wounds. She'd suffer because she was Howell's wife. Just as he had made others suffer. Better this life be ended.

Revenge hardly passed through his feverish mind as he stepped up to the bed and took the pillow from behind her head. Kindness—that was the true motive —Christian kindness. He owed her that much. Warren Howell would get no such consideration.

He laid the pillow across her abdomen, his left hand across her bristly stitches, his right awkwardly wrapped around the plastic, and began withdrawing the tubes from her nose. Then as tears welled in his eyes, he placed the pillow over the discolored face and began pressing. He neither saw nor felt any sign of struggle and was grateful this would be so painless for her, the gaunt, pitiful wife of the devil incarnate.

And, true, the only visible sign of struggle was a feebly quivering hand. All the thrashing and screaming took place in that most horrible of places—in Beth's terrified mind.

Mark left Poole at the nurse's station. Poole said he wasn't family and didn't want to see another battered patient anyhow after his visit to Darnall's mystery ward. "Besides . . ." he said, winking and tossing his head in the direction of a brunette nurse, who had just fingered Mrs. Beth Howell's room number on her chart.

So Mark left him to plot against her. He pushed into the room, steeling himself for what he might see and what he might have to do to keep from passing out if that old feeling of queasiness came on.

He saw the back of a white coat, somebody tending a patient.

"Sorry, Doctor," he said. "Should I wait outside?"

The startled man turned, showing a pair of frightened—and frightening—wild eyes. The man had greasy, unkempt hair. He needed a shave. Mark decided this place was as bad as Darnall with its quasi-military doctors.

The doctor walked toward him, veering at the last second to slither out of the room, leaving behind his scent of decaying flesh.

Mark watched him leave; saw the three-fingered deformed hand as it slid through the doorway. He looked to his sister, expecting to see the bandaged face of a mummy. Instead, he saw a crumpled pillow where Beth's head should have been.

He dashed across the room and pulled the pillow away. The face wasn't Beth's, thank goodness. Stitches, teary swollen eyes, blood trickling from the flattened nose . . .

But, God, it was Beth. It had to be—with those ears bent in just the Payne children's way, the Payne father's way.

And somebody had just tried to kill her.

He ran out, skidding on the floor at the door and

again in the hallway. He shouted for help, babbling that somebody had tried to kill his sister. The pair of nurses froze, unable to comprehend what they were hearing from this crazy soldier with the bandaged finger.

"Goddammit, he tried to smother my sister. Get in there."

They inched away.

"Move."

One of the nurses spoke urgently into a telephone: "Code Blue," she said. "Room eleven fifty-seven. Code Blue"—she looked up at Mark—"and send security—stat."

In the room, the brunette was clearing Beth's breathing passage. She stopped to stare at him. She had the look of fear, worried Beth might—

—No, she was afraid of him.

"No," he said, raising the palms of his hands, "you see, I came in here and found her being smothered by some greaseball in a doctor's coat." He stepped forward. The brunette stepped away.

"I'm her brother," he said, pleading. "I came in here and found a guy trying to kill her. . . . Shit." He wheeled and left the room so the nurse would go back to work on Beth.

In the hall, he mashed the elevator button and shouted for Poole to take the stairs.

Poole shrugged. "What the—"

"The sleaze with the greasy hair and a couple fingers missing. Get him. He tried to . . . hurt Beth."

Poole bolted down the stairwell. Mark smashed the elevator button until the doors finally opened.

When the elevator arrived in the lobby, he ran into the belly of a bloated cop, who first cursed him, then, eyes lighting up, pulled a pistol with a giant bore. Mark froze as ordered. The cop slammed him, face-first, up against the closed door of the elevator.

A crowd immediately began to gather, oohing and aahing in unison. Mark saw Poole's wild face coming through. Mark steered him off with a shrug and a shake of the head.

Mark said, "Sheriff, do you know me?"

"You bet your ass, punk. You're Payne, remember? The guy who run off from the army hospital. The douche bag who's under arrest for suspicion of murder and arson in the death of Albert Kiser—"

"Who?" Handcuffs pinched his wrists. He looked over his shoulder.

"Don't play dumb with me. You're coming with me, Payne." He shoved the barrel of the pistol into his back. "One way or another."

Mark shook his head. This had to be a dream. He blinked and shook his head, but when he opened his eyes, the stumpy sheriff was still there.

A security guard ran up to the clutch of people, asking if the prisoner was the man who had been trying to kill the patient in 1157.

Beard grabbed Mark's shirt and pulled him around, yanking the bewildered face down to the level of his own. "Well, well, well. And how about that, Payne?"

"She's my sister, Sheriff. Why would I—"

"Why the fuck not? She's the only witness to what you done out there at the clinic."

"Kill her, Sheriff? I saved my sister's life out there,

and I saved her again a couple minutes ago when some fake doctor tried to smother her."

"Fake doctor. And just when I thought I fuckin' heard 'em all."

He yanked an elbow. "Come on, Payne."

"Don't I have any rights here?"

"You bet your ass you got rights," said Beard. "You got the right to remain silent, asshole. Exercise it."

7

Pandemonium had erupted at Dodson's zoo.

Deputy Britton pulled his John Deere cap down to his eyebrows and put on a stern face to fend off some of the reporters pressing in on Mack Dodson. The more insistent ones he just had to shove back.

Dodson kept trying to tell them that one bobcat had returned to its cage and that a second one had been hit by a VW Rabbit near The Grove, but they didn't want to hear about bobcats killed by Rabbits. They wanted to hear about lions and tigers. They wanted to see them. They wanted more than an illiterate Texan; they wanted flowing blood and steaming guts.

Britton answered the rapid-fire questions in his drawl, slowing the inquisition's pace. He told them artillery observers had spotted the carcasses of a lion and a tiger. A hired veterinarian had flown out to investigate in an army chopper. They had found the lioness wounded. They tranquilized her and moved her back to the zoo. She needed four hundred-plus stitches but was far from dead. Already she was up pacing and complaining in her enclosure.

Britton paused as the lioness let loose a coughing roar as if on cue.

He continued, saying that the tiger had been torn apart, apparently by the lioness in a fight. Yes, the tiger was dead. Dodson chimed in to say the tiger weighed at least one hundred pounds more. No, tigers and lions are not natural enemies. Sometimes they even mate in captivity, producing offspring called ligers, he said.

And Dodson was off on a tangent—coaxed on by some of the amused journalists who thought they might get an ironic touch from the simple, sincere Dodson. Others of the mob asked more pertinent questions.

Britton answered them. "We've still got us a wolf and a grizzly bear on the loose. The bear's probably the most dangerous of all the excaped animals still out."

"Are you investigating reports of killed livestock and where are these incidents and what progress have you made?"

"We're looking into all reports. They're some from areas to the west and some from places to the southeast and others from along the Leon River. Not all the stock deaths can be shown to come from the escaped animals."

"What do you mean?"

"I reckon you know some stock die of natural causes. Some are killed by spotlighters looking to put a side of beef in the fridge. Nowadays with so much attention, every bobwire scratch is being laid to the feet of these escaped animals."

"How could the smaller lion tear that tiger up?"

Britton hesitated. "Nobody knows." He looked at Dodson. Dodson's expression said he sure as hell didn't know. "Nobody was there but the cats," Britton said. *And a goat*, he thought. *Or were they deer tracks, or what?*

"Why patch up the lion—Lisa? Why not just put her to sleep like a horse with a broken leg."

Dodson's face went blank. He'd never considered killing her. "I raised Lisa from a kitten. I love that cat."

For a moment there was silence as the pack tried to digest the simple emotion of this simple man, but as always happened they moved on to the next shouted question: "Any word on the missing teenagers?"

It was Britton's turn to go blank in response. A trio of teens had gone hunting tigers yesterday after the "carnival" at Walker's. A worried mother had called this morning after she woke up in her chair by the door; her sawed-off, attitude-adjusting broom handle still across her lap. Britton might not have been so concerned if they had just been three boys out on an all-night lark, drinking and hunting. Mostly drinking.

"Two boys and a girl. All I can say," he murmured, "is we're looking into it."

As Beard dragged Mark into the sheriff's office, they met two suited men on their way out.

Riley shot up from the sheriff's chair, sheepish at having been caught trying out the throne of power. "Is this Payne?" he muttered.

"Yeah. Who was that?"

"Insurance men. They want to take a look at the Pinto we hauled in from the Howell's." He nodded at Mark. "What's he cuffed for?"

Beard crowed. "Arson. Murder. Attempted murder. I got him dead to rights." He sneered into Mark's face. "Nabbed the somebitch after he tried to croak his sister and run away."

Beard stabbed a finger at Mark's face. "Now whyn't you tell us about the first time you tried to croak her, the night out to the clinic?"

All eyes followed the stabbing finger to Mark.

"It's about time somebody asked me what was going on. The other night I got hit on the head and almost blown up. End of story. Today, I was chasing the man who tried to kill my sister when I ran into you, Sheriff. I walked into the room and caught a little greaseball shoving a pillow into her face. He was dressed like a doctor, so I didn't know what was up at first. But then I saw he was missing two fingers on his right hand. My buddy and I—"

"What buddy?"

Mark was telling him that Poole could support his story when the two men in suits entered the office with Britton, just back from the zoo.

The older man, tall and lean said, "Sheriff, I was just telling your deputy here that somebody's smashed the window on that Pinto and rifled the car."

Beard sneered. "Your mother ever teach you it's not polite to innerupt? Who the hell are you, anyways?"

"Oh," said the shorter man, proffering a business card, "didn't the dispatcher tell you? We're from Empire Insurance. Investigating the losses and estimating the worth of the Howell estate and so on."

"I don't give a shit if you're from the evil empire. I'm interrogating a prisoner and you're getting in the way over a piece of shit Pinto that ain't worth two bits." He looked at Mark. "And I suppose you don't know anything about the Pinto either, Payne?"

The two men glanced at each other, then focused on Mark.

Mark said, "Sheriff, I haven't had time enough since leaving the goddamned hospital to commit every unsolved crime in your county. Besides, I'm heir to my sister's estate and beneficiary of her insurance." He looked over at the taller man. "Isn't that right?"

"Why . . . yes, of course."

"So why would I have to break into anything of my own, especially that raggedy Pinto? Sheriff, you've been with me most of the day, for chrissake. Now, what do you say? Are you going to charge me with something? Let's get it over with if you are, because I want a lawyer if you charge me. And if you don't, I want to get my car and go home."

Beard took a step. Britton eased between him and Mark. He spoke in low tones close to Beard's ear.

Beard whirled on the pair in suits. "You guys get what you come for?"

The taller man nodded.

"Then get lost."

The shorter man stared at Mark. He returned the

stare. Each took the measure of the other. Mark felt as if the man knew him . . . but then he couldn't have.

When they had gone, Riley whispered into Britton's ear. The deputy leaned over the sheriff to talk in his ear.

Beard reddened, then burst. "Riley . . ."

The dispatcher shrank.

"Why the hell didn't you tell me this somebitch called here before he went to the hospital?"

Riley shrugged. "I didn't think—"

"Shit, that's the trouble with you." He waved his handcuff key, then threw it at Riley. "Turn him loose. Sonofabitch. Goddam sonofabitch."

Linda Fontaine. Eighteen. Called Lucky. And why not? She had everything: Body, brains, wealthy parents, an academic scholarship to the university in Austin next month. And she had boyfriends. As many as she wanted. Two of them, Bobby Lee Harwood and Lester Shields, had practically grabbed her off the Gatesville main drag with the invitation to go tiger hunting.

The two didn't actually grab her. Their excitement and the words "tiger hunt" did the grabbing. And the promise of a couple cold ones. And cigarettes. Maybe even a joint. Shoot the guns.

They picked Preachers Creek, three miles east of Hubbard Lake. The boys guzzled beer as fast as they could, stoking up their courage, hoping the fox would be encouraged to drink as fast. For appearances, they let her shoot the rifle at a distant herd of cattle and

blow away some beer cans with the shotgun. Then
they sat in the cab of the GMC, passing a joint and
gulping three fresh beers. The twelve-gauge rested
on the dash with the box of shells and three backup
beers growing beads of condensation.

Suddenly Bobby Lee had an idea. Les thought it
was a great idea. Lucky didn't exactly mind being
kissed by two jocks at once. At first, she resisted the
fondling, fighting them off with shrill giggling and
squealing. Nobody in her position could afford a reputation of being easy. But she wasn't too reluctant.
Even if she had been reluctant, she might not have
been able to stop them once they pulled down her
tube top and got a good look at her magnificent
breasts.

When they started playing with them, she didn't
want to stop. They dragged her cut-offs down to her
ankles and unzipped their own pants. *Pretty well coordinated,* she thought. They began masturbating her
and themselves at once. It was almost as if they'd
planned it.

Lucky's eyes were closed, the better to feel the
sweaty bodies scorching her own. She knew this kind
of thing made a reputation, that it might get around.
But the mouths and hands were awfully persuasive.
She decided to go a little while longer before asking
them to stop.

As she came closer and closer to orgasm, she reasoned that this wasn't really a really bad thing, not if
she didn't "do the dirty deed." And, at the moment,
even that didn't seem all that horrible a prospect. As
she began moaning involuntarily, she decided it was

she who was using them, that she would use them up.
She gripped their heads and threw her hips up, crying out in her pleasure.

The beast, caked in drying blood from its struggle
with the cats, might have passed by the GMC two
hundred yards upwind. But Lucky was squealing.
The sound drew it like a shark to a blood scent. It
began the stalk immediately, circling to get down-
wind. It had learned so much so soon. From below, it
picked up the musky odors from the pickup. There
was the acrid scent of spent gunfire and the oily fragrance of the truck, but the odors of young, laboring
bodies were the most powerful of all. The beast crept
the last hundred feet on all fours—right up to the
grill of the rocking pickup—before it stood on goat
legs.

Lucky was lost in a fantasy, dreaming and living it
at the same time. Pressed back against the seat, two
heads bobbing against her chest, two hands sliding in
and out of her crotch, she had headlocks on both
boys. Her orgasm came intensely; her moaning
turned shrill.

They breathed ragged and heavy, pounding their
penises faster and faster, trying to catch up to achieve
a three-way orgasm. Talk about a story. This was better than tiger hunting.

When the shadow passed across Lucky's face, terror struck her heart still for a beat or two. The worst
thing in the world had happened. Somebody had
caught her in the act and had caught her enjoying it.

When she opened her oversized blue eyes, she saw her fantasy become a nightmare—something worse than the worst thing in the world.

Her scream taught the jocks the meaning of curdled blood. They turned and saw it bearing down on them, scrambling, shrieking, scratching across the sheet metal, denting it deeply. Bobby Lee wrenched his back, twisting beneath the steering wheel. They filled the air with obscenities. Full of surprise, fear, anger, confusion, they shouted orders at each other, asked questions that had no answer, called for help from heaven and hell.

The beast smashed the windshield to frost. The boys, for some reason, found it imperative to pack their softened members back into their jeans. Until a goats horn came through the glass fragments. Then Les grabbed the shotgun off the dash and tried to turn it. The muzzle caught on the steering wheel. He jerked it free, jerking the trigger as well. Bobby Lee's all-American head vanished like an exploding blood balloon.

The horn pulled back through the glazed windshield.

Lucky had not stopped screaming; it seemed as if she never would.

Les somehow kept a shred of composure. He locked the doors and got the windows up, reaching across her and the corpse of his buddy. He poked the shotgun through the hole in the windshield and fired.

But the beast was gone.

Lucky still shrieked.

Holding her tube top up to her chin, she inhaled

deeply and exhaled another scream. Les dragged her hips toward him, toward the passenger door, making a space so he could get to the steering wheel. He shoved Bobby Lee against the door. The spurting remnant of his buddy's face fell over on Les's shoulder. Les turned the ignition key and pulled ahead. Angrily, frantically, he threw his shoulder into Bobby Lee's corpse to get him out of the way. Les was crying. Lucky was screaming. The beast was not to be seen.

Les pressed his head against the blood-smeared door glass, peering out the front quarter. He could see enough to move the GMC forward.

He couldn't see the hulk coming from the side.

The beast's head rammed through the side window, driving irregular crystal fragments into the shattered left temple of Lester Shields. His last act was to stiffen, mashing the gas pedal to the floor, sending the truck lurching out of control. It rolled into a ravine, engine roaring, throwing two dead boys and a screaming girl around inside the cab. The GMC landed upside-down wedged into the bottom of the ravine—engine screaming, then coughing, then dying—trapping Lucky inside the crumpled cab. She was still trying to scream, as bad as it hurt her crushed chest.

The beast could find no way to get to the bodies. It dug around awhile and battered the door on the driver's side near the bottom. Finally it gave up after the whimpering inside turned first to feeble coughing, then ragged breathing, then went silent.

It dragged its own wounded body away, leaving Linda Fontaine to die untouched, lucky to the last.

8

The red Camaro roared to life at the flick of the ignition key. *The car is the one thing that has gone halfway right*, Mark thought. *And even it wasn't too right.* The fiery grill paint had literally been blistered by the explosion and fire that night—when was it? Could it have been only two nights ago?

When the lawman had finally taken the cuffs off, Mark told and retold the story of the fire. Beard could find no inconsistencies in the telling. All Mark could do was speculate that Howell had set it up.

Then he told and retold the events at the hospital.

Poole phoned, interrupting Mark's story with his version of the day's events. He agreed to come up and give a full statement the next day.

Beard was fast running out of reasons to hold Mark in custody. He called the hospital. The floor nurses confirmed what Mark had told him.

So, as dusk neared, Beard had to admit he had no evidence. He gave Mark his keys and told him to get lost. "And stay fuckin' lost. And stay away from the fuckin' hospital," he ordered.

So he fired up the Camaro and headed toward the Cove. He wanted to talk about his vision, his nightmare, that monster. But Beard wouldn't have listened. He would have used the crazy story as grounds to hold him longer. Of that Mark was certain.

At home Mark saw a Tempo in the driveway, so he parked the Camaro at the curb. He couldn't place the car till he peered over the cyclone fence and saw the figure in the Nomex flight suit wrestling with Shep in the backyard. She was on her knees, holding the dog around the neck. Shep braced all fours, waiting for her to make the next move. She threw a hip into him. He leaned on her. She dropped, pulling him down.

The dog yipped. She laughed—a good, clean, healthy, hearty laugh.

The dog froze; muzzle lifted. It spun to confirm with its eyes what its nose had discovered and bounced across the yard.

Mark's own eyes watched the woman. She stood and brushed herself off. She smiled, eyes downcast, cheeks reddening. She said, "I . . . was . . ." She waved toward the food and water bowls.

"Thanks," he said. "I asked the major to find somebody."

There was a long moment of silence.

"He's a nice dog," she said lamely.

"Yeah. Shep." The dog perked up at its name.

"Yeah, I know."

They were both looking at the dog, unable to meet each other's eyes. The dog looked expectantly from one to the other as if wondering why neither paid any attention to him.

"Well, I'd better go now," she said. "Sir."

Mark gulped. "PJ, would you . . . come inside for a few minutes?"

She cocked her head.

"I mean . . . I'd like to thank you for taking care of Shep."

She cocked it again.

"No, I—I'd just like to talk. With a decent person. It's something I haven't done since . . . since I can't even remember."

She hesitated for a second. Then she smiled and went through the gate as he held the disappointed dog back.

"I'd like that," she said. "I really would."

The pair sat silent for fully half an hour, having exhausted the news from Texas, groping for an explanation to the apparent loss of that damnable research journal.

Beneath his calm exterior, the silvered aristocrat felt a rush of panic. The loss of that book was not a mere setback. It was a catastrophe. His career—maybe even his life—depended on recovering that book.

To the hulking giant, overflowing in the black leather chair, he said, "Where is that damned book?"

The hulk put an unlit cigar between his teeth and chomped down hard, knotting his temples. His only reply was a grunt.

Every hour or so throughout the night a feverish pair of red-rimmed eyelids would fly open, momentarily released from the interminable nightmares.

Finding no monsters outside the head to compare
with those inside, the eyes would peer at the darkened house just north of Hog Mountain. At four A.M.,
the eyes saw a light from inside. Finally. Thankfully.
Now Bradley Nathan Spellers could awaken fully,
temporarily escaping the dreams.

Spellers was not particularly adept as a sleuth. It
had taken him most of the day to realize that the soldier who had surprised him in Beth Howell's hospital
room was the same Captain Mark Payne who had
escaped the clinic fire according to the newspapers.
Even after he'd gotten the address from the phone
book it had taken him till after midnight to find the
house with the Camaro and Tempo parked in the
drive. He cruised by once with headlights and another time with the 1975 Grand Prix darkened, a
technique he'd seen in a television cop show. Then he
parked where he could watch.

A woman left in the Tempo at about twelve-thirty.
The house was dark by one o'clock. He took up the
vigil, knowing that he would find the answer to his
troubles in that house. He would finish his mission
after all.

Spellers saw the Camaro leave at four thirty-eight.
His heart sped up as the car's lights disappeared
around Hog Mountain. He clutched a twelve-inch
screwdriver in his lap, fondling the sharpened instrument. This was the closest thing to orgasm he'd experienced in the three years since Howell's shots had
destroyed his manhood. Maybe the shrink was right
about having a reason to live. Revenge was a reason,
wasn't it? And sensual too. Why, he'd felt the first

twinges of titillation as he began honing the screwdriver blade back and forth against a rock. He could
imagine the climax to come from plunging the foot of
metal clear through Warren Howell's starched body.

With the exception of the headlights far behind
and an occasional oncoming pair, Mark owned the
road. He nudged the Camaro to cruise at seventy,
windows down, T-top open, breeze swooshing loud,
building a shield of white noise around him. He
wanted a smoke; craved one, in fact. But now was the
time to quit. For the moment—because of the dumb
thing he did last night—he had no choice. He was out
of cigarettes.

He thought of her.

Pamela Jane Larson. PJ. She had actually accepted
his invitation to come in. He was grateful for that.
He needed somebody to talk to, and even his closest
buddy, Poole, was not the right somebody.

Mark had gone to the refrigerator and taken two
cartons of Marlboros from the freezer compartment.
He filled the sink, slit both cartons with a knife on
each side, cutting into every pack of the twenty.
Then he submerged the cartons for a few seconds,
letting the packages gurgle themselves out before
throwing the dripping mess into the trash.

"Looks like you're serious," she said.

"I'll have to empty all the ashtrays too—while I'm
still strong. Otherwise I'll be poking through them in
the morning. Maybe I can make it this time. It was
easier in the . . . in Marble Falls."

* * *

The Camaro dashed through Pidcoke, unnoticed by the still sleeping inhabitants of the thirty or so houses. And Mark barely noticed Pidcoke. He was remembering how she made him feel even though they'd barely gone beyond small talk. A reputation for not caring doesn't abide too much idle small talk —it ruins the rep.

She let him know his stay in the sanitarium should never embarrass him. She asked how he was recovering from his injuries. Standing by the sink, he showed her the finger, now barely swollen, hardly tender. He wiggled the pinky and shrugged.

"You looked so much worse off in that room with all the . . . zombies."

He remembered. "I felt like a zombie when I woke up. My face felt starched. . . ." He remembered the fragrance. "You were there. Your perfume woke me up, but nobody was there."

"Yes, I was there with the platoon."

They shared a gentle, warm moment of laughter. Then she pinned him with her eyes. Serious, caring eyes. "What happened?"

He told her of the night's drama and his suspicions of his brother-in-law. He described his self-dismissal from Darnall. He told her of the three-fingered man, his arrest, his confusion. He told her that nobody had believed him. That he felt like a criminal.

"I believe you," she said. And that was that.

He checked her eyes. She did believe him. He nearly blurted out the story of his dream or vision or sighting of that monster outside the clinic. Would she believe *that?*

"What's on your mind?" she asked.

"I . . . uh, nothing."

The Camaro's headlights glittered back from a set of eyes ahead. Mark stood on the brake pedal. A cow? The bulk disappeared into the brush. Not a cow. A bear. He slowed to a roll, passing through the dip. The remains of a raccoon were smeared on the pavement. One of the escaped animals was a grizzly. He made a mental note that he'd just barely crossed the pipeline.

Just then a pair of headlights caught the Camaro from behind. The lights dipped. Mark cringed. The beams weaved left and right as the car swerved, then sped by.

Mark felt a momentary twinge of embarrassment. He was surprised the driver didn't honk and flip him the finger. Then the cruise control took over, leveling his speed at seventy. And PJ took over his thoughts again.

She seemed to know he needed to talk. She asked him about his family. He simply started talking. It was so easy.

He talked for an hour about his childhood, his family, Vietnam.

She sipped her Pepsi, widening her eyes now and then, encouraging him to go on.

He told her about Beth, the brat kid who was always his and daddy's favorite and how she had grown away from them both.

"She refused to make peace with him even when he was dying," Mark said. "So I told him she loved him." Tears welled up in his eyes. He couldn't help it. Yet he didn't feel embarrassed. "He said he knew it. He said she'd get over it when she understood her feelings better. When she grew up."

He wiped his eyes. "This is a hell of a way for a hardass pilot to be acting. I don't even have the excuse of being falling down drunk."

PJ smiled at him but didn't say a word. She let him talk, and her own eyes filled up.

When he had finished, there was a long silence as he regained control of his emotions. She broke the mood with a change of subject.

"How come you never married?"

He pulled a bit of the shroud down between them. "Who says I never married?"

"I—I'm sorry. I—"

"Don't be sorry," he said with a smile meant to reassure her, to lift the shroud again. He looked at the clock on the wall above the dinette. "It's after midnight. No time for that story now. Later we'll trade stories about previous lives." He showed his best grin, a smile warmer than he'd let himself experience for a long time. "Maybe I'll even let you talk next time."

Mark showed her to the door and watched her until the Tempo pulled away. He went to bed right away—after emptying the ashtrays from his bedroom into the toilet—but didn't go to sleep until one-thirty or so. Yet when the alarm went off just two and a half hours later, he awoke refreshed. He actually bounced out of bed, eager to get on with the things he had to do before he went to work, before he might get to see her again.

He turned the Camaro east on Bald Knob Road on the very northern boundary of Fort Hood. The road would take him to Route 36 through North Fort, down toward the clinic and house where his sister once worked and lived. If he'd been paying attention to the rear view instead of the view of the lightening horizon through the windshield, he might have noticed headlights again—the same headlights—this time about a mile behind.

9

The man with three fingers on his right hand waited barely fifteen minutes after the Camaro's lights disappeared. He knew he had to move in on Howell before the sky lightened. He crept toward the house.

Even at six-three, slinking befitted him. Ever since the shooting—the fatal shooting as far as he was concerned—he seemed to be shrinking. Lacking a reason to stand tall and preen for the women of the world, he slumped, his once fluffy blown-dry hair gone greasy, his complexion running to blackheads and pimples. He belonged to the shadows much as a jackal belongs to the night.

He vaulted the fence and was at the back door when a cyclone hit him from behind. Shep burst from the hole under the house, attacking the rancid scent that had spooked him throughout the night. Shep's jaws closed on him from the side, piercing his calf with the top canines and sawing into his shin with the bottom fangs. Spellers stabbed downward with the screwdriver as if he were a veteran of a dozen commando raids. Again and again he stabbed. Shep held on, tossing the leg back and forth like a rag, working the teeth in deeper, until Spellers went down.

Spellers threw his forearm across his throat and waited. The attack never came. Shep had died with his jaws locked in place on the leg.

The three-fingered man sweated heavily as he worked, prying the jaws apart, breaking teeth with the screwdriver. He waited for the sirens to start wailing, for the lights to spot him lying in agony in the backyard. Maybe even Howell would burst out the back door, gun blazing again, and finish the job he'd started three years ago. The Labrador. This is what he had come to. It took all his will to fight back nausea. Dogs. His life—his life's potential—squashed by a dog. His leg now mangled by another damned dog. Ruined by fucking dogs.

Inside, he left a trail of blood from room to room, leading the way with the point of the screwdriver, forming pools at the doorways and corners where he'd stopped to listen before stepping beyond. His shoe squished as he walked.

But there was no Howell.

He searched again, this time without stealth, tearing through the house like an enraged tornado. Only when he passed by a window and noticed the brightness did the rage subside. He collected himself. He tore a clean sheet into bandages. He lifted his trouser leg and wrapped his puncture wounds tightly. Mesmerized by the sight of his own blood, he took off his shoe and poured it out on the carpet.

He limped out boldly into the morning and started driving aimlessly in his Pontiac, unsure how he

might go about finding this man Payne—the only
man who might lead him to the object of his search:
Howell.

An exhausted Paul Winston stared through binocu-
lars from nearly a mile away. He was too tired, too
upset—and it showed. His mind had drifted. He had
almost mated his car with the rear of the Camaro on
the way up. Imagine what his superiors would say if
he crashed into the man he was tailing. Not that it
mattered. He knew his career was over.

He'd driven past the access road to Howell's—no
way to approach during the day without being seen—
and parked below Bread Tray Mountain, the twin of
King Mountain. After climbing up the crumbling
side of the bluff, he hunkered down like one of the
junipers, his back to the hill, and trained the binocu-
lars on the charred area near the Leon River.

For a long time Payne sat inside the Camaro. Then
he'd gotten out and stood leaning on a fender. Every
once in a while the green-clad figure, small and indistinct even through the Nikon glasses, would turn to
the pecan tree, then back to the ashes. Payne was remembering, splicing the facts. Winston lowered the
glasses and rubbed his eyes. He lowered his head to
rest on his knees. He remembered too.

Winston's fatigue compounded the feeling of defeat
that kept swamping his consciousness. But more than
that, he truly felt depressed, and for the first time,
guilty. He'd been through an operation like this before, going days without changing clothes, bearing
the heat and the boredom during the day and endur-

ing the task of interrogation and reporting at night. So that part wasn't particularly new, either. What was new was that, as he watched Payne, he found himself feeling compassion.

Payne was just an ordinary citizen. He'd done nothing to deserve this—the worst thing in his file was a juvenile conviction for possession of beer. All he did was enter the army at a time and place when and where the service did a few drug experiments on people without their knowledge, let alone their consent. Then Fate doubled up on that accident by allowing Payne's sister to marry a psychopath who would try to engineer the stuff of life itself for profit, manufacturing a generation of . . . things that would work for room and board and never complain or resign, or be late, or cry or reproduce or anything. They'd be programmed to do windows, shovel walks in winter, cut grass. They could be made in any color —a concession to the egalitarians, perhaps. They'd be cheaper than robots and more docile than Mexican illegals. They could become a permanent underclass. They could become a standing army of infantrymen who never challenged orders or demanded promotions or suffered from fear. They could be anything that people like Howell engineered them to be, that is, once he got past the current little glitch, the stage where they turned into raging monsters like the one now on the loose.

And Payne's final mistake was to drop in the day the monster got loose. Just as he and Buchanan tried to destroy the evidence of its existence.

Winston thanked Payne. Had it not been for his

heroism, Winston would be a murderer. He thanked God (someone he hadn't thought of in a long time) that he was only an accidental murderer. Howell was truly accidental. How was that stupid Buchanan to know a double dose would burn out Howell's brain. All they'd wanted was information. At least Howell was a bloody ruthless bastard who almost needed killing.

Payne was another matter, an innocent.

His superiors would call Winston's reticence a loss of nerve, a lack of guts—because he'd never been tested in a murder situation before—and that's what it was, dammit. Murder, not elimination or termination or discontinuance. Murder.

Winston had learned a couple of things from Mr. Payne. First, that he wasn't cut out to be a killer. And second, that honor was important and that whatever shred of honor and decency remained in him would go into the unmarked grave with Army Captain Mark Payne if he killed him.

A lump formed in Winston's throat. *It is the fatigue*, he told himself, trying to keep a grip on his emotions. *Just the fatigue*. He lifted the glasses and saw Payne squat down beside the gas meter.

Mark's brain raced through a dozen recollections, emotions, reactions. The heat made him dizzy. Or was it the turmoil in his head, the tempest in his chest?

A blackened wrench lay under the meter. He put the jaws on the valve and replayed his movements Friday night. He had pulled that valve shut. Now it was open. Though somebody—probably fire fighters —had turned off the gas at the main, somebody else, before the fire department arrived, had turned the gas back on that night. The fire had been set. Somebody had tried to kill him and Beth.

Questions. Why would Howell want to kill Beth? Why would he try to kill his brother-in-law? Who was that three-fingered man? Why would he try to kill Beth?

Answers? Where the hell were the answers?

All he knew for certain was that somebody had tried to kill him. Somebody had tried to kill Beth— poor, pathetic Beth—and for all practical purposes had succeeded. Warren Howell had disappeared.

And a lot of the blame for things seemed to keep coming back to Captain Mark Payne—by default if nothing else. Maybe it was his fault. It could be. For no other reason than that he had no control. Thirty-three years old and still couldn't control his life, himself, anything.

The world won't pull the strings for you, said a little voice. *You have to do it yourself. You have to see the strings. Recognize them, identify them, untangle them. Pull the right ones. Accept the consequences of pulling the wrong ones. The worst thing you can do is stand by and let others yank on every string from your dental floss to your vas deferens.* The voice told him what he already knew—he spent his whole life watching what was happening to him as if he were a bystander . . . to his own destiny.

The voice began to shriek at him. It set goose flesh percolating on his sweaty neck. It started shrill and ended in a cough, then began again on the high note.

He opened his eyes. The daydream was gone. But not the shrieking.

He rose to his feet and looked to the corrals in back. A pony. A little Shetland mare tossed her head, her ears barely clearing the top plank of the fence, beckoning him. For a moment, the edges of his vision went black. When the dizziness subsided, he strode to the rear stock pens.

He felt ill when he saw her. Great black gashes down her ribs and flanks were scabs and open sores filled with flies and boiling rice beds of maggots. Hay and filth from the corral caked over the wounds. She held her left rear hoof off the ground.

He saw her water trough was dry. He turned on the faucet above the trough and her belly swelled as she drank deeply. The fetid odor rising from the dead animals in other pens kept convulsing Mark's stomach. Probably the fire fighters had seen the mare's wounds and assumed she was dead as well.

But she was anything but dead. Three days with those wounds. In this heat. Without water. He found a bale of hay and tossed it in. She tore at the bale, went back to the water, went back to the hay. She was bent on surviving. It probably never occurred to her to do otherwise.

The mare was a fighter. Mark vowed to help her live. And he vowed to begin taking care of somebody else he'd been neglecting too. Himself. He'd commanded other men. Time he took command of himself. Time he became a fighter too.

First the mare. He'd ask Dodson to take her in at the zoo. Then he'd better get to Britton. The deputy seemed like a sensible man. Maybe he could help answer some questions.

10

Sheriff Jacob Zebulon Beard was on another tear, storming through the office. After slamming the phone receiver down in its cradle on his desk, he tossed a pencil against the front door. It clattered feebly on the floor.

"Jesus H. Christ. Why me, Lord?" His face had gone pale after the phone conversation. He threw an ashtray that resounded against the door with a much more satisfying crash.

"What's up, Jake?" asked Britton. Riley left the room before Beard began flinging dispatchers instead of desk furnishings.

Beard picked up the telephone. After a moment's hesitation he put it back down. Hard. "Any more of this shit and I'm gonna start my ass back to church. First the fire, then the animals, then the tiger hunts up the ass. No sooner do we get the lion put away and three tiger hunters disappear. Next we get bear hunts up the ass."

Britton said, "Jake, that call. The three teenagers?"

Beard swallowed his Adam's apple and lit a cigarette. "Down by Preachers Creek. Truck overturned in a gully. Been dead for more'n a day by the smell."

Britton was silent. More frantic families to notify. More panic. Searchers had found more and more dead animal remains. Nobody knew whether the animal deaths could be attributed to thirst, starvation, or escaped predators, because varmints and vultures had worked the carcasses over. Nobody could even say whether the number of carcasses was more than normal or just seemed more numerous because of the quantity of searchers. And in the morning another hunter, a Temple man out for bear, had disappeared —last seen near Owl Creek.

Mark Payne entered and stooped to pick up the ashtray. He looked quizzically at Britton, whose expression warned him to be careful.

"Good morning, Sheriff. Deputy."

"My ass, Payne. What the fuck you want up here?"

"I just came by to have a word with the deputy, Sheriff, on my way to work."

"What you got to tell my depitty you can't tell me, punk?"

"Nothing, Sheriff. I didn't think you'd want to listen to me."

"Now where'd you get a fuzzy notion like that?" He pulled his hat brim down and crossed to the door.

"I just thought you'd be busy. But if you're interested—"

"You're right." He threw a sneer as he passed by.

"What's that, Sheriff?"

"I ain't got time for none of your shit."

And he was out the door.

Britton stood up behind his desk. "He takes some getting used to."

"Easy for you to say."

"He's got a lot on his mind. He's on the way out to the south of here to see a pickup full of dead teenagers. Don't tell anybody. Sheriff would be mad."

Mark rolled his eyes back.

"What'd you want to tell me about the Howells'?" Britton said as he motioned to a chair. Mark sat.

"I found a few things that raise many more questions. If we can come up with a few answers, maybe it will help find Howell or whoever's responsible."

"First, somebody set that fire. I'm sure you're right about that. I told you I went out with Howell to shut off the gas valve at the meter before checking around the clinic. That's when I got hit on the head. You know the story."

Nod.

"That night I turned the gas off. I remember shutting that valve. This morning I found the valve open again. Somebody opened it before setting the fire. That's what caused the explosion."

Britton sniffed. "I been more or less sure it was arson since Saturday when I seen the place in the daylight. The smell of gasoline in the dirt between the house and the trailer was too strong to have come from the burned pickup and van. That fire was too quick, too hot, too . . ."

"Thorough?"

"Yep. Somebody didn't want any sign of anything found."

"Who?"

"You think Howell?"

"I thought so at first, but the more I think about things the less I think so."

"Why not?"

"He was a selfish s.o.b., but I think he loved Beth. He was truly shocked at the destruction at the trailer when we went in. He was worried about her. I'm sure he wasn't faking. He didn't set it up."

"You're right."

"Huh?"

"I checked in town. He'd been to the bank till closing. Then he bought a beer he didn't drink and made a couple dozen phone calls on the pay phone—spent a lot of money in quarters. Barkeep remembers. He didn't start back home till near dark. It fits with the story you told."

Mark cocked his head and surveyed the lanky Britton with new respect.

"So where did my brother-in-law disappear to?"

Britton wagged his head and raised an eyebrow. "Dunno. You hear any more from those insurance agents?"

"No."

"I'm not surprised. They weren't insurance agents."

"What?" Mark sat up.

"I wondered how the company would even know about the fire. Nobody'd make a claim but you and you were out cold for a long time and never mentioned it later. I also wondered why a company would be so anxious to send two men to check out a beat-up old Pinto. Then I noticed when the sheriff mentioned your name, these two zeroed in on you like a couple hawks. So I checked out the Empire Insurance Company."

"It doesn't exist?"

"Oh, it exists, all right. And they had two agents by those names, but neither of them has ever been to Texas."

"Who were they, then?"

"I don't know. But I do know who your three-fingered man is."

Mark's pulse picked up. Britton was thorough. And sharp.

"His name is Bradley Spellers. Used to be a grad student at A & M. Worked for Howell. He lost his fingers in a lab accident and Warren Howell accidentally shot him in the gonads."

"What?"

"Officially, Howell was cleaning a pistol and it went off. Slug hit Spellers in the family jewels. Spellers went in and out of the nuthouse. Tried to kill himself a couple times, last time quite a while ago. His doctor says he's not violent anymore. . . ."

"But he tried to kill my sister."

"You think so. And so do I."

Mark had to smile. It was a relief to have someone believe his story. "Do you think he started the fire at the clinic?"

"That's my best guess. I've put out a bulletin and I been looking. In between hunts for bears. And teenagers. And bear hunters."

"Do you think Beth is in danger?"

"Yep. Sheriff asked the hospital to put extra security on her—because of you. So she's pretty safe."

They sat silently for a few awkward seconds. Then Mark stood up.

Britton said, "By the way, you got a gun?"

"Yes. You want it?"

"No. You ought to think about carrying it. This three-fingered guy might come after you."

"Why would he do that?"

Shrug. "Why would he want to kill your sister?"

Mark shook his head. He remembered the black form he saw on his drive around the north horn of the fort this morning. "I'm sure I saw your grizzly bear beside the road from the Cove. Just north of the pipeline."

Britton squinted at him. "We haven't had any sightings or livestock reported missing over on the west side. I'll make some calls to the ranchers on that side."

Mark stuck out a hand. "And I'll fly over that way today."

Britton gripped the hand and smiled. "I'm going to check it out myself the first minute I get time—right after I get the provost marshal off your ass as a suspect."

Mark called Poole from a Gatesville phone booth. The operations officer's excitement infected him.

"Hey, asshole, where are you? We gotta get going before the rest of these turkeys find that bear."

"What's up?" asked Mark.

"Governor asked for some help after two days of not finding the three teenagers and another hunter turned up missing over near Preachers Creek. They

think maybe we got a man-eater for a goddamned
bear. So now the Newnited States Army is in on the
action. And guess what? We're the fucking cavalry. I
mean they're issuing weapons from the arms room
and everything.

Mark felt a surge. "I saw that bear this morning on
my way toward Gatesville."

"Are you sure?"

"Does a bear shit in the woods?"

"Anybody else know?"

"The deputy sheriff up here. But he's got his hands
full of other stuff."

"Well, forget him. I'll pull the preflight and file a
flight plan. You just haul your ass in here. You can
use my three fifty-seven."

Payne sped toward Gray, unmindful of the ancient
Grand Prix steaming along behind, trying to keep up.
He urged the Camaro in a final sprint to the flight
line and parked behind the operations shack. As he
gathered his flight gear from the trunk, Poole came
out and leaned against the rear fender, arms folded,
head hanging.

"What's up?"

"Might as well throw that shit back."

"Why?"

"DePree won't let me fly."

"Why?"

"You think he explains to me? All he said was for
me to tell you to drag your ass up there before you go
out."

"Bullshit. After we get back. We got bears to hunt
down."

Poole shook his huge, greasy head. "Fucker is getting too smart. He's got us figured out. He said if I let you fly before he talks to you, he'll send me to battalion too. . . ." The head came up with the admission.

"Battalion? So he did tell you what he wanted. You mean he still thinks I'd go?"

"He didn't act like it was open for discussion."

"Fuck him. Let's go bear hunting."

Poole sighed. "Mark, you know I would. But he told me directly. You're my asshole buddy, but I ain't going to a staff job for nobody. I'd sooner go bear hunting with nothing but a hard-on for a weapon. Besides, I already gave the aircraft to Mills and Barnett. Theirs went inop for radios."

Mark put a hand on the slumped shoulder and squeezed. "Get avionics down here to fix the radios on that bird Mills and Barnett left dead on the line. I'll go up and shake the drops off DePree's wiener."

While the platoon was bear hunting, PJ had drawn the task of inventorying forms and records so new stocks could be ordered. Odd number of pilots. So she was odd woman out. She sat idly with a lap full of blank forms, thinking about last night. She had called Maggie after getting home.

"What?" the drowsy voice had asked.

"Maggie, I said it's me, PJ."

"I heard that, Peej. I mean what the hell could any friend of mine be doing calling after one o'clock in the goddamned morning?"

"I'm sorry. It was thoughtless of me. Maybe I should let you get back to sleep."

"Are you bullshitting me? No way now. Now I'm dying to know whether you got laid."

"Come on, Maggie."

"Okay. So why *did* you call? Certainly not to correct my foul mouth."

"No. I just had a long talk with Mister Hard Guy Payne. I found out he's a human being."

"Translate please. Is this anatomically speaking?"

"No. He's one of those people who wear a shell to keep people away. But now he's having a tough time personally, and he doesn't really have anybody to turn to. I mean, he does have friends—Poole—but he's not the kind of friend you talk to."

"Let me get this straight. Payne's best buddy is now Pamela Jane Larson after all these hours she's known him."

"Yes, I guess so. You know, it's just . . . different talking with a woman—with any person of the opposite sex. I just spent hours talking to him . . . listening really."

"And he didn't make a move on you?"

"No. Come on, Maggie, I'm serious here. We talked for a few hours. Nothing went on."

"Hey, kid, I'm happy for you. But at this time of morning, what can I say?"

"I don't know. I'm worried because I like him. I know it can only lead to liking him more. And that can only lead to trouble."

Payne burst into the platoon shack, rattling her from her reverie.

"C'mon," he growled.
She stood up, forms flying.
His voice softened as their eyes met.
"Let's go flying."

11

Wilbur Waskom stood munching half a salami sandwich and surveying the upper reaches of intermittent Riley Branch, which during the rains flowed into the Cowhouse. The deputy had said to be on the lookout for a grizzly. Waskom decided there was little chance of a bear traveling across the artillery ranges to his property. Probably another of those phantom sightings. He left his Chevy pickup, door wide open, at the cut bank of Riley Branch and jumped the dry ditch. From the high ground a quarter mile from where he left his pickup, he could see most of his spread. Just as he thought. No bears. No nothing.

Mark couldn't remember the last time he'd felt liberated, captivated, enraptured by army aviation. After flight school, yes—because he'd achieved something: the wings he polished every day for the first weeks, then monthly, finally only for inspections. In Vietnam? Yes.

But after he returned from Vietnam that second time, friends dead and the country he came home to almost unrecognizable, flying ceased to be fun. Mark took a discharge to go back to college. And the army was happy to release a surplus pilot.

Four years later, the reductions in aviation had been only too effective. So the army asked certain separated pilots to return to duty. Mark, having forgotten some of the bad times, took a commission as a first lieutenant and returned to flying.

It had never been as much fun or as worthwhile as Vietnam again. But today was coming close. Maybe it was because he had Poole's loaded .357 strapped under his armpit. For the first time since he could remember, he was on a mission. Or maybe . . . just maybe . . . he was enjoying the opportunity to fly with the green-eyed blonde who listened so well.

Not-So-Gentle Ben picked up the scent of salami, his favorite meat—often shared between him and his pal, Dodson—and a tidbit eminently preferable to greasy, musky raccoons, armadillos, and possums lying squashed on the asphalt. He found the smell emanating from the pickup and climbed into the cab to dine. Half a sandwich hardly tingled the boa of his tongue, so he scratched for more in the crevice of the seat where the smell was strongest.

It was the truck rocking on its suspension that first caught Wilbur Waskom's attention. From a hundred yards he could only guess that somebody must be trying to steal the pickup. He ran toward the Chevy, shouting, until he saw the hulking bear. Waskom would have left well enough alone if that damned bear hadn't been throwing something out of the cab. If that something hadn't been the stuffing of the seat.

Waskom was one of those Texans who hold their horse—and by extension, their pickups—sacred. If Ben had been mauling on Waskom's wife, he might have run for help. But the bear was screwing with his pickup. So he began pegging rocks at the bear. A lucky shot rattled around in the longbed and startled the grizzly.

Ben piled out to investigate and ambled toward the tailgate.

Waskom still might have left things alone. But he figured a little success could be stretched with a couple more well-placed rocks. A third dreadfully unlucky stone hit Ben on his humped shoulders.

The hungry grizzly spun, swiping at the phantom assailant that had rapped him from behind.

Still Waskom would have escaped trouble if he had stood quietly, if he had not shouted, if the breeze had not carried his scent to the lumbering giant.

But Waskom roared a few Texas obscenities at the bear and whooped, waving his arms to frighten it.

Ben's dim vision picked up the waving signals coming from the direction of the whoops and hollers. Then the scent of salami wafted to his nostrils. It occurred to Not-So-Gentle Ben that a giant salami sandwich was trying to attract his attention, volunteering to be eaten. The bear lumbered off to oblige.

No helicopter pilot flying visual flight rules will resist following the roads, power lines, and rivers. A pilot will go out of the way to pick up one of those features rather than navigate by dead reckoning—flying given headings for specified times.

So PJ simply followed the road north at one thousand feet and at Mark's signal, turned left abruptly at the pipeline, banking the Huey forty-five degrees on its side. The blades began popping against the air at this maneuver. Mark looked to his left—down—to begin his search for the grizzly.

And there below him, the entire scene unfolded: brown and beige pickup, loping bear, scrambling man with a fifty-foot head start.

"Holy shit," he exclaimed. "There it is."

"Come on, Captain."

"No joke. I've got the controls." He dropped the collective.

She may not have believed him, but she instantly acknowledged the positive transfer of helicopter controls. "You've got it." She looked out of the cockpit and whispered, "Holy shit."

"Call in our location on FM," he commanded. "We're west of Old Georgetown Road, where the pipeline crosses the road to Gatesville."

Concentrating on the scene below, he heard her talking. She asked for *Lifesaver* to be launched—*a good head on her shoulders, that one.*

The grizzly closed fast. Waskom, running uphill, had begun to tire. His arms flailed. He stumbled and nearly went down. The bear closed to twenty feet.

Mark made the animal his approach point and dove. At ten feet, he pulled in an armload of power, swamping the bear in a hurricane of downwash and noise. He momentarily lost the bear under the belly of the craft. The tail swung right. He backed up to see the effect of his maneuver.

It worked. The bear's attention was diverted. Ben began spinning. It swiped at the craft above it as if fighting off bees.

It worked only too well. The rotor wash also flattened Waskom. He lay groveling; forearms up to fend off an attacking bear. Less than fifteen feet separated the bewildered pair.

Mark hovered ahead, putting the skids between bear and man. "I can't see the bear, Peej, you take the controls."

"I've got it."

Mark looked for the man to be readying himself to clamber aboard if they landed. But no. Waskom had curled into a fetal position, beaten down by the rotor wash.

PJ shouted, "The damned bear is coming for us."

"Lead it away."

He needn't have told her. She pulled away, hovering sideways, keeping low enough to interest the grizzly. It followed.

Waskom had regained his composure and movement of his feet and started stumbling toward the pickup. It looked as if he might make it.

Ben lumbered after him. Waskom made the mistake of looking back. Either the sight of the grizzly or the movement of his head and shoulders set him off balance, and he fell again.

"Put the bird between them again." Mark pulled his pistol, lowered the window, and aimed a bouncing arm at the bear.

PJ, frantically working pedals, cyclic and collective, and slid into the twenty-foot space. Again the bear attacked. This time it lost interest as soon as she backed away.

Mark let loose a shot that missed by half an acre.

The man on the ground was gasping. Or was it retching? Or was he having a heart attack?

"I'm going down," he said.

"Are you crazy?"

"Let's get him away as far as we can, then dash toward the guy. Hit the deck like a touch and go and let me out. I'll get him up to the pickup; you lead the bear away."

"No. I won't let you."

"I said put this thing down."

"*Shoot it,*" she shouted. "You don't have to land to shoot it."

"I tried that. Dammit, PJ, do as I say or give me the fucking controls and I'll do this myself."

The Huey danced as she fought him for the cyclic. "Okay," she said. "You are crazy," she muttered as she began a descent.

Mark started to say something to calm her. But her lips were working as she concentrated on the maneuver. She was cussing him out under her breath. Just then it seemed funny.

He unstrapped himself. The skids bounced on the slope, and Mark was out. He latched the door and PJ drifted the aircraft toward the bear, keeping between it and the men.

Mark ran to the downed man and looked back. The bear had followed the Huey. Waskom was struggling to his feet, holding his throat.

"Can't bree—"

"Forget it, old-timer. I'll help. Here." He took a thin arm and draped it over his neck. A few steps, and he looked back. So far, so good.

"Can't bree—"

"Shut up and save your breath, mister."

Waskom gargled again and slumped.

"Shit, mister." Mark turned and pulled the man over his shoulder. He looked back. No longer so good. The bear had given up on the helicopter. It rambled directly at Mark, closing the fifty-foot gap in five-foot bounds.

He took off, running toward the pickup. No use.

He dropped the man and spun on the bear.

Twenty-five feet.

He went for the .357.

Twenty feet.

It was almost as if he was an impartial observer. The helicopter was closing in on him as well. He brought up the magnum, cocking in one motion.

Fifteen feet.

The stairstep sight covered a crease between pig-like eyes. His finger took up the trigger slack.

The pistol slammed his stiff arm into his shoulder joint.

A puff of dust exploded on the bear's hump.

The bear skidded at ten feet and abruptly stood up, letting out a moaning bellow. The huge paws dog-paddled the air in front of its muzzle.

The bear began to topple forward. If it fell, it would be on Mark's face.

The gun roared, jolting him again. Ben's head tossed back. Mark fired three times more, and the

bear continued to toss its head as if catching peanuts back at the zoo.

A skid of the Huey sailed by Mark's ear and bowled the bear over.

The .357 followed Ben to the ground. Mark staggered, fighting the rotor wash.

Ben sat up on his haunches. He bellowed, but the sound was literally drowned in his throat. Muzzle down on his chest, he swayed in large circles.

Mark started to back away. Waskom groaned and sat up. Not ten feet away sat the bear. The man gasped and grabbed Mark's legs.

"Let go, mister," Mark shouted.

Ben perked up, seemed to remember why he was so angry, and made a half-lunge at the men. Waskom recoiled. Mark went down.

The bear loomed not three feet away from Mark's face, literally casting a shadow on him. Mark thrust the .357's muzzle into the frothing mouth and squeezed a last shot between a forest of teeth, into the roof of the mouth. The last thing he remembered was a warm shower before the stinking hulk of the grizzly knocked the wind out of him.

PJ had, in the vernacular of warrant officers, been busier than a one-legged man in an ass-kicking contest. Every pilot listening in on the Vulture frequency heard her announce the bear sighting and call for help. Every one called back to ask one stupid question or other until Poole entered the radio net and silenced the jabbermouths with a simple "You people shut the fuck up." When the frequency was quiet, he said, *"Double-oh-eight*, this is *Vulture Three*, where the hell are you?"

She hadn't answered because she was swooping on the grizzly. She felt the skid hit. She prayed it was the bear and not Mark. She swung the tail around and saw them through the chin bubble between her feet. All three were down. The man grappled with Mark. The bear sat up, then lunged.

"It's on Mark," she screamed over the air. "Shit," she said, fighting for control. "Send *Lifesaver*. The bear is on them."

The effect of her report was electric. The radio was quiet for a full thirty seconds. Long enough for PJ to land.

She didn't know what to do. Everybody, including the bear, seemed to be dead. What if the grizzly came back to life? Her indecision on what to do was maddening to her. But in the next few seconds, she learned firsthand the dynamics of heroism. Angry, indecisive, worried sick about somebody else more than herself, hating herself for feeling so helpless— she just acted. It wasn't rational, wasn't smart, wasn't planned, probably wasn't right. But she did it. She twisted the throttle back to idle, shut the fuel and electric switches off and locked down the controls. In seconds she was out on the ground, .38 pistol in hand, ducking under the whispering, whipping blades, striding toward the grizzly bear and the two men.

Nolan Parish was upset, even alarmed. He had monitored the standard emergency radio frequencies, both UHF and VHF. There should have been a crash an hour ago—he had listened to N95777's takeoff on the UHF tower frequency. No crash on takeoff. And no crash an hour later. He hated "hit and miss." He especially hated "miss." This miss was a matter of life and death—if that helicopter didn't crash and if Payne lived, Parish was dead. And he knew it. Now here was this woman calling in an emergency and using the name Mark and the call sign of a platoon leader—and they were in a helicopter with the tail number of 008, not 777. For the first time in his career, he was shaken. Badly.

PJ strode up to the bear and kicked it in the ribs. It was like a fur-covered brick, numbing her ankle. She had half expected to have her ankle torn off. But the bear didn't attack. It didn't move.

She sobbed in relief and put the pistol aside. The bear's muzzle covered Mark's bloody head and shoulders, and seeing that shook her with another sob. She felt for Mark's pulse: it was slow and steady. She touched the old man's neck, and he jerked to life, his eyes and mouth wide as if in a silent scream.

"The bear?"

"Dead."

"What about this soldier?"

"Help me," she ordered.

Together they tried to pry the bear's muzzle away from Mark. But when they lifted the massive, bloody head, the flight helmet came up, too.

The man got down on his knees. "I see the problem. The jaw is clamped down on his helmet. Maybe we can pull him clean out of it."

PJ held her breath as they worked.

When Mark came free of the bulk, PJ gasped. His neck and head were soaked in thickening scarlet. But Waskom probed the skull and neck and turned Mark on his back.

"The skin ain't broke. His clothes ain't tore up. This is all bear blood. I'll get me some water from the pickup and bring him to."

Mark was dreaming again. He felt his world closing in blackly, crushing the breath from him.

The water hit him in the face and slapped him awake instantly. He looked into her eyes. PJ's shocked eyes. Waskom was draining a plastic gallon milk jug full of ice water on them from an altitude of four feet. Mark sat up, blubbering and gasping. She shrieked as the water poured into her lap.

The helicopter is the world's undisputed champion vibrator.

The smoothest of these machines buzzes, jumps, and wobbles on a thousand different frequencies. Flying in one belongs to the realm of the erotic. The body absorbs the vibrations, resonates in tune with the whines, sops up the rhythms—it's like lovemaking with a familiar, experienced partner. In hovering flight especially, and at low altitude and high speeds, the body picks up the pulse of the craft, anticipates the turns, the drops, the climbs. The passenger becomes contemptuous of gravity as soon as he realizes that centrifugal force will press him into the seat in a banking turn so he can sit horizontally, looking down at Earth without feeling its pull. The vibrations of the craft become the body's rhythms. The body becomes an organ within the craft. The eyes become mere portholes for looking outside the belly of the beast that is the throbbing helicopter.

The most obvious sources of vibration in the Huey are the rotor blades. At cruise flight, the main rotor blades make three hundred twenty-four revolutions a minute. They set up a characteristic bounce because getting them perfectly balanced is nigh impossible: little rocks tossed up in the air by the rotor wash at hover are pulled down and each dent in one blade makes its aerodynamics different from the other. Park a helicopter with one blade in the shade and it will fly a variant track because of temperature differential. If one blade flies above the track of the other, it pitches the nose up a fraction with every rotation. Because the blade advancing into the wind meets more resistance than the retreating blade, main rotors literally flap up on each backswing, creating enough resistance to equalize that of the front-swinging blade. The result is another vibration. Abrupt banking turns and even routine descents set the blades to *wop-wop-wopping*, the characteristic sound of an approaching Huey.

The nearly invisible tail rotor sets up a high frequency vibration, which, if excessive, is enough to drive a pilot nuts tickling his feet on the pedals. The tail rotor drive shaft has its vibration, however slight, as it turns through its bearings delivering torque to the tail.

The turbine engine delivers six thousand six hundred revolutions a minute to the vibrations. There is the generator, fuel pumps, inverters, gyrocompasses, gear boxes, and transmission gears. Not to mention the effect of wind passing over the fuselage, hydraulic pressures stiffening and relaxing lines, humming radios, and a thousand other singing parts of the helicopter.

These vibrations add to the magic of helicopter flight. They are also the reason every movable, screwable, adjustable, fastenable part would jiggle loose and fly off the craft within an hour of takeoff were it not for half a dozen types of positive-locking safeguards. Latches are two-stage snap-and-lock affairs. Dzus fasteners—part screw, part spring-loaded catches—secure inspection access doors. Locking rivets hold the skin joints together.

There are no simple screws or nuts or bolts. Cotter pins hold nuts in place. So do special castellated nuts, designed for slip-free, one-time use. Special washers have bend-up collars to keep bolts from turning.

The most common form of securing threaded connections and nuts and bolts is the ubiquitous safety wire. Stainless steel strands of various gauge twist and wend their way throughout the airframe and engine like baling wire on a Texas jalopy. Nuts and bolts are drilled. Wire is threaded and twisted to take up the slack. Then the whole affair is anchored to an immobile part, preventing the movable part from loosening.

It requires no special talent to sabotage a helicopter.

* * *

The first pilots at the scene saw two men, a woman and a dead bear. The people were passing a milk jug, washing themselves, laughing, hugging—in general, acting like idiots.

Warrant Officer Stanley Mills was flying around the southernmost tip of West Fort when he heard the call about the bear. "Finally some action," he said to his copilot Andy Barnett. "Goddammit, we're lucky."

Mills, a twenty-one-year-old high school graduate with a loaded pistol under his arm, sitting at the controls of his half-million-dollar flying machine. As far as he was concerned, he was the luckiest man alive.

In less than eight minutes he had 777 at the pipeline.

Mills and Barnett began circling at a thousand feet. Their attention was on the cluster on the ground. Stambrough had tethered himself by a monkey strap to tie-down on the deck. He was hanging out the side of the craft; his feet on the skid. Nobody saw the master caution light illuminate on the instrument panel of N95777. Nor the oil pressure light nor the oil hot light illuminated on the caution panel. They couldn't have seen the snipped safety wire or the hose fitting blast loose from the transmission. They might have felt the rattle if their attention hadn't been riveted outside. But they didn't see or feel a thing for precious seconds.

When Mills dropped the collective, the Huey slewed violently as the smoking transmission gears mis-meshed for a second. Three sets of eyes went to the segment lights to diagnose the problem.

Mills should not have—had he been a more thoughtful professional, he would not have—dropped the collective and twisted the throttle down to idle, entering an autorotational glide. He should not have done so because bad as the transmission condition was, keeping engine drive on it might have kept it in one piece for a few seconds longer. But once the power to the transmission was unloaded, it simply froze up.

Barnett knew. He screamed "No!" and reached for the controls.

Too late. Even if Mills hadn't acted incorrectly, it might not have made a difference, since the transmission had run dry minutes ago.

Mills screamed, "Mayday!"

The center of the fuselage disintegrated.

"Mayday. . . ."

Other Vulture pilots had landed at the bear scene asking a hundred questions at the same time.

N95777's blades *wop-wop-wopped* as it began its descent.

Nobody paid attention. Until it exploded. Then everybody on the ground locked into freeze-frame, their heads skyward.

It wasn't a true explosion as if fuel or dynamite had blown the helicopter apart. The transmission gears seized, welding themselves together. The main rotor blades, four hundred seven pounds apiece, refused to stop so suddenly. So they wrenched the transmission

out the side of the fuselage, tearing the helicopter in
two, bursting two fuel cells, and drenching the
wreckage in JP-4. One rotor ducked down through
the cockpit, nailing Barnett to the seat, bisecting him
diagonally across the chest. The other blade snapped
off and went spinning across the sky like a blade of
grass in haying season. The engine oversped, flamed
out, and disintegrated. The front half of the fuselage
hit the ground and burst into an orange and black
fireball.

The only man with a chance for survival was Sergeant Willie Stambrough, who fell or jumped from
the fuselage when the transmission lurched free of its
moorings. He hung outside on the monkey strap like
an astronaut on a space walk. As the fuselage tumbled, he swung around in a giant arc like a yo-yo in
the trick "around the world." Those on the ground
marveled at the feat, whispering obscenities in awe.
When the fuselage hit, Stambrough was on an up-
swing. Slow motion, he belly-flopped into the earth.
The tail section came down last, drilling him where
he lay.

The crowd of pilots took off, running toward the
crash.

Mark swooned and almost went down. PJ grabbed
his arm.

"You'd better lie down," she said.

"No," he shot back. "Forget the dizziness, PJ."

"Forget it? How can I—"

"You just forget this. You don't mention a thing,
understand?"

She nodded.

"I'm not going back to the hospital."

She wondered about the abrupt mood swing. For a second this afternoon, she had seen some more of that warmth and vulnerability he'd revealed last night. She could still feel his touch from minutes ago. He had laughed, congratulated her, applauded her flying, and praised her bravery. He had thanked her. And he had hugged her.

But now the man seemed to be spurning her. Again. She liked him better when he was unconscious. She felt like taking the butt of the .38 and rapping him on the head. It was this anger that tipped her off. For chrissakes, she was falling for him.

As they neared the crash site, the fire held them back with a wall of heat. There could be no survivors. The men settled in to watch the ship burn itself out into a pool of molten metal.

More helicopters were approaching. The one with the red cross on the nose compartment was *Lifesaver*. The group began to hail it, waving arms and Day-Glo orange panels taken from various pockets in pants and survival vests. PJ did not join in. There were enough rescuers. Too many, probably. She turned to say as much to him.

Mark wasn't paying attention to the fire. He had stopped at the tail section where Stambrough had been pinioned. Awestruck by something in the wreckage, he knelt by the tail fin. He stared at the black letters on olive paint: N95777. He was to have flown it.

He would have died in it.

12

Winston and Parish continued to follow the saga of the bear by eavesdropping on the tactical FM radio and the universal aviation emergency frequencies. The news of the crash hit them hard. Winston was shaken because he had been party to the murder of three innocent people. Parish was shaken even worse because he knew this error would end everything he ever wanted to achieve.

"How the hell did he get in zero-zero-eight?" Parish finally said. "He was scheduled to fly seven-seven-seven."

Winston grimaced. "How the hell should I know?" he said. "Maybe you could have that goofy DePree chew his butt for not taking the one that was supposed to kill him."

Parish went gray. "We have to report this fuck-up."

"No need."

"You think we're under surveillance?"

Winston answered with silence.

Parish said what they both knew, "They've had somebody on us ever since that monster escaped, ever since the press jumped in on the animal escapes and the fire, haven't they? That first day at the hamburger joint I knew it. I saw your face. You knew it too, didn't you?"

Winston answered with more silence.

Parish began to breathe harder. "We've done nothing but screw up by the numbers, and we both know what happens to major screw-ups."

Winston heaped on the silence. His gaze seemed to go right through the dingy walls of the motel room to stare at a distant planet.

"You think we can recover?" asked Parish.

Silence.

"Paul?"

"Hmmm?"

"Can we get ourselves out of this?"

Winston sighed. "Maybe."

"Maybe if we jump right in and kill Payne?" Parish asked hopefully.

Winston smirked—weakly.

"I know if we get that book, we can recover. Maybe we can get a line on that fucking monster on the loose. Yeah. If we bring that thing back alive to Washington, I know they'll give us a break."

Winston perked up, eyes snapping back into focus inside the room. "Maybe you're right, Nolan. Maybe there is a way."

The man with snake eyes approached the flight line from the west. At the south tip of Seven Mile Mountain, he took a jog up Radar Hill, which gives a commanding view of the flight line about a mile to the east. The sun had begun slinking toward the horizon. The voice snarling down the phone line had told him once and for all that Payne was too smart to be left alive to ponder the events of the past few days on into old age. Ditto Britton.

First his orders were to find Spellers, get the book, and vanish some people. It was no longer even necessary to create accidents. Unsolved homicides were just as effective and much simpler.

And it did look as if it might be simple. Below him was the Grand Prix in the gravel pit overlooking the flight line. That it was Spellers, he was certain. Beyond that was the flight line. Two figures were in animated conversation beside the red Camaro.

"Captain, you should get yourself checked out by the surgeon."

"PJ, that idiot is the last—"

"Suppose I tell him?"

"Like hell you will, Larson. You ever heard of loyalty?" His hands went out, as if to retrieve the words. He opened his mouth as if to vacuum up his angry utterance and tone.

She saluted briskly. "Forget it . . . *sir*." She spun on her heel and strode off toward the platoon quonset.

"Oh, the hell with it." He adjusted the pistol under his armpit and slumped toward his Camaro. He wished he had the guts to follow her and apologize.

Poole and Maggie Anzola stood in the doorway of the quonset. As PJ approached, Poole slid into her way.

"Lovers' quarrel?"

"If you think that, Captain, you're as—"

Poole opened his mouth.

"—crazy as he is, sir. Now let me by . . . sir."

Maggie said, "Admit it, Peej. You kind of like the guy."

"You too, Maggie. Certifiable."

Poole inspected his nails. "He's sure got the hots for you anyways."

"What?"

Maggie said, "It's written all over his face, Peej. Yours too. You're both just blind to it."

"But he's so—"

"Fucking crude?" said Poole. "And old. Drinks too much. But he told me himself. And he was even sober at the time."

PJ's lip quivered. She glanced at the Camaro, then at Maggie, whose expression said, "Why not?"

PJ ran up to the Camaro as it started. The driver's window slid down, and she bent over to speak; hands flying nervously. Mark leaned across the front seat. PJ ran around and slid into the passenger seat.

"You're such a damned liar," said Maggie. "We're gonna get blamed for contributing to the fraternization between a captain and a warrant officer, which is a capital offense around here."

"That's what I like about it. Let's go get laid."

Mark turned from the gravel onto the asphalt leading away from the flight line.

PJ said, "Instead of a drink, maybe we could just . . . go to my apartment for a talk. The club is so . . . noisy and un-private."

A pair of lights played off his rearview mirror and hit him in the eyes.

PJ hadn't noticed the intense look on his face yet. She continued trying to sort things out for herself aloud. "If we go to the club, everybody is going to want to hear war stories about the bear. It will be like before—we won't even get to talk. Besides, with those three guys killed today in the crash, it would seem kind of irreverent to—"

"Somebody's following us."

She started to turn. He held her shoulder.

"Why would—"

"I don't know. Humor me. I was supposed to fly triple-seven today. Yes, the one that crashed. Last night somebody broke into the operations shack. Last week somebody tried to burn me down. Today my bird crashed. Tonight somebody is behind me in a car. Maybe I'm a little paranoid, but why don't you just humor me."

His left bicep pressed Poole's .357 against his ribs reassuringly. He took the turnoff to the club. The lights swung around the corner and followed. No big deal. Somebody going to the club. PJ sat stiff and silent.

He turned short of the club parking lot and drove into a residential area. The streetlights twinkled through the leaves of live oaks. The headlights came around—still following. But still no big deal. A resident of the housing area might be coming home this way.

Mark abrupty swerved left to the curb and got out of the Camaro. A houseboat of a car went by. He tried to look inside without seeming too obvious. The car, one tail lens leaking a triangle of white light, went on by without hesitation. It was a Pontiac, one of the big ones from about ten years ago. That was all he could tell. Then the car was gone.

Back inside, he looked over at PJ and smiled sheepishly.

"Sorry if I scared you."

She let out a chestful of air.

The Camaro turned out of the residential area onto the West Fort access road. The headlights of the Grand Prix hit him again.

PJ looked at him and stiffened again.

The lights followed him onto Highway 190 toward the Cove. He sped up to ninety before easing back to sixty. The lights kept pace.

"He *is* following," said PJ. "What are you going to do when you get home?"

"I'm not going home."

Mark moved the car to the left, traveling south; abreast of Seven Mile Mountain. The lights followed. He hit the gas pedal. The Camaro issued a throaty, satisfied growl and leapt down the road, instantly opening a gap between the red car and the tagalong lights.

Mark knew the road that lay ahead—a dirt road that connected to the left and ended dead against the base of Seven Mile Mountain. There was a little turnaround at the end. It was the same turnaround he and Poole had passed through on their wild ride in *Shitbird*.

A pair of headlights hit him from ahead. Then, just ahead lay the dirt road.

He hit the brakes and spun the Camaro hard left, off the asphalt, rattling gravel behind and leaving a cloud of dust to mark the trail. The lights, a quarter mile behind, exploded into the cloud.

"I've got the son of a bitch."

"What can you do? Shouldn't we call the police?"

"Later."

At the turnaround, he jerked the wheel to the left and floored the gas pedal. His car spun, grinding a mushroom cloud. He turned off his headlights and parked by the bottleneck of the cul-de-sac, leaving the engine to idle. He stepped out, smiling wickedly.

"Stay inside."

"What are you going to do?"

"You keep asking that. I'm not sure. I'll let you know if you can help."

The Grand Prix hit the turnaround at fifty miles an hour. Spellers locked the brakes. The Grand Prix took out four junipers and skidded sideways, bouncing to a halt.

It wasn't a crash. Just a sudden stop. The Pontiac's downhill wheels lifted a foot, hesitated, and crushed two of the junipers.

Mark rushed the car before it had stopped bouncing on its worn shocks. He tore open the driver's door and yanked on the figure sprawled across the front seat.

The man hit the dirt and moaned.

"My leg, please my leg is hurt."

For a second Mark's heart leapt. *Was he the right man?* He grabbed the right hand and felt the stumps.

"You sonofabitch, why'd you try to kill my sister?"

Either the grunt or the glint of metal sparked a reflex in Mark. He jerked back. His cheek stung as if a match had been struck on his face. Blindly, he threw a punch.

Spellers grunted in pain. Mark found the wrist and wrenched it, bringing another cry. He had to restrain himself from jerking the arm loose from the socket.

"Stop, please don't hurt me. I . . . wasn't going to hurt you."

"Sonofabitch." Mark pushed the tip of the sharpened screwdriver at the sniveling face. "Then what's this for?"

"I just wanted you to lead me to him."

"Who?"

"Howell. I wanted you to take me to him."

"What are you talking about? I don't know where Howell is, and who the hell do you think you are, giving me the first degree? You tried to kill my sister. You've been following me. You take a stab at me with this . . . Now you want to give me hell for lying or something. You must be fucking crazy."

The greasy thin man went limp. "You don't understand."

"You bet your ass I don't. Suppose you explain it to me."

"You don't know about the experiments, the monsters, do you?"

"What's this got to do with your pushing a pillow into my sister's face? And burning down the clinic?

And sabotaging the helicopter, for all I know. If there's any monster around, you're it."

"Burning the clinic wasn't me, Payne. And I don't know anything about any helicopters. And I wasn't trying to hurt your sister."

"Looked to me like you were trying to kill her."

"I was."

Mark tightened up on the arm. "Bastard," he whispered.

Spellers groaned.

"Please," he whimpered. "Don't kill me. Let me talk. Let me prove to you I wasn't trying to hurt your sister."

Mark slugged him in the ribs. Instantly he was sorry to be letting his emotions get the best of him. "Let me get this straight—you weren't trying to hurt her? Just kill her?"

"Yes," Spellers wheezed.

Unable to pull the punch, Mark rapped him in the ribs again. "Bastard."

"Please," he begged. "Just let me prove it."

"Okay, mister, you prove you weren't trying to hurt her."

"I have to show you."

"Show me what?"

"A book. A research journal that Howell has kept for years. It's under the front seat. I'll get it."

"Like hell you will. You climb into the backseat. Lie on the floor belly up. I'll search under the front seat." He reached under his Nomex and withdrew the .357. "You make any sudden movements back there and I'll just start shooting through the seat."

"I'm sorry, Payne. I never wanted to hurt you. I never wanted to hurt your sister. I didn't want to kill anybody or anything—except Howell for what he did to me."

"Knock it off, Spellers. Get into the backseat."

Mark groped under the driver's seat and the fingers closed on a hardcover book. He riffled its pages with a thumb. *Big deal.* "Come on, Spellers, get your butt out here. We're going to take a little drive up to Gatesville and talk to the sheriff."

He put Spellers in front of him for the walk to the Camaro. The three-fingered man limped ahead.

A set of headlights played through the trees. Mark took his captive's arm and moved him away from the center of the turnaround in case the driver went out of control when he saw the disabled Pontiac slumping sideways on the incline.

The large yellow sedan skidded a few feet on the gravel before the driver pumped the brakes and turned the car. The headlights swung, circling the perimeter counterclockwise.

Mark, holding the journal in his left hand, took Spellers by the elbow. He pivoted in place, following the car around, waiting for the driver to see them. He guessed it was a carload of teenagers looking for a safe place to drink or pet.

The headlights dipped the moment they illuminated the two men, and the tires scratched at the gravel.

A voice came from behind the headlights, "Are you all right?"

"Fine," shouted Mark. Thirty feet separated the bumper of the sedan from their knees.

"Are you sure?"

"Yeah. My friend here just bumped his head on the steering wheel. I'm taking him to the doctor."

"Did you have an accident?"

Mark clenched his teeth. The last thing he wanted to encounter at this time and place was a good Samaritan.

"Look, mister," he said forcefully, "I better get this fellow to the hospital. Thanks for stopping."

Mark heard the snap of a door latch. In the dome light, he saw a thin shape step out.

"Mister—you, the one who got hurt. Do you need any help?"

"I'm already helping him, mister," said Mark. Under his breath, he murmured, "Tell him we're okay, Spellers. . . . I've got a pistol pointed in the middle of your back."

Spellers spoke up, "We're okay."

Mark guided Spellers toward the Camaro.

"What'd you say, mister? Are you okay?"

Why the good Samaritan was so insistent, he couldn't imagine. Why he suddenly felt a tingling spot between his shoulder blades, he couldn't fathom. The one thing he did know was that he and Spellers weren't going to make it into the Camaro—let alone the sheriff's office—without a lot of trouble.

Mark released Spellers's arm to reach for the door handle. Spellers must have known that, with the book in his left hand and the elbow in his right, Mark could only be bluffing about a gun. Spellers spun away and clutched at the book. Mark jerked it away. The man behind the headlights shouted. The book twirled from the grasping hands and fell under the Camaro.

Mark shoved the frail man away and crouched to retrieve the book. He saw the kick coming a mile away. The shadows cast against the Camaro showed it to him in plenty of time to duck.

A week ago, Mark would have been horrified to watch a dent kicked into the side of his car. But when Spellers yelped in pain, he was merely gratified that the bastard had hurt himself.

He was horrified that a bullet hole appeared in the dented door panel. The slap of the slug and the report of the gun sent him diving as it had dozens of times before in Vietnam.

He became aware that the voice behind the headlights was shouting, "Freeze. FBI. Don't move or I'll shoot."

"You *are* shooting, asshole. Stop. We give."

PJ scrunched down inside the Camaro. "Mark, what's happening."

"I don't know." He lay flat, rocks poking his knees and chest, watching Spellers's feet, waiting for the man to kick him. Great. An FBI man. He hoped he would not fire another warning shot so convincingly close. He knew he was in trouble. Deep trouble. Who would believe that he was not kidnapping Spellers? And who would blame Spellers for stomping his head this very moment as he lay helpless at his feet.

But Spellers bolted. Mark heard the uneven footsteps biting for purchase into the loose gravel.

The pitch of the FBI man's voice changed. "Stop," he shrieked.

Another shot. He heard Spellers yelp.

He cringed. "Hey, I give," he shouted. "Don't shoot." Blinded, he looked imploringly toward the headlights.

PJ opened the Camaro's door, illuminating the dome light.

The FBI man shot twice more, and two more rounds slapped into the Camaro. PJ shrieked. Mark pushed the door shut, extinguishing the light.

"Stop shooting, you sonofabitch. I said we give up. . . . PJ, are you hurt?"

In answer another round sparked the gravel in front of him, spraying his face with stinging fragments, slapping into the Camaro on the ricochet.

"Stop shooting, you asshole. . . . PJ, are you okay?"

"Stop calling him asshole, for cripes sake."

"Thank God. Duck, PJ."

"I'm ducked."

Mark pulled the .357. FBI or not, the bastard was definitely not taking prisoners. The realization dropped a load of adrenaline into the bloodstream. All at once it occurred to him to get the hell out of there. He could turn himself in to Britton and get this mess straightened out later.

He aimed and shot out the right headlight. It brightened, then dimmed to red. The second light took two shots. A return shot splashed gravel in his face. He remembered the book and found it under the car.

Something extra in his awareness told him to be prepared to use the .357 again if he heard footsteps rushing the car. What a fix to be in. Was it ever justifiable to shoot a cop—an agent of the FBI, for crying out loud? Would he be allowed to give up? Or would he be gunned down as an escapee? He tried to recall the number of shots fired from behind the headlights. Must have been six, weren't there? He felt like a punk in a Clint Eastwood movie. Maybe the FBI man was reloading. Maybe not.

Crouching, he rested his hand on the door handle and readied himself for the spring, rehearsing the steps of throwing the Camaro into gear and driving out of the dead end in the dark.

"PJ, knock out the dome light and get ready to get the hell out of here."

"How? With what?"

He handed the pistol through the window and felt her cold hand as she took it.

Another shot sang off the Camaro's wheel. From inside the Camaro came the sound of a muffled shot. For a second there was silence.

Mark grabbed the door, threw himself in, tossed the journal on the floor, stuck the car in gear and dropped the clutch. Immediately, two more rounds slapped the Camaro.

It took forever to get in motion. Too fast on the clutch. The Camaro raised a hailstorm of gravel but barely moved.

Mark eased up on the accelerator. The tires caught. He spun the wheel and was gone, barely missing the sprawled form of Spellers, an indistinct black shape lying broken in the dust. He couldn't tell whether it was gravel or bullets raining on the Camaro. But he was moving.

He hit eighty on the straightaways, following the ribbon of white dust, leaving a rooster tail behind. Finally, once on the asphalt, he thought it safe enough to turn on the lights.

He looked at the smoking headliner and dome light. "I meant break the bulb, Larson, not shoot my car."

"I thought, hell, what's one more hole? You know, this car's going to the dogs."

He burst out laughing.

"What's so funny?" she said, starting to giggle. "We should be crying. That guy was trying to kill us."

"Knock out the light . . . *blam.*"

She mocked him back, hardly able to talk, breathe, and laugh at once. " 'We give. . . . Don't shoot. . . . We give. . . . *pow.*' "

He mocked her. "Well, 'stop calling him asshole.' "

They laughed awhile longer, then abruptly sobered. He turned toward the Cove and home. *No, that's the wrong move.*

"I need to find a telephone and call Britton. He has to come for me. He'll turn me over to the FBI alive so we can sort this out."

"It's too dangerous to stop at a pay booth in the Cove. Better to take the back streets through town and head toward Killeen. Nobody will look for you at my place."

As the adrenaline level dropped with the excitement, he felt the edges of black closing in on his vision. He fought back the edges, but they insisted. He was simply too weak to argue.

13

Nolan Parish cupped his right hand over his left wrist and touched a button on his wristwatch, illuminating the dial: 10:37 P.M.

Finally things had begun to cool. Parish sat with all the LaBaron's windows down, the tiniest of cross currents fanning his face. He watched Payne's house and the street through the three rearview mirrors aimed so he could slump down with the headrest between him and direct observation from the rear. The right-door mirror he adjusted to watch the house. The windshield mirror covered the driveway and street. The left-door mirror covered the two houses on the other side of the street in this half-developed area. His eyes never stopped checking in a circle: the three mirrors in turn, then out the left, the front, the right; keeping a constant tab on the neighborhood houselights, barking dogs, prowling cats, and the blue glow of televisions.

His heart quickened when a set of headlights on high beam swerved onto the street. The lights passed by Payne's driveway, cruising purposefully past the LaBaron as Parish ducked. After the car went by,

Parish eased his head up enough to make out the essential details.

A light yellow Crown Victoria, the large luxury Ford with Texas plates, but Bell County, not Coryell. It turned in at a darkened house a block away. The Ford followed the driveway out of sight beyond the house.

Parish began counting mentally, allowing for the normal actions of somebody going into his house at night, waiting for the lights to go on.

Eight, nine, ten. . . . He checked his mirrors.

Still no lights in the darkened house.

Twenty, twenty-one, twenty-two. Parish tensed, his hand on the automatic under his left arm.

A horn honked from ahead.

The Ford backed into sight again. He stopped counting at thirty. The driver's action explained the Bell County plates in a Coryell County neighborhood. A visit. Nobody home.

The lights still on high beam, the Ford retraced its path. Parish scrunched down, both hands on the steering wheel, waiting for the lights to pass so he could pull himself up enough to watch the Ford in the mirrors.

But the Ford did not pass. Its heavy tires grabbed the street and yelped. A door flew open, bashing into the side of the LaBaron.

Parish instantly knew this was trouble.

His hand jerked on the automatic already fitted with silencer. A mistake. Two mistakes.

He knew that he should have had the pistol in his hand from the start. He knew that he should not have let the silencer catch on the holster—he had practiced his quick draw a thousand times with the silencer mounted. But those thousand times he had been standing, not slumped under a steering wheel.

And he should not have looked up to peer out of the open driver's window of the LaBaron to see the snake-eyed man coming for him. He should have rolled to his right, to the passenger side. He should have turned and come up firing.

Maybe, just maybe, that would have saved him from getting Holt's ten-inch ice pick in his left eye and out his right ear.

A sharp spit of sound—more than a clap, less than a crack—accompanied the hot blast that puffed out Parish's coat and left the expensive jacket fuming with the spent gases of the 9mm.

Holt calmly extracted the ice pick and tossed it into the backseat of Parish's car. He shoved Parish across the seat. The corpse obediently turned over on its knees and knelt beneath the dash, its head draining blood and other fluids onto the passenger seat

Holt smirked, his dark eyes unreadable. Parish, the rising star, had suffered the final indignity. Like some hapless country deputy in a television sitcom, he had shot himself in the gut; his pistol still stuck in the holster.

Two down.

Mark shook his head.

"Are you getting dizzy again?"

"No." He picked up the phone, striving to keep his

head from weaving. The fatigue kept creeping in around the edges of his consciousness. Encroaching. Threatening to engulf him like a tide. He couldn't give in to it.

"Coryell County. Deputy Sheriff Britton."

"This is Mark Payne, Captain Mark—"

"Don't say another word—"

"They already called you—"

"Goddammit, shut up, Payne."

Mark was stunned by the vehemence of the soft-spoken deputy.

"Don't say another word until I tell you. And hang up when I tell you. Whatever you do, don't say where you are or who you're with. Understand?"

"Yeah."

"You're not home, are you?"

"Uh, you said not to say where I am."

"If you're home, hang up now and get the hell out of town. Call me from a pay phone."

"I'm not home."

"Good. Just listen. I don't know what's going on, but it ain't good, whatever it is. I don't know what the hell you're involved with, but you've apparently made some enemies along the way."

"You're right about that. People and things have been trying to kill me for the past few days. Even the FBI. That's why I called. They're after me."

"No, they're not."

"Bull. I just had an agent shooting at me."

"It wasn't the FBI. They don't know anything about you."

"But who—"

"Maybe Spellers . . ."

"No. Spellers is dead. The FBI—impostor—shot him tonight. Tried to shoot me. My car is full of holes. I thought it was a trigger-happy fed shooting at me. I was afraid to try to give up after they kept drilling my car. That's why I called."

"You're not wanted by any police agency. I've just confirmed that. The real FBI will be interested in checking out whoever's been impersonating one of their own."

"Who, for chrissake?"

"They weren't telling. And I found a bug, a listener, under the edge of Jake's desk. About where those two insurance men were standing the other day. There might be more. That's why I don't want you to go home or tell me where you are."

"Christ, Bob, I've got to go home. Hell, I don't have a place to hide."

"Don't go home until I give you the word. And don't go to the base either. I'll get your house checked out. Call me back in an hour. From a different phone. I'll be here to tell you where to meet me, or else I'll leave instructions with the dispatcher."

"I have to go home eventually, Bob. I need clothes, a bath. And I need to get this mess straightened out." Mark felt his eyes closing involuntarily.

"Hang up, Mark."

"I'm so damned tired."

"Hang up."

* * *

"Hungry?"

He sat up abruptly. "I . . . took a little nap. How long—"

"An hour. I took the chance to shower and change. Grilled cheese okay?"

He took the sandwich. The lamplight reflected off her eyes. Green eyes. There was not a pair like them in the world. Blond hair unfurled, falling over the shoulders and framing the face. Silky green blouse, a pullover feebly trying to match the fiery eyes, hung loosely, exposing one shoulder.

He, a slovenly drunk in his flight suit, rank as it was from the evening's exertions, sat speechless, in awe of the vision before him. Suddenly he was aware of his body odor, his greasy face, matted hair, the itch under his armpits and between his legs, the hot dampness in his combat boots, the dirt and bear blood. The scratch across his face.

"What did the deputy say?"

He started wolfing the sandwiches and downing a tall milk, speaking in snatches. When he finished all she could say was, "Why?"

The question jogged his memory. "Spellers. He said he had to show me something that would prove he wasn't trying to hurt my sister even though he was trying to smother her."

"What did he show you?"

"This." He held up the book and riffled through the pages. "Howell's research journal." He tossed the book aside. "Tonight I'll go through it looking for a clue to what's going on. Right now, I have to shower.

Later I've got to call Britton, and maybe go to the Laundromat and wash my flight suit."

She directed him to the bathroom and offered to get his clothes started. She handed him a terrycloth beach robe of hers.

Back in the living room, she picked up the journal and riffled through as he had, stopping at an early entry. She read a section a couple of lines long, a simple description of a set of implements and conditions for a laboratory experiment. Nothing interesting.

Her thumb riffled into the center of the book, stopping where the ink color changed. She began to read —with difficulty. The writing was feverish, the work of a harried man. As she deciphered the hieroglyphics, her grip tightened on the book's cover, her knuckles turned white.

The scratchings described an Irish Setter bitch brought to the clinic for destruction. The entry described the form of destruction in detail—gruesome detail.

After the beast finally gave up trying to reach the bodies inside the crushed cab of the GMC, it limped along painfully, feverishly following the streambed of Preachers Creek southeast, scaring up half a dozen head of deer. Already it had learned not to bother with them, for they were too wary to stalk and too agile to chase. The effects of its wounds and exertions had begun to wear it down.

Just after moonrise it crept up on a stock pond fed by the creek. At the edge of the water it left an un-

wary cow suffering and bellowing and had chased
her persistent calf away half a dozen times. But it was
not hungry, so it left the cow in its agony and the calf
in its confusion. It dragged itself eastward toward a
set of yard lights three-quarters of a mile away.

Mark, toweling his hair, wearing the robe that
barely reached his knees, found her sitting rigid on
the sofa. "Hey, what's up?"

She didn't answer.

He reached out and pried the journal from her
porcelainlike fingers.

Effie Finney found her solace on the radio dial,
where she could tune in the gospel. Saturday nights,
though, were the times she depended most on the
broadcast word of God. They were the times her husband found *his* solace at Bingo's Bar and BBQ Grill.
He didn't begrudge her the word of God, and she
didn't really begrudge him one night out. Old men
had to have some outlet, and better he drink than try
to engage her in pleasures of the flesh—something
she hadn't permitted for the dozen years since her
reborning.

Only when she heard the commotion in the hen-
house did she wish he spent more of these Saturday
nights at home. Why, she would even have allowed
him to keep a bottle around for the purpose. She ignored the racket at first, concentrating her attention
on the radio preacher, reading along with the eighth
psalm of David: "O Lord our Lord, how excellent is

thy name in all the earth who has set thy glory above the heavens."

Nina, the Jersey cow, joined in with the commotion. The chicken coop was a lean-to on one side of the barn, so whatever disturbed the poultry bothered her too.

Effie prayed aloud, becoming truly afraid. Ever since the frightening news of escaped animals—Even if the lion and tiger *had* been found, even if the cougar *had* been shot, there was still the wolf. . . .

By now Nina's urgent bellowing was too loud for prayers to drown it out. Effie went to the back door. The security light illuminated a storm of feathers flashing wildly inside the pen like a thousand pillow fights gone awry. Suddenly Nina's bleating was cut off.

"For thou hast made him a little lower than the angels, and hast crowned him with glory and honour."

Effie shouted "shoo, shoo" a couple times into the blackness, but she dared not step off the back step. From the sitting room came the radio's unreassuring message. She went for the phone. Bingo's number she knew by heart.

The beast finished the cow. It killed the chickens for the sake of killing. It tore up those it could snatch from the air and herded the rest into a corner before smashing half a noisy dozen. It derived no pleasure from killing these animals, but killing was better than not killing.

Yet unsated, it went for the house. Through the

window it saw the woman. Her scent was laden with
fear. And the smell of fear ignited a special brand of
hatred in the beast. Fear in humans had brought it
instantly to the brink of explosion when it was in
captivity. Effie's fear drove the beast to rage now. It
remembered those first humans it had known. Its fevered brain made the simple comparisons. It had begun to discover that battering and tearing and killing
humans was the closest thing to satisfaction it had
known.

As the phone rang insistently at Bingo's, Effie
watched the back door as the beast came through the
front.

Literally.

A blizzard of splinters and glass preceded a whirlwind of teeth and claws, a cloud of stench and a triumphant roar.

Foxy Ervecker, bartender, picked up the phone at
Bingo's with a hearty, "Yup, you got Bingo's—" He
heard the sounds of snarling. Or was it grunting?
And from the background came the unmistakable
booming voice of a preacher: "O Lord our Lord, how
excellent is thy name in all the earth."

Foxy slammed the phone receiver down in its cradle. "Imagine," he said to the bleary-eyed Rob Finney. "An obscene phone call from a goddamned Bi-
ble-thumper."

Mercifully, God had answered Effie Finney's final
prayer. She was indeed dead—of a heart attack—be-

fore the beast could tear into her frail crumpling body.

Spent, the beast found another streambed and began moving southwest, back toward the artillery impact area. It passed clear of the incessantly active artillery firing points on the east side of the fort, tracking into the wind with its overpowering human scent blowing from Fort Hood and Killeen.

14

Mark set the journal aside. Stunned, he looked at PJ. For the past hour his only reality had been the words in the book. The words that became a picture of what he had seen at Beth's that night.

"Is it for real?" she asked.

"I saw it that night at the clinic. . . . I thought it was just a dream. Those deaths—those attacks on the livestock—they weren't all caused by lions and tigers. My brother-in-law created a—"

"Monster."

"No wonder he dropped out of sight. It was another of his monsters that made Spellers a cripple. He actually threw live animals into the cage with that thing. *He* was the real monster."

She held up the palm of a hand. "We can talk about that later. Right now, we know there's a beast loose out there that's worse than all the lions and tigers and bears combined. Plus, you've been shot at, chased, blown up, beat up, and burned. And we still don't know why. Do you think that's connected to Howell and this . . . this thing?"

"I'm sure of it. Britton said the FBI was interested

in what he told them about an impostor. This thing is way bigger than we know."

"What do we do first?"

First, he told her, they must try to distinguish among all the incidents. He asked her to collect newspapers of the recent days chronicling the incidents of sightings, animal shootings, and bestial killings. She produced a stack of *Killeen Herald*s and *Austin American-Statesman*s. He asked for her 1:50,000 scale training map of the Fort Hood Military Reservation. She took it from inside her flight bag. Together they circled the site of every incident from the afternoon's bear hunt backward to the site where the tiger's carcass was found to Preachers Creek, where the three teen tiger-hunters died. Then they began Xing off sightings clearly traceable to the escaped zoo animals.

As they worked, he began to notice her more than ever. Concentrate on his work as he might try to, he couldn't ignore the perfume she wore, light and enchanting. It seemed he had always encountered the fragrance while coming out of a stupor: coming to from his drunk, recovering from the blackout in flight, awakening in the hospital room, regaining consciousness today after the bear knocked him out. The scent had been permanently etched in his olfactory memory. Now that he was awake, it and the silk blouse that simply refused to cover both shoulders at once made him wonder whether he might not still be in a stupor. He tried not to look, but when she leaned over, intent on the map, and her blouse exposed a clear line of sight to her breasts, he felt dizzy, almost as if he'd downed one Tequila too many. He would have walked away but for the erection growing beneath the robe.

Finally, mercifully, they had Xed all the circles they blamed on Dodson's animals or on drought or hunters.

Mark colored in red marker the incidents lions and tigers could not definitely account for. "These also happen to be the most savage incidents," he said.

PJ spread one hand on the map. Her polished fingertips traced an arc that nearly touched every red circle. "They're all in one place," she whispered. "West of the impact area . . . between Flat and the grove . . . all within miles of the Howells'."

They looked at each other. "But what do we do now that we know?" she asked.

"We know where to begin looking for this thing. So tomorrow we take a helicopter out and find it."

"Alone? I mean just us two? Just like that?"

"No," he said, clearing his throat, "not the two of us."

Green eyes snapped wide-open, angry. "You're not leaving me out of this one, Captain."

Distracted by those angry eyes, he said, "No intention of leaving you out, Warrant Officer Larson."

She blushed momentarily. "Sorry. Who else would believe this . . . incredible story?"

"Only one person." Mark went to the phone and dialed the sheriff's office. As it rang, he looked at his watch. "One A.M. Probably too late. Even for Britton to . . . Hello . . . I'm calling for Deputy Sheriff Britton. . . . No, I don't want to talk to . . . Hello, Sheriff, this is Payne. . . . No, your deputy asked me to call—he said he would leave a message. . . . Well, let me leave one for him. . . . Well, I'm not at my house, I—"

Mark looked helplessly at PJ as he pulled the phone away from his ear. Beard's obscenities arced across the room—little lightning bolts of sound. He shrugged at PJ as the line went dead.

"Guess he didn't want to chat." He dialed another number and waited fifteen seconds. "That's funny."

"What?"

"My phone is busy."

"You left it off the hook?"

"I didn't use it. Haven't used it for days."

"It's out of order?"

"Maybe so." He shook his head. "Beard said Britton went over to my place. I can call him tomorrow from the flight line. I, uh, have to thank you for your help. I'll meet you at the flight line. Early."

"You're not going home. I mean . . . the deputy told you not to go home until he cleared it." She averted her eyes.

He uttered an anemic protest. "It wouldn't look so good for me to spend the night."

She put her finger to her lips. "You can sleep on the couch."

"I don't want to drag you into this."

"I'm already in," she said.

" 'I'm already in.' " The words traveled through the tiny speaker into the ear of the man outside and put a glitter into his snake eyes. He sneered and holstered the 9mm automatic pistol under his left arm.

"You bet you're in, sweetheart. You're in up to your ass."

The red digits flicked from 3:28 to 3:29. PJ wasn't sure whether she'd blinked and missed it or it had been there all along like an optical illusion. Didn't matter. What mattered was, she should have been sleeping. Big day tomorrow. Make that today. Didn't matter either.

Why couldn't she sleep? She'd seen three men die, a helicopter crash, and had been shocked by the wave of emotions when the bear fell on top of Mark. Make that the captain. How much could the mind endure in a day? How many tears, how much laughter? All in one day. She should be exhausted.

Yet she could think of nothing but the man in the next room.

Why did she want him at all?

He needed something, no doubt about that. He was not well, what with the blackouts. He needed friends. Needed support. Needed somebody to track down that beast. Needed somebody to believe in him.

If he was half a man, he needed somebody to make love to, too.

So where was he?

Probably asleep by now. Too decent to take advantage of her? Too proper to engage in an affair with a subordinate?

Yes, and probably not merely because it was against regulations, either. Probably for nobler reasons—foremost among them that it was simply wrong. Indecent. Immoral. Bad for morale.

Bull. Nobody was that decent. Certainly not her. Least of all him. So why hadn't he come into her bedroom? Maybe he was a homosexual. Maybe that's how love worked: First a mad, exquisite rush of infatuation, then trading "I love yous," then dread as the middle of things began to settle for lack of support, then the exquisite pain as things fall apart, then simple anguish in the aftermath.

But this man seemed so indifferent, so nonchalant. That intimidated her.

It had to be that he had that beast on his mind.

Or else he was definitely queer.

When next the digits flicked, they read 6:01. The radio disc jockey told her to get her tail up and moving before she was late for work.

Yeah, she said to herself, *just another day tracking down Frankenstein's monsters and stuff.*

She could not have been more relieved for the end of a night. Though her leaden limbs resisted, she tossed them out of bed and dressed them in a flight suit. As she scrubbed her face, getting some color back in her cheeks and trying to wipe away the itch in her reddened eyes, a radio newsman switched from banal chatter with his female co-host. He cleared his throat and adopted a somber tone to report a murder-suicide. ". . . report the woman, Effie Finney, was found in her demolished, ransacked rural ranch, battered and bloodied, obviously beaten to death and slashed. Her husband, Rob Finney, a retired rancher, was found outside, shot in the head, with his own rifle, which was lying beside him on the ground. Coryell County sheriff's officers investigating the incident three miles east of The Grove just northwest of the Bell-Coryell county line suggest a long history of . . ."

PJ ran into the living room, toothpaste foaming at her lips.

"Mark," she said to the stacked pillows and folded blanket, the robe hung over the arm of the sofa.

"Payne, you sonofa—"

There was a note.

PJ:

Couldn't sleep. Too much excitement yesterday, I guess. Left at 0430 to get Poole for today's mission. Though we hardly know each other, already you mean too much to ask you to take such a risk. Poole and I are already on everybody's shit list. So if we have to do something slightly illegal, it won't cost us as much as it would you.

You—Another reason I couldn't sleep. I can't get you off my mind. How long has it been since we met? A couple days? Seems like we've known each other forever. I hope I'm not out of line in saying so. And I hope you'll indulge me long enough for my crush to go away.

Honest, I haven't written a note like this in years. I hope you do not find it too unprofessional.

Later today—after all this is over—maybe we can talk. I'll try to be more like an adult.

    Sincerely, P.

"You sonofabitch," she said, spewing tiny globs of toothpaste. "You stupid sonofabitch."

Droplets of dew jitterbugged down the windshield in time to the bouncing craft. The sky had the dull shine of unpolished silver. Mark sat strapped into the vibrating Huey, letting the "paint shaker" unjell his blood. Anxiety about what lay behind him and the uncertainty of what lay ahead excited him, but fatigue had begun to numb him.

About time for Poole to get his butt out here, he thought.

Poole had slurred a greeting into the phone at five o'clock. Mark explained his urgent need of assistance and when he had finished, he asked, "Okay, Ken?"

" 'Kay what?"

"Ken, you'll meet me at the flight ops in thirty minutes, okay?"

" 'Kay."

"Okay what, Ken?"

"Meet that horses ash Payne atta flight line in a hour . . . even if I am off sick today."

"Half an hour, Ken, half an hour."

"Nope, thirty minutes . . . and not a minute sooner."

"Ken, no bullshit, this is an emergency."

"Who'sh booshittin', assho?"

"Ken, forget it. You're too drunk."

"Twenty eight minutes, assho."

And he hung up.

Poole had not arrived by the time Mark finished his preflight and called in a flight plan from the operations quonset. He went back to the aircraft and

started the engine. It was 6:19, and there was no
Poole.

Hell with it. He twisted the throttle full on, set the
RPM with the inker-dinker, and finished the runup.
He switched his communications control panel to the
UHF set to ground-control frequency.

"Gray ground, this is UH-1H 98258, south ramp,
clearance to taxi?"

"Huey 98258 is clear to taxi for south departure.
Wind two-niner-zero degrees at five, altimeter two-
niner-niner-five, tower time zero-six-two-one."

"Two-five-eight roger."

"Two-five-eight contact tower when ready for departure. Good day."

Mark pulled pitch. The helicopter rocked backward and broke ground. Good day indeed. Long as he
didn't have one of those blackouts.

"Two-five-eight roger. Also, I'd like to amend the
flight plan I filed for this craft."

"Roger, ready to copy."

"Two-five-eight roger. Delete the name of the copilot . . . wait." The black turbo Nissan appeared,
its wheels locked, its tires biting into the dust in front
of operations. "Ground, this is two-five-eight. Never
mind the amendment. Here comes my late copilot."

"Roger, contact tower when ready. Good day."

Like hell. It would be anything but a good day
judging from Poole's staggering walk across the concrete. *Not again*, he decided as he set the bird down.
Once was too many times to fly with a drunk.

Poole opened the left-side door and smiled the combination wicked and sheepish expression known by pilots as a shiteating grin.

Mark waved him off, mouthing the word no. He knew he should have pulled pitch and taken off. It would be useless to peacefully refuse the seat to this drunk now.

Poole gave him the finger. He licked white flecks of spittle from the corners of his mouth, spat on the palms of his gloves, braced his hands inside the door frame, and was . . . dumped on his ass on the asphalt.

Another frame filled the doorway. Poole staggered to his feet. The other pilot strapped in. No doubt about that fragrance, no question about those lips. Mark could almost feel two piercing green lasers shooting darts at him from behind the black sun visor.

The other pilot plugged a helmet cord into the craft's receptacle, "Warrant Officer Pamela Jane Larson re—"

Mark looked over her shoulder as Poole stepped up on the skid and pulled the cords apart, separating the words of her sentence as well.

PJ whirled, bringing a petite fist in motion, unloading the roundhouse blow into the center of Poole's visor, snapping the helmet back.

Poole hit the tarmac again, flat on his back, his helmet bouncing on the pavement. He struggled up onto propped elbows, but his neck gave way and the helmet bounced again.

She shut the door and replugged into the intercom system.

"If you'll wipe that shiteating grin off your face and fly, we can unass this place, Captain."

15

Except for radio calls, UH-1H 98258 flew mute. The aircraft's racket was tumultuous enough, but that only served to magnify the pitch silence on the intercom. Mark flew toward the east side of the fort. He had decided the best place to start would be near Preachers Creek, the site where three teenagers had been found dead. The incident was blamed officially on a hunting accident that led to a driving accident. The piece in the local paper was so brief that it could only mean that the authorities were confounded.

About as confounded as Mark. He kept searching for something to say. He thought it might be best to simply begin talking business, telling her his plan. Then he decided he should apologize for starters. Then he undecided. Nothing seemed an appropriate transition from his actions as a perfect jerk to words he could say to put his foolishness behind them.

She folded and refolded a training map across her knees. After studying the square she had made she said, "Head for a spot somewhere in here. . . ." Her gloved finger indicated a grid square.

"Why there?" It was a relief to have something to say.

"There was another incident last night at a ranch southeast of the grove. A woman was killed. The barn and house vandalized according to the latest reports I heard on the radio."

"PJ," he said.

"Forget it, Captain Payne." The lips beneath the visor were set.

Her words hit him hard. They were simple; they were polite; they were understated; they were properly formal. And they ripped into his solar plexus like an uppercut. Clearly, she didn't want anything to do with him except the business of flying. He knew that they'd probably never have an informal word together again. Of course, he also knew that formality was all he had a right to expect from a warrant officer in his command. The other warrants should be so respectful. The words hit him hard, he realized, because he didn't want formality. He wanted intimacy. But he'd insulated himself from companionship for years—the friendship he'd never had in his family and among friends, except for three exceptions: One brief moment died with his father; another died with the betrayal of his divorce; Beth lay comatose in a hospital. He saw in P. J. Larson the chance for it to happen again. He longed for it, but now he'd blown it.

Yet he couldn't let it go so easily. "I can't forget it. I have to say I'm sorry."

"For what? Sir." The lips turned into a smirk, up on the left corner, down on the right.

He winced at the "sir." "For leaving you behind. For writing that absurd note."

"Apology accepted for leaving me behind. But I didn't find the note at all absurd." The tight set of the lips relaxed, filling out with color. "I found . . . that it . . . pleased me."

A pair of snake eyes watched the Huey. From five miles back and two thousand feet above, Holt's position in the white Bell Ranger was almost as invisible as a shark cruising above a grouper on ocean floor.

Holt watched, giving orders to his hired pilot when necessary, but saying little. He didn't even know the pilot's name. He didn't want to know. All he wanted was to keep tabs on the Huey, listening in on flight-control frequencies and watching with darting eyes.

As the Ranger crossed Belton Reservoir, the Huey to the north dropped lower and began to circle. Below it were sparkling red and blue bolts of light. Holt ordered the nameless pilot to veer right, taking a line that would close the distance between helicopters, though not on a direct line. Reflexively he squeezed the nesting 9mm between his elbow and his ribs. The perpetual razor burn on his neck seemed particularly angry this morning. His eyes had grown harder, darker, smaller—the eyes of a viper poised to strike.

The Huey leveled off its approach five hundred feet above the emergency flashers of an ambulance and two police cars. Mark circled the site and began widening the gyre clockwise. A knot of officers below stood, hands on hips, engaged in conversation, barely bothering to look up.

"There's nothing to see here," he said into the intercom half to himself. Then to her: "See if you can tune up a newscast on the ADF."

PJ went to work tuning the automatic direction finder to an AM radio station. "Nothing now," she said. "I'll stay tuned. Maybe at seven."

Mark eased back on the cyclic, raising the nose, and lowered the collective, reducing power so the Huey would maintain altitude while slowing to fifty knots.

"Traffic at two o'clock high," said PJ.

Mark looked high and right and saw the Bell Ranger on a heading toward the northeast. "News chopper, probably. Looking for some ambulances to chase."

"I wish I knew what to look for."

"Me too. I imagine a shaggy black goat with heavy black arms like an ape. Keep your eyes open for artillery firing points so we don't blunder into a gun-target line."

He looked at her. She had raised her visor, revealing her face, unshielding the glow of her eyes. To him, her face looked friendly, warm—even inviting. He smiled tentatively. She smiled in return.

For Mark it was pure catharsis, a purification of the emotions, a draining of the swamp of tensions. No matter what they would find, or not find, on this search, he had come to terms with another human being—a decent one at that—and himself in one silent moment of warmth, an emotional symphony amid the cacophony of the helicopter's noise. He knew he would be all right after all. After today—no, after the flight—he would start another rehab program. He longed to be a decent human being again.

For a moment he wondered how long it had been. When he couldn't recall right away, he returned his attention to flying. And the search. He didn't have time to rummage through his psyche looking for that last, rare moment of decency. There was the monstrosity in his imagination that kept intruding. He needed to find it, to bring it down to size in reality, to dispense with it intellectually and actually.

Second Lieutenant Blaine Holmes was pissed. He was grateful to be off the observation post, happy to be on the way back to hot chow and coffee, glad to be feeling the stir of a breeze in his face as his jeep bounced along, whining engine wrapped tight. For two days there had been no breeze on the observation post. Nothing warm to eat but the dust. Nothing to drink but the lukewarm, plastic-tasting water from his canteen. And there hadn't been any firing either.

That's what had him pissed off. Some of these dumbass bear hunters had gotten their asses lost. Probably they were just camped out with some whiskey, hiding from their wives. Firing had been held up, so instead of directing artillery, Holmes had had to wait, ear glued to his radio-telephone earpiece, as the flyboys cleared the impact area. Then there was an ammunition malfunction back at the Cold Springs firing points where his battery had set up its six 155mm self-propelled howitzers. By nightfall the bear had been found and killed on the opposite side of the impact area. But the hunters were still lost. So firing was suspended through the night. Now his relief was on the observation post. And he was a mem-

ber of the search party scoping out the road at the
base of Owl Creek Mountain. He wished he could be
the one to find the bastards. He'd like to personally
kick each of their asses for ruining his chance at a
little action.

He looked around at the two men in the backseat.
Asleep and bouncing like rag dolls, cuddled up
against each other. Some searchers. The only reason
they volunteered for the search was to catch some
sleep and get out of work detail.

The beast lay on its breastbone, goat legs bunched
beneath it, muzzle on its forepaws, nose snuffing ir-
regularly into the dust. The animal seethed. Fever
had taken over its uncontrollable brain. The wounds
on its legs oozed blackly. The gashes on its forequar-
ters shone red as fresh blood continued to flow from
the inch-deep cuts. Swarms of flies hovered above its
wounds, and battalions of them trooped through the
stinking flesh to get trapped in the stickiness and the
matted fur. Already maggots percolated through the
dead flesh, falling off now and then like slimy puffed
rice when they became too exuberant in the filth of
the monster.

The animal no longer raged at the insects. It lay,
greatly weakened by all its exertions of the past days,
hardly able to gain strength from its blood-rich
meals, plentiful as they were. It snuffed the tickling
flies from its nostrils when they walked too deeply
into the sticky tunnels. Every half an hour it would
roll over in agony, bathing its injuries in dust, making slimy mud.

It was too exhausted to growl at a cottontail that passed within a few feet of its nose. It would take much more than a measly rabbit to arouse it from its silent, raging delirium. Maybe if one of the half-dozen range cattle a hundred yards across the open, sloping pasture came closer . . . maybe if one of them strayed across the deep wash twenty feet away . . . maybe if one of them continued across Cold Springs Road into the vicinity of the dust bath at its edge where the beast lay . . .

It heard the whining of a motor. The sound rekindled its anger. The sound meant humans. The beast found new strength and braced for an attack.

PJ saw it first: Her screaming declaration electrified the cockpit: "My God, it's attacking that jeep."

Second Lieutenant Blaine Holmes never saw it coming. He was looking left, bitching at his jeep driver.

"Slow this thing down, soldier."

Holmes expected a comeback, a sarcastic, disrespectful, "Yes, *suh.*" Instead, the private's eyes opened wide in genuine fear. *That's more like it,* thought Holmes. *A little fear wouldn't hurt anybody in the ranks of the enlisted swine.* But the soldier wasn't looking at him in fear. He was looking past him, gawking at something over his shoulder.

Holmes swiveled in his seat. The driver jerked the steering wheel left. Still Holmes did not see the attacking beast. He saw the dusty roadbed coming up at his face. Just before he belly-flopped and rolled at forty miles an hour.

On one of the rolls he knew the jeep was somersaulting off the road. For a fraction of an instant he almost felt sorry for the sleeping enlisted men in the backseat. Then he was out.

Mark bottomed the pitch, setting up for a steep, hot descent. He picked his spot across the wash, a sloping V-shaped piece of ground between the gully and a streambed. There was no time to worry about wind direction. He just hoped it was as calm as it has been in the morning.

Smoke and flames rose from the wash where the jeep tires continued to spin and the bottom of the chassis was outlined in gray like a pressed plastic model from Revell. The men inside must be dead. But a figure was on his knees in the roadbed, resting his head in the dirt. The beast staggered upright toward the man.

At ten feet, Mark pulled in an armload of collective. The Huey rattled down, tap dancing on its skids, coming to rest rocking from side to side on the slope between the brushy streambed on the left and the wash on the right, raising a white whirlwind of dust.

"Take it," he commanded.

PJ took the controls, looking past him at the beast, its attention diverted to the noisy intruder from the heavens. Suddenly the beast attacked, its huge jaws gaping as if trying to outroar the helicopter.

"Mark, it's coming."

He saw it. He had unbuckled and flung his door open. He had Poole's .357 magnum out. He pointed the pistol, tried to settle the bouncing muzzle, and squeezed the trigger. He felt it wrench his wrist. An explosion of dirt erupted a hundred yards up the side of Owl Creek Mountain. He lowered the muzzle and fired again, hitting the near bank of the wash. He tried to bracket between the short and long rounds, but the beast dropped out of sight into the wash bottom below the near edge.

In a second he was out of the craft, kneeling and aiming. As his helmet cord came unplugged he heard her shout at him. The words didn't register. Though the temperature must have been in the nineties by now, he shuddered. The blades stirred the air, chilling his sweat.

He swiveled left and right on his knee, covering the edge of the wash from left to right. *Where was it? It should have been up by now.* If only he could hear.

He turned to PJ and waved her away, a thumb pointed skyward, telling her to take off.

She set her lips, gripped the controls, and shook her head. Her lips formed the words "No way."

He spun back toward the wash. Still nothing. His knees ached. *How long has it been? A minute? Less? More? Where the hell is that thing?* Suddenly he felt surrounded. Had it had enough time to travel down the wash into the ravine on the left and come up behind? Was it smart enough to stalk him like that?

But, God, it was every bit as horrible as the nightmare at the clinic. Worse. He kept thinking: *This should be night, and dark, and a nightmare.* But he was awake. In the unbounded daylight, hot and white. He had seen the thing—the beast—attacking.

But now it was gone.

And time seemed to be standing still.

There. A movement. No, a puff of silent black smoke from the wash. Fast-rising heat currents. The jeep was burning fast. He was grateful for the helicopter's noise. There might be the screaming of men rising with that heat for all he knew.

Another movement. The man in the road had regained the use of his feet. His face was blackened by mud and blood. His arm dangled. Actually both arms dangled, though one seemed half a foot longer, as if dropped out of its socket. The man staggered toward the helicopter, the wash—the beast.

Mark shouted. For naught.

The dazed figure tottered, zigzagging his way.

Mark stood up waving, trying to direct the man away.

Like a punch-drunk fighter, the man kept coming.

Mark strode up the slope, waving with his free hand. He watched the edge of the wash over the sight of the pistol in his other hand.

PJ's last words nagged at his subconscious. He froze. "Blades." She had been saying, "Watch the blades." His knees buckled instinctively. He looked up from his crouch and felt the breeze emanating from inches away as the rotor blades passed over his head. Although on level ground each main rotor tip passed more than seven feet above at its lowest point, he had been walking upslope. Into them. Another step . . .

He glanced back into the cockpit. PJ held one hand across her chest. In the other she had pulled the cyclic as far as possible into her left thigh, raising the upslope blade. If he had kept walking . . .

The lurching man with the injured arm reeled at the edge and pitched headfirst into the wash.

Mark ducked under the blade, then waddled, his pistol still held in front. Once clear of the rotor disk, he ran up to the edge, prepared to fire into the monster as it tore into the injured man.

But there was nothing in the wash below. Nothing but a broken rag doll dressed in green camouflaged fatigues. His heart pounded, and he began to worry about the dizziness that always seemed to follow his bouts of excitement. He couldn't afford to black out now.

A glance to the right showed him the orange-black bonfire of the jeep. To the left the wash doglegged left and disappeared into the brush. In the dry silt of the wash's bottom beneath him, Mark saw the deep, scuffed tracks of the animal disappear to the left with the wash.

It hadn't been attacking after all. It had been fleeing. He hopped over the edge and began skiing down the near slope of the wash to the bottom eight feet away.

16

PJ couldn't believe what she saw him do—unless the beast were dead at the bottom. She cursed the suspect intelligence of this man and her own stupidity for caring. She tried calling for help on the radio again. Range Control did not answer her call. No doubt the mountain blocked her call.

She tried the emergency frequency. She switched the UHF radio to T/R Plus G, the VHF to 121.500 MHZ and the FM to 40.50. When all were equipped to work on guard, the universal emergency frequencies, she went to work transmitting, first on UHF.

"Attention all aircraft, this is UH-1H November 98258 calling an emergency on guard. Two-five-eight is down near Cold Springs north of Owl Creek Mountain near Fort Hood, Texas, at the site of an accident—burning vehicle, people injured, possibly fatal. Request you relay to Fort Hood Tower and launch *Lifesaver*. Over?"

She repeated the call on VHF and FM. Before she'd finished the last call, the receivers crackled to life.

American flight 279 responded from high over Austin asking her to repeat the call. Delta 325 en route to San Diego at thirty-five thousand feet told American

279 he would relay to Fort Hood on guard. Two air guard tactical fighters, F4s inbound to Dallas NAS, promised to follow up by telephone on the ground. And a scrambled rush of helicopter pilots on Fort Hood's north and west training areas said they were on the way.

In seconds a white flash streaked overhead, not fifty feet off the deck. It was a Bell Ranger.

A wow formed on her lips. She was astonished. And deliriously happy. Help was on the way. The captain would be safe. . . . She thought she might cry in happiness. . . . Until she saw the beast emerge from the wash on the far bank—like a creature scrambling out of a tunnel from hell—and dash along the rim to where the accident victim had toppled.

The Bell Ranger saved his life.

Mark had found a strong pulse in the accident victim's neck, a second lieutenant of field artillery, he could see by the collar insignia—Holmes, by the dusty name tape above his breast pocket. If there were no internal injuries, he would probably survive with no worse than bruises and the dislocated shoulder. He shoved his pistol into the shoulder holster and tried to rearrange the man's limbs. Although unconscious, he groaned loudly when the right arm was touched. So Mark left him lying still and loosened his clothing.

The Bell Ranger shot by. Mark barely caught a glimpse of it before it disappeared from the slice of sky above the rims of the wash.

But the helicopter led his attention to the pebbles and dirt clods rolling down the slope of the wash to the left.

Mark snatched out the .357. How many rounds were left? He stood up and backed into the center of the wash, training the muzzle on the bank, leading the avalanche of pebbles working its way toward him. He cocked the hammer for a quicker shot.

A black cloud appeared above the rim. What the hell? Flies? Swarms of flies . . . ?

When he saw it face to face with only a few feet intervening, he flinched. The beast's black eyes were rimmed in bloody red and rivers of yellow pus were draining down its face. It drooled strings like white syrup from its matted muzzle. Flies swarmed in and out of the gaping maw full of teeth. Mark was so startled by the terrible apparition that he jerked off the shot into the bank, blasting dirt into the animal's face.

Then it was gone.

The swarm of flies lifted and dropped out of sight with it.

Mark recocked the pistol and pointed it above the bank. He had a vision of the monster leaping at him.

Then the stench hit him. His stomach lurched. He coughed and choked back the imminent eruption of his belly. He remembered Hemingway's description of the smell of death—the breath of blood-drinking hags from the slaughterhouses. He remembered the smell he had discovered for himself in the breath of a well's mouth outside that Vietnamese orphanage.

His locked knees grew weak. He tried to steady

himself, bracing against the slope at his back. But the pistol trembled. Suddenly he knew he should not be in this spot. He broke left. Wrong decision. He should have gone right toward the jeep fire, to use it as a shield if necessary—all animals feared fire, didn't they?

He braked and moved right. He saw the flies rise above the rim. His adrenaline launched him over the second lieutenant of artillery. He felt the shadow and pivoted in the air.

The beast was fully splayed out, hanging in the air above the wash, flying toward the spot where Mark had just stood.

He brought up the magnum and fired twice. A puff of dust exploded from the beast's side. At least one hit. The beast crashed into the opposite wall of the wash.

And Mark's momentum, carrying him backward, took him over a limestone boulder that snatched his heels and brought him down hard. In an instant he was sitting, the pistol trained on the heap of stinking, black fur. But it was immobile. Thank God, it was finished. He rose to his feet. Adrenaline spent, he felt a wave of dizziness and another burst of nausea as the odor hit him again. The flies, tracking in the wake of the stench, found their idol again and descended in hordes. But no sooner had they settled than they lifted again, above the horizon of the wash.

Mark's skin stung with the shot of adrenaline his body gave him. The pile of fur was assuming a shape. The thing was bellowing. The vision was stark, horrid, mesmerizing—complete with stench and sound and goddamned flies.

The beast was coiling for a leap, a form with teeth dripping red syrup and a tongue sluicing blood from the throat out the mouth and down the dusty chest. It was a form whose dilating, pumping nostrils, like miniature whale spouts, sprayed blood into the air to water the dust in the wash. The blood that did not spray bubbled up into scarlet foam, deadly soapsuds dropping down into its muzzle.

Mark shook off the hypnotic effects of sight, sound, and smell. He brought the pistol up, hoping he had one more round.

The beast roared. Instead of a shriek, the sound ended with a cough and a jet of blood spewing from the throat, followed by black vomit.

Mark saw its abdominal muscles working. The beast had been mortally hurt. It seemed galvanized, unable to move. Its head dropped and its jaws worked as it licked the black mass from its stomach, chewed it, and swallowed it again.

Mark's stomach turned and he almost puked too. He saw the muscles gathering. He actually saw them tightening into knots through the deep gashes in the shoulder fur, opened like zippers. He drew a line with the blade of the front sight between the bloody, black eyes.

The gun.

The beast.

The man.

The three exploded at once.

Mark fired and jumped to the left as the beast leapt.

He saw the dust cloud and blood fountain erupt high on the forehead almost between the horns. It should have been a fatal shot.

He didn't wait to find out, knowing he'd be crushed and torn to pieces even if only in the death throes of the beast. The pistol forgotten, he hit the wash's slope and scrambled, throwing fistfuls of dirt behind. He kept waiting to be stabbed and ripped, to feel the jaws closing on his neck.

The stabbing didn't come.

Just one more handful of dirt.

And then the death-grip on the grass on the rim.

Then both hands pulling him over.

He rolled and came to his feet, running toward the helicopter. He wanted to look behind, to reassure himself the thing was gone, but he was scared as hell that he'd see it closing in on him. It was a time to let his imagination fill his mind with a vision so horrible it would spur him to the fastest sprint he'd ever achieved.

So he did, and gained another burst of speed. As he closed the distance to the craft, he chanced a look at PJ. Maybe her reaction would tell him something about what was behind.

Her face was a mirror of terror.

Her left hand was again pulling the cyclic into her left thigh. Her right hand, palm open, was trying to push him to the ground from twenty feet away. It was a signal a third base coach would give to a runner when the play was to be close. Her wide-open eyes and mouth told him the beast was behind and . . .

The blades.

He did a "Pete Rose"—a headfirst, diving slide into third, a belly-flopping, rolling, dirt-eating, star-raising, bruising plunge toward safety.

He thought he might have taken a rap on the helmet. But then his knees, elbows, and chin hit in a five-point landing followed by hands, arms, chest, pubic bone, thighs, feet, and head again on the second bounce. And he couldn't tell whether the rap on the back of his helmet came from the beast or a blade.

Then the world blew up in his face.

PJ had begun lifting off the Huey. She was going to fly over the wash and take a look for herself because she could no longer stand the tension.

But then he pulled himself over the edge and rolled. *Thank God.* She dropped the collective. He jumped to his feet and ran as if chased.

And, yes, the monster sprang over the edge of the wash close behind. It closed the gap to the man in two leaps. One more lunge.

The blades.

She jerked the cyclic left and waved. He was going to blunder right into the blades.

He looked up at her frantic signal and dived under the rotor plane.

The beast leapt into the space—the open door between earth and rotor blades—after the man she—

She threw the cyclic toward the right, toward the slope, slamming the door shut.

There was still a couple of feet of space between the blade tip and the ground. But the door was shut enough so the beast could not have fitted through even if it had seen the rotors.

It didn't. And everything disintegrated.

The beast was first, one blade hitting it beneath the left ear, exploding its head like a blood blister, the second blade catching the jackknifing body in the chest, outdoing the first in pure gore.

PJ's impressions were first of the blood, a shower of it darkening the windshield like red raindrops. Next the helicopter lurched, rearing up and to the left like a startled horse. Rising, she saw the broken body of the beast fly by and smelled an unspeakable stench as a bent main rotor blade entered the cockpit, an intruder from above smashing into the radio console, showering the interior with sparks. As the helicopter began falling over onto its back and left side— her side—she heard music on the ADF. Then silence filled her headset as the helicopter hit the ground and she fell on her left side, losing her breath and passing out before she could muster a scream.

Mark rolled into the right front skid strut with his ribs. It stung him, but he hardly had time to think about the pain. A shower of blood hit him, soaking him with the smell of the animal. The Huey rolled up and left. His left arm, draped over the toe of the skid, caught and he was jerked first to his feet, then lifted onto the rolling aircraft.

He was thrown free, somersaulting over the fuselage and practically into the brushy streambed on the left. He sat up and watched the transmission rip itself free of the airframe. From inside the engine access doors, the turbine disintegrated in a bomb-burst of shrapnel.

A torrent of JP-4 jet fuel poured onto the ground. At first it was soaked up by the thirsty earth, but then it began running. He heard the *poof* of what sounded like a gas barbecue grill starting.

Fire. The nightmare of every pilot. They called the fuel systems "crashworthy." *Shit.* This was the second fuel fire he'd seen in as many days. He went to the front and knelt to look inside the cockpit. He saw her lying limp inside. He could climb up and go in the pilot's door—but how would he get her out?

A secondary whoosh came from the belly of the craft. He could feel the heat now. He kicked at the windshield with a boot. Nothing would come of that but a broken foot. He looked around for a rock and found a fist-sized stone. He bashed at the greenhouse windows on top of the Huey.

The third blow cracked the greenhouse. The fourth and fifth gave him a hole to work with. He stood and kicked the shards, shielding his face from the inferno crawling toward them along the craft's skin.

Smoke began to pour out.

He thought of toxic fumes.

He thought of PJ, the woman he . . . God, he cared for her.

Then he was half inside, fumbling, holding his breath, closing his eyes against the hot, powerful fumes, shucking her lap belt and shoulder harness.

There was an incongruous moment of embarrassment as his first grip closed on her brassiere and her breast. Then he began pulling, backing out, hauling her along by a grip on the collar like a bitch moving a puppy.

His flight suit caught on the edge of the opening and he felt a breeze—a hot breeze. His Nomex must be torn. He felt the tickling of blood running down his back. He knew he was in danger of being burned. He didn't care. He needed to return the day's favors. He needed to save her life at any cost.

When Holt heard the responses to PJ's emergency calls he asked his pilot, "How long before help comes?"

"Maybe twenty minutes. Yeah, twenty minutes tops for *Lifesaver* to get here—figure they're already running to the helicopter. But if there are other pilots in the area who can find this place, expect a flock of them to start landing inside five minutes. After the first guys make their calls, other guys will be homing in like flies to shit."

"How come you know so much?"

"I'm retired army. Warrant officer pilot."

"Take us in."

The veteran pilot made a quick reconnaissance on his first pass over the scene.

"What the hell is that animal down there?"

"I don't know."

"I never seen anything—"

"Just fly the helicopter, dammit."

"Whatever you say."

"You bring the tools, the rope, the sling?"

"Yes."

The snake-eyed man watched in fascination as the beast pounced after the rolling figure of Mark Payne and was caught in mid-pounce by the helicopter's blades and chopped into chunks. The Huey began to beat itself to death on the ground, raising dirt and smoke and throwing parts of itself everywhere. In slow motion it raised itself up and toppled backward.

"I better go around," said the Ranger pilot. He started pulling power.

"No," shouted his passenger.

"But them pieces is going to hit into our blades if we—"

"No. Land."

"If that thing blows—"

"You land this sonofabitch."

"I'm in command of this bird and I say—" He looked into the muzzle of an automatic pistol.

"All right, but I'm making a full report about everything that happened here. Your people ain't going to like it."

"Land beside that animal. While I'm checking out the other helicopter, you rig your net around it so we can sling it out of here. You be sure and gather up all the parts."

"Christ," whispered the pilot. "I get all the good fucking jobs."

By the time he had dismounted, the Huey was engulfed in flames. The rotor wash of the Bell Ranger fanned the fire. Snake Eyes left the pilot to his grisly work and went looking for Payne and the woman.

As he approached the Huey, it erupted into a higher intensity fire. The heat forced him back. Anybody inside must be dead. But he had to be sure. He started a wide berth around the blaze and down the dry streambed, pistol at the ready. This time there would be no mistake.

A voice called to him. Two voices.

The Ranger pilot was waving to him and pointing. He followed the point to a tottering soldier staggering toward the Ranger. He was crying aloud, babbling.

He ran back to the Bell Ranger. The pilot told him, "I got this smelly thing ready to sling. You going to help this guy? You better hurry if you're so damned worried about somebody coming and finding us."

"You got an ax?"

"In back with the rest of your shit."

He dug in the back and produced it. "Get this helicopter ready to go," he ordered.

He ran to the figure standing dazed in the sun. He took the man by an elbow and gently led him to the blood-muddied spot where the beast had been struck by the blade.

The soldier protested, mumbling about the heat.

Snake Eyes took a step backward and raised his pistol to the center of the mud-streaked face.

"Good-bye, Payne," he said, and flicked off three 9mm soft slugs into the face.

Before the dead body had hit the ground, he had put the pistol away and raised the ax.

Two strokes took off the head.

Half a dozen strokes more pulverized the cavity between the shoulders. Blood gushed liberally over the earth already muddied by the beast. He bent over the torso. He slapped a cloud of dust from the name tag above the breast pocket and spat in disgust. HOLMES, the name tag read. He looked around, toward the fire. The Bell Ranger's pilot waved and pointed at the sky.

He picked up the head by the hair and tossed it into the center of the blast furnace, white hot in places. He ran back to the Ranger and took his seat, throwing the spattered ax into the rear of the craft.

"Did you see anybody get out of that fire?"

The pilot shook his head. He looked as if he might throw up.

"Get the fuck out of here."

The Ranger labored a moment, then lifted off.

"Forget you saw that."

The pilot nodded solemnly, dumbly.

"Land on top of the cliffs above the lake."

Minutes later, they were lugging rocks the size of bowling balls and loading them in the netting with the beast. The veteran pilot complained continually. "I'll never get this fucking smell out of my clothes," he shouted over the turbine noise.

He got no answer.

"I guess we're going to throw this thing over the edge?"

"No, drop it in the middle. Cut it loose."

The pilot nodded.

Snake Eyes handed him a thick envelope.

The pilot opened it and riffed a thumb across its contents. "Looks fair—more than fair. You ready to go?"

He waved at the brush behind. "I've got a car stashed here."

The pilot nodded enthusiastically. "Can't say it's been a pleasure. And you can tell your bosses I won't be hiring on anymore."

"I'll tell them."

"You got anything left in the chopper?"

"There's a little small change—a couple hundred cash in the knapsack. You keep it—a bonus."

"What is that thing?" asked the pilot, pointing at the netting.

"You don't want to know."

As the Ranger lifted off, the man on the ground pulled a box of Marlboros from his shirt pocket. As the craft labored away, he opened the cover and extended an antenna two feet from the box.

When the Ranger reached the center of the lake, he threw a safety switch and mashed the button on the tiny transmitter inside the box.

And the white Bell Ranger turned into a fireball, arcing like a meteor into the lake, tracking a black plume into the water.

The cool breeze of flight awakened PJ. As soon as her eyes opened, she asked for him. The medic pointed and unstrapped the belts across her chest and thighs.

She watched his eyes come open. The first sounds from his mouth were her initials. They locked eyes gratefully and smiled.

She unstrapped him.

Against the medic's orders, they sat up and hugged all the way back to the landing pad at Darnall Army Hospital.

17

Forgetting came so easily. Forgetting was insulation from the stark realities of the day. The beast was dead. That was one certain reality, for he had seen the dismembered carcass flying through the air. And only hours ago.

Yet so far away. If it weren't for the lingering smell of the beast's blood on him. . . .

PJ Larson sat up on a stainless steel table across the cold interior of the emergency room at Darnall. Two men worked on her. One daubed at a clot of blood above her eyebrow. Another held her hair out of the way and probed a bruise on the long, fine neck.

They exchanged smiles every time the medics let their eyes meet.

His memory of their embrace in *Lifesaver*—the press of her arms, the grateful clutch of her hands, the pressure of her breasts, eased the terror further and further away. Rough hands worked Mark over, as though the medics resented tending him when they might have been examining the blonde across the room.

His injuries were many but apparently minor: scrapes on the knees and elbows, bruised ribs, a

wrenched shoulder that he knew would stiffen, slight
burns on the neck and back, face stiff from yesterday's scratch.

More serious were a collection of deep scratches on
his back. They stitched on him awhile, and he felt
impatient little tugs on the flesh, but no pain. He
didn't know whether the beast had swiped at him or
the greenhouse shards had done the damage. His
neck was stiff. His helmet lay on the floor. A scuff
mark showed yellow on the back where a blade tip
had nicked it, leaving paint and flattening him. It was
a wonder it hadn't taken his head off or at least
knocked him out. It was a miracle, actually. Had he
been out, he would never have been able to save PJ.
And he might have perished lying next to the helicopter, literally going up in smoke with it. But he had
passed out later in the streambed, after pulling PJ out
of the burning Huey.

"Anything else wrong?" asked the tending medic.

"No, just a little stiff in places. And tired, I'm awfully tired." He looked across the way at PJ, who was
having her eyes probed by a penlight. She glanced his
way, nailing him in the midst of his lie, the beam of
the penlight highlighting the green anger in the iris
of one eye. He narrowed his own eyes, pleading for
her complicity until they could talk about his dizziness in private.

It wasn't necessary to ask. A sudden commotion
broke out in the hallway outside the emergency
room.

The commotion burst into the room in the forms
of Sheriff Jacob Beard and Provost Marshal Colonel

Wayne Rice, followed by Forman, the battalion commander, and DePree, the company commander. And by Riley, the dispatcher from the sheriff's office, and Poole, along with Anzola and half a dozen pilots. And several military police officers and sergeants, who crowded into the doorway keeping even more commotionants in the hallway.

With many a "What the hell?" and "What the fuck?" from the ER staff, the throng gravitated to the table where Payne sat.

Finally Rice outshouted the group to order.

"Now, Payne, I've got a few questions for you. Everybody else out of here."

Nobody moved. Except Beard. Mark's eyes were drawn to the sheriff, who kept edging forward, hand on his pistol. There was no mistaking the hatred in those eyes.

"Why did you land in the impact area, Payne?" demanded Forman.

DePree nodded his approval of the good question.

Rice demonstrated his mastery of the situation. "I'll ask the questions here. Why the hell did you land in the impact area, Payne?"

"It wasn't the impact area, Colonel. You ought to be able to find several dozen pilots to confirm that . . . or to join me in the blame, because half the fleet of Three Corps was there when I left on a stretcher."

The group mumbled assent to the truth of this observation.

Rice looked to Forman for help with the new development.

Forman said, "Well, it *was* in the way of the Cold

Springs firing points. Why the hell did you land there?"

"I landed to save the soldiers."

"From *what?* The evils of drinking? They all died in the jeep crash anyway."

"Not the lieutenant, for chrissake—he didn't die. Didn't you see that goddamn monster chopped up by the blade?"

"Monster?" Forman sneered. "I admit I've seen some pretty raggedy second lieutenants in my day, but other than the absence of his noggin, I wouldn't call the guy a monster."

"Guy?"

"Yeah, guy. What's with you, Payne? You nuts or something? There was three barbecued soldiers in the jeep, the lieutenant who flipped his lid walking into your main rotor blades, and you two . . ."

"That lieutenant didn't walk into the blades. I tell you he was alive last time I saw him, alive and in the ditch."

"Tell that to his next of kin, Payne. The sonofabitch is laying in a body bag in a meat locker right now, and half the fucking fort is on a search for his head even as we speak."

Mark's mouth could hardly close around the words. "But what about the—"

"What about *what?* What is this fucking *what?*"

"That animal, the beast, the monster with the horns, that . . ."

"I saw it too," PJ said, capturing all eyes. "There was a horrible beast out there. If the captain's crazy, so am I."

The sheriff found his cue. "Now that we got that settled, I got some questions to ask about my deppity. I hope you have some answers, Payne." He seemed to be wheezing worse than usual.

"Maybe you'd like to tell us why he happened to be found in your house with a—fuckin' ten-inch boning knife stuck through his head." He pulled the half-inch butt from his lip and dashed it to the floor.

"No," Mark whispered.

"Payne, you somebitch." He reached for Mark's neck, thumbs cocked to throttle. Rice and Forman held him back.

"I talked to him on the phone. Sheriff, I swear. . . ."

"He went out to see you."

"He told me not to go home. He said to call later. I did. Your dispatcher knows . . . hell, you know . . . I talked to you that night. Didn't Britton talk to you about his suspicions?"

"Suspicions my ass."

Suddenly he was very tired, even defeated. The tension rose up behind his eyes, above his soft palate. Salt came to his throat. His eyes itched. He thought he might become ill right there.

Beard snapped, "So where the hell were you last night?"

Silence. Half a dozen sets of ears waited for the answer.

Mark stiffened. Suddenly his worries about nausea were gone. This was another kind of trouble. A thousand plausible lies rolled across the screen of his consciousness as he searched desperately for one that couldn't be checked out. Anything but the truth. Any way but in front of all these people.

He sought PJ's eyes through the crowd so he could again ask for her silent cooperation until they could talk this out.

Too late.

"He was with me," said a thin voice from behind the mob. "We were together until late—no, that's not exactly true—actually, we spent the night together. And I was with him when he tried to call the deputy. About midnight. I heard the conversation. And then we stayed in my apartment. We didn't leave until . . . until it was time to go to work this morning."

Beard spat an obscenity.

But now it was Forman's turn to smile. "Payne, we have rules against such behavior," he said quietly. "It's improper for an officer and his subordinate to socialize after work, let alone to the extent they sleep together," he added with a snicker. "Did you know that?" he asked with the smug look of one smart mountie who had, as always, gotten his man.

In the melodramatic pause that followed the pronouncement, Mark looked for something reasonable to say to protect PJ. The only thing that occurred to him was the truth: That they had not slept together at all; they had stayed in separate rooms; they had not touched or kissed or anything. But the truth was so absurd it would only prolong the agony of the moment. And provoke laughter. And a million stories would be added to the billions already being formed in the minds of the mob. These million stories would describe the incredulity with which the captain's feeble excuse was received. And the laughter it provoked.

So he said nothing.

Hearing nothing, Forman said, "I'll have to remove you from your platoon, Captain. Larson, I'll deal with you later. First thing in the morning. Yes, I'll see both of you first thing in the morning." He waved his arm into a bystander's chest. "Now let's get the hell out of here. This is an investigative matter for the police and accident board. For now."

It was well after dark when Ellis Buchanan stopped at the gate of the Virginia country estate. He leaned out of the cab to stare at the left concrete pillar, waiting for the video camera to recognize him, to scan the vehicle. At night the cameras were switched to infra-red to probe the darkness illuminated by invisible floodlights. Deeper inside the estate, passive systems monitored the approaches—Starlight systems that magnified the faintest ambient lights.

The gate swung open, and he drove through. Out of sight of the first gate, he encountered another. Through a wrought-iron door to the left a uniformed guard approached him warily.

Buchanan flashed his ID and said a few words of nonsense code that made sense to the guard, who relaxed not a bit and opened the van to search with his flashlight.

He had driven straight through from Texas. He wanted out of that mess. Winston and Parish could keep on screwing it up if they wanted. He was going to come in from the heat and ask for . . . what? Forgiveness? A sabbatical? Yeah, forgiveness *and* a sabbatical.

From nowhere another uniform came, with a leashed dog in one hand and a long-handled, lighted mirror in the other. After a walkaround with the mirror held under the van's carriage satisfied the pair, they disappeared behind the wrought-iron pedestrian gate. The vehicle gate slid aside and Buchanan drove to the next, more thorough checkpoint at a gate half a mile on.

He saw chain link fences—two perhaps forming a dog run, others indicating who knew what. Mine fields? Electrical fences? He didn't know. He wasn't permitted such knowledge. All he knew about was the existence of at least two more checkpoints. At each he would be asked to get out and stand still for a patdown. At the second, he would be separated from his vehicle, weapon, and cargo. He'd be asked to change clothes and shower in an electronically monitored safe room—he'd be x-rayed for anything hidden internally and examined by a physician, a psychiatrist actually, for signs of abnormality. His fingerprints would be checked. Then he'd pass through more gates inside—how many he couldn't guess. He'd be debriefed. And then, because the case had reached Yankee, he'd probably get the ass-chewing of his life from somebody very important.

Instead of a patdown at the third station, three men approached him. Two threw him roughly up against the side of the van. He was disarmed and cuffed— handcuffed and struck alongside both temples.

"Hey, fucker," he said to the bristly gray fireplug who hit him.

The hulk responded by clapping his hands savagely with Buchanan's ears between the palms. Even as Buchanan sucked wind for screaming, the hulk followed with a driving right hook deep into his solar plexus, emptying his lungs and stopping his breathing.

Buchanan doubled up over his fat gut and toppled. He saw the shoes move to the side, letting him go to the pavement. He hit nose-first and tasted blood immediately from where his cracked front teeth lacerated his lip. He felt blood gushing from the broken nose into his throat. He would be permanently disfigured from this one, and that was bad news. Awfully bad news. They didn't care apparently. They were pissed at the way things went down in Texas. Pissed enough to kill him.

A drop kick to the kidneys emptied the considerable contents of Buchanan's considerable stomach. It also blew a renal artery.

It hurt Buchanan so horribly that he couldn't feel pain anymore. He marveled at that. And the fact that this big computer-driven sophisticated hi-tech outfit would resort to gorilla tactics. This was the eighties, dammit.

In seconds his gurgling lungs emptied for the last time.

18

Nightfall seemed to be the only force able to prevail against the relentless sun. And not much at that. The temperature dropped a dozen degrees. The insects thrived in the respite of the night. But the humidity still lay on heavily. And temperatures in the eighties still made the body grease ooze. In the distant north sky, perhaps as far away as Dallas and Fort Worth, the horizon sparked feebly now and then as if to taunt the parched Fort Hood region with the vague memory of rain.

They walked in silence from the parking lot to her apartment door, she rubbing her neck, he dictating their slow pace with a stiff-legged limp. For hours they'd told the facts about the accident to police and investigators.

But the questioners insisted they stop mentioning the beast.

"Let's take it from the top. This time tell the story without this . . . alleged monster. Let's hear what it sounds like that way. Not that you would lie or hallucinate, mind you. Let's just leave the dragons out of this next version and see if we can help each other put together the pieces of this puzzle."

When the civilian cops were done, the military police took over.

"Enough," Mark finally said. "If we're not under arrest, we're going home—like your own boss did hours ago. There's nothing new here. We can finish this up another time."

"Not yet," said the major.

Mark simply walked away, into a waiting room where PJ lay with her head on her forearms. "We're done here," he said. Gratefully, she grabbed for her flight helmet bag and left with him.

"So," she said at the door.

"So?" he answered.

"So we're not sleeping in jail tonight. At least."

He snickered. "Don't make me laugh. The local is wearing off and I can feel each stitch in my back. I feel like a snagged salmon."

"So. What will they do to us?"

Us. To Mark it had a nice ring coming from her lips.

"Flight eval board. Accident investigation. You might get your wings suspended for a while—slap on the wrist. I'll get it good, maybe lose my wings. Forman might want to court-martial me too. I doubt that will happen unless somebody higher up starts screaming for heads. He'll probably banish me to the crappiest job on the staff, trying to wangle a resignation out of me. He wouldn't want an ugly trial around his neck like a toilet seat. . . ."

"Too bad. Be a great story in court. 'Yes, your honor, we did spend the night in my apartment, but we didn't have sexual relations.'"

"Any idea what that would do to my reputation if it got around? A woman like you—"

"Plato would have been proud of us."

Mark changed the subject abruptly. "We need to take that journal in to the sheriff. We may be crazy for not sleeping together, but that goddamned monster was for real."

"Where in God's name did the carcass of that animal disappear to?"

"And why?"

"Why?" she echoed. "Why on earth?"

"Maybe I can find a clue in that research log of Howell's."

She handed him her flight helmet bag and fumbled for the key.

"You are coming in?"

"I was afraid you wouldn't ask."

She brightened and heaved the door open.

Transfixed by her face, her smile, her everything, he gazed at her affectionately until a pained expression contorted her beauty.

The instant he saw the disarray inside the apartment he shoved her aside and darted in at the ready, momentarily forgetting his wounds. He sprinted through the rooms, completing his search in a minute.

"Nobody," he said, ushering her inside.

"Burglars?"

"You know better than that."

"The book?"

"Gone."

"I'm scared," she said.

He was silent for a moment.

"Me too," he said finally.

"What next?"

"Next, we fight back."

"Against whom?"

"Finding out is part of fighting back."

"Let the police do the . . ."

"Come *on*, PJ, for crying out loud. What police? Beard? Rice? The only cop worthy of the name was Britton, and he's . . . gone. No, we have to do this ourselves."

They were silent for a long moment.

Her head came up. "When do we start?"

"Tomorrow . . . I . . . the cops have sealed off my house. . . . It's a crime scene."

"No matter. You'll be staying here."

"I . . ."

"Strictly business, of course. To protect each other."

He searched her eyes, looking for the mirror of his own passions now being stoked.

She stood up in front of him, stepping into the personal space reserved for intimates.

"What now?" he asked.

"A drink. An omelette."

"I'll stir the drinks, you break the eggs."

"Later. First you need a bath."

He blushed. "Yeah. Badly. I'd forgotten how rank I am."

"I'll scrub your back," she said.

"You. . . ."

Her hand covered his mouth.

"Then, like it or not, you will scrub my back. Partner."

Her eyes, her lips, her voice—another daydream almost.

"I love you, PJ. So help me, God."

She took his hand away. "Don't swear—"

Her words were stifled by his lips.

The omelettes and brandy came very much later, after they were already intoxicated by the gentle lovemaking of exhausted, wounded bodies taken to heights where only slow, painstaking, exquisite ecstasy can go.

At last they slept. It was the sleep of the dead, two nude bodies entangled, two minds dreamless, unable to respond even to the crashing thunder and stark lightning of the first rainstorm in fifteen weeks drenching the distant world outside the apartment.

"And the first beast was like a lion, and the second beast like a calf, and the third beast had a face as a man . . ."
—Revelation, Chapter 4

BOOK III

NEVER BEGINS

1

Shitbird bounded across the hills and ground up the south side of Manere Mountain, throwing up a plume of dust tinted orange in the setting sun. Atop the hill, Poole parked so they could watch helicopters depart the flight line for night training. He took a swig from a brown-bagged bottle and held it out.

"No thanks."

"You need your nourishment."

"Not tonight."

"What's wrong with you, boy? Din't you get your daily ass-chewing from Forman?"

"Worse. I endured the ultimate humiliation today."

Poole pulled on the bottle and gasped. "So," he hissed, "who knocked your dick in the dirt?"

Mark told him about his latest order to begin organizing an officers' ball.

"Shit," Poole whispered when the story was done.

"I'm going to resign."

"What? Get serious."

"I'm going to give them what they want. I quit."

"Fuck you," said Poole, suddenly not only serious but angry. "Don't give them the satisfaction. Don't give them dogshit."

"I'm grounded. I'm on staff doing shitty little jobs. Hell, yesterday I spent three hours after work counting stupid damn Conexes. I'm dying the death of a thousand cuts."

"Shit, a lousy three months more of groundation. That's a slap on the pecker compared to what they coulda done if they went to court on fraternization. They didn't have the guts to go to trial. Now you don't have the guts to stick it out. You're giving in to those bastards. Why do you think the people in the Vultures care about you? Because you don't quit. So it's my duty to see you don't quit now."

"Those guys have treated me like an outcast. They don't even talk to me at the club."

"They think you're avoiding them. They don't want to cause you any more grief."

After a long, thoughtful silence, Mark said, "You're probably right."

"Bet your ass I am. You'd see it plain as day if you weren't so pussy-whipped. Listen to you. Just listen. Right now, the best thing could happen to you is get a set of orders and get the hell out of this place."

"They'll get me somehow. You don't think they'll let my promotion go through, do you?"

"They'll stab you in the back on your next rating, but you'll have a few years to recover before being considered for light colonel. It's too late to do anything to stop your promotion to major. Unless . . ."

He stopped and stared.

"Unless what?" Mark, knowing what the unless was, couldn't meet the stare.

"Unless you get caught doing something illegal—

like dick-dancing with that woman after they told you not to."

He snuffled in her ear.

"What's so funny?"

"Nothing."

"Then why are you laughing?" She pushed at his head, trying to get a look into his eyes.

He nuzzled deeper into the nest of hair between her neck and shoulder. "Just an expression I heard today."

She shifted her body beneath his, the better to feel the fullness of him inside her. "What expression?"

He started giggling. She followed his lead. The jiggling intensified their sensations.

"Come on, Mark, what was it?"

"Wanna dance?"

"I don't get it."

He could barely get it out for the laughing. "Dick-dancing."

"You call that funny?" Suddenly he was very heavy, and the sensations were not all that enjoyable.

"What's the matter?" Now he looked into her eyes. She saw he was struggling to compose himself.

"Your heart's not in this—come on, Mark, stop making a joke out of everything."

"Okay, I'll be serious."

"You don't have to. You don't have to do me any favors."

"PJ, this is not a favor. I love you."

"Okay, then. Keep your mind on loving me."

He kissed her on the neck, subduing her anger

with passion. She let the matter slide. She knew him
very well now after three months of almost continual
lovemaking, as if on a never-ending honeymoon. The
mystery and adventure had not diminished. It was
not so much that they weren't married, not so much
that they were keeping it a secret from everybody,
including Poole and Maggie—they had even kept separate living arrangements, sometimes sneaking into
his house, at other times her apartment—but because
it was illegal. And because she loved him, because
their togetherness was more important to both than
their careers. She meant it when she said it. She
needed him. And he had convinced her he needed
her. If for no other reason, he needed her to awaken
him from those awful nightmares. Oh, yes, he was
utterly sincere about loving her—a little reluctant to
talk about marriage, but utterly in love. As time had
passed without a single substantive clue to the mystery of the beast and the shadowy men who had come
and gone like mirages, he had devoted himself more
and more to her.

She asked for no conditions and he offered none.
They loved each other. It was as simple as that. They
had exposed their previous lives and loves to each
other. She did so more freely, talking about the men
who'd stood her up enough times so she was reluctant to love again. He couldn't understand anybody
standing her up. He told her of his ex-wife—reluctantly. And children—even more reluctantly.

"Don't you want to see them?" she had asked.

"Oh, yes," he said. "But it hurts them both so
much."

She didn't say a word for a long time.

"And me," he finally admitted.

"I love you," whispered PJ urgently, nearing her climax.

The selfish concern for his daily misery vanished with PJ's words. He found himself elevated above it. To PJ, the woman he loved. "I love you," he said and clutched her, catching up to and joining her explosive release.

Though drained, he could not sleep. Would not. Only consciousness kept the nightmare away.

She might have been a starving African woman except for two things: the whiteness of her skin and the absence of flies promenading across her face. Otherwise, she displayed the classic signs of starvation: bug-eyed appearance, lids unable to close all the way —only the ooze of weepinglike tears kept them from drying out—gaunt cheeks, teeth visible even through closed lips, stick limbs tucked into the fetal position, distended belly.

"She has lost the will to live," said one nurse, the one who always clucked and pronounced.

"She doesn't know she's alive. How could she lose her will?" retorted the other woman.

"Looks like she's crying all the time."

"She can't cry, dammit, she's brain dead."

"She'll need life-support by week's end. She's visibly deteriorated."

"She'll never get life-support. Her only kin is her brother, and he doesn't care enough to visit."

"Oh, you haven't heard?"

"Heard what?"

"He tried to kill her. Only way he can come is with an armed escort from the sheriff."

They left the room, clucking about the tragedy of it all.

Behind their backs, the woman began quaking. Swimming eyes flew wide as if bursting from their watery sockets. From deep in the chest a silent scream arose, fighting to climb up the tubes. No use.

But the eyes—they wailed, screaming for succor.

The Shetland mare pierced the night with a shrill screech that raised Dodson from his bed instantly. He knew it was a scream of trouble. Then the lioness let loose a yowl as if to punctuate the trouble.

"What's wrong?" murmured his wife.

"Dunno. Something's into them animals, maybe the wolf's come back or something."

Clad in blue jeans and moccasins, Dodson patrolled the pens and cages, his shotgun at the ready. He arrived at the mare's corral in time to see her drop to her knees and roll over, legs quivering.

Behind him the lioness paced, emitting distressed squalls and displaying her fangs.

The smaller animals were going insane, as if their frenzy were coordinated by some sort of ultrasonic whistle, some unseen force or scent or command.

A chill crept up his back, and Dodson began backing toward his trailer house, shotgun covering the areas of darkness his security lights didn't illuminate.

* * *

Mark romps on a high plains Montana meadow with Shep. Hereford cattle graze the tall grass below the Rockies, moving nearer and nearer to the dog and man. Shep dashes in mad circles around Mark, tightening the spiral until the man dives for the dog, missing, landing in a laughing heap in the fragrant grass. The dog turns and attacks, rearing up at the last instant to trample his laughing master with front paws until Mark drags him down into a headlock. Suddenly the cattle stampede. Or is it attack? Bleating and bellowing, they come on, wide-eyed. As if stumbling over a trip wire, the cattle herd is cut down into a writhing mass before the man and dog. Shrieking and screaming, the cattle flail the sky with their hooves until they quiver and go still. Before he can run, Mark is transfixed by the sight of them changing from cattle carcasses into . . . monsters. Shep bristles, advancing stiff-legged toward the first of them. They are beasts reincarnated. They smell even worse than he remembers the other. One takes Shep out with a swipe of bloody claws. Mark turns to run. They are upon him.

Mark sat up in bed, startled awake. God, another run of that nightmare.

He was relieved that he was only dreaming, but then he realized the ringing phone awakened him before PJ got to him as she usually did. His heart was pumping as he leaned across her to pick up the phone. The digital readout: 3:32.

As he talked, PJ sat up and rested her forehead on her knees. As his tone grew more concerned, she stiffened.

Mark dropped the phone in its cradle.

"What is it?"

"Dodson calling about my—Beth's Shetland mare having trouble."

"Oh? Did he call a vet?"

"He says it's past that. He might have to . . . put her to sleep."

"Oh . . . I'm sorry."

"Forget it." He stood up and stretched before finding his pants on the chair beside her bed. "Peej?"

"Where are you going?"

"I'm going to ask you to marry me."

She laughed. "You don't have to get dressed to ask me, and you don't have to go anywhere, silly. And the answer is yes."

"I didn't ask you yet, woman. Don't be so forward. I want to do it more romantically than this."

"Then where do you think you're going?"

"Out to Dodson's."

"Why? What can you do?"

"Comfort Dodson. He's frantic over the mare. I owe him that much for taking care of the horse."

She bounced out of bed. "I'm going with you."

"You don't have to."

"I know. But I'm not letting you out of my sight now that you're on the verge of proposing. You might pick up a woman hitchhiker or something."

"Hardly. I love you, Peej. And you don't have to go."

They kissed, lingering over the feeling of bare chests.

She pulled away, a distressed look on her face. "There's nothing more going on out at Dodson's, is there?" He shook his head. "Then," she said, "we'd better go before you get something started here."

As she dressed, he went to the entry closet. From inside a coat pocket, he drew a .38 caliber pistol. He snapped the cylinder out, checked that it was loaded, and tucked it into his belt beneath the shirt. Another grab into the coat produced a fistful of loose cartridges.

He was warming up the Camaro when she pulled the door to the apartment shut.

The drive to Dodson's was all small talk, mostly hers, mostly animated, mostly about the possibility of marriage. It was as if she had bottled up such waiting for the moment it could gush free.

As the Camaro's headlights swept into the zoo parking lot, she said, "Something's really very wrong out here, isn't it?"

"I'm not sure."

"You're sure enough to be carrying a pistol in your jeans."

Two shots from inside the zoo saved him the trouble of explaining. He killed the lights and stepped out into the darkness. She was beside him in seconds. He turned.

"Save your breath," she said. "I'm coming with you."

They found the gate open and crept inside, the .38 pointing the way. At the walkway to the trailer, Mark hesitated, crouching low in the shadow of the picket fence. There was too much light from the porch fixture and from lamps inside for him to feel comfortable stopping here. Yet he didn't want his back left uncovered.

"Why don't you wait here and warn me if somebody comes out of the trailer?" he told PJ.

Automatically, they looked toward the trailer door. A crack of light broke out around the edge of the door and widened. A figure stepped down one step as Mark swung the pistol. The startled figure screamed and sat down hard.

"It's a woman," said PJ, rushing up the walk.

"Don't shoot," she begged.

"We're not going to shoot," said Mark. "Where's Mack?"

As she answered her voice rose at the end of every sentence as if she were asking questions. "He . . . I don't know. He come out here with his twelve-gauge and then come running back in to the phone and then run out again. I din't hear nothin' for the longest time until a shot. And just now I just heard two more. I'm Rhonda Dodson, y' know. I'm his wife."

"Yes. Did he say where he was going?"

"That female lion. He . . . *aaaaaahhh*." Wide-mouthed and wide-eyed, she was staring over Mark's shoulder.

He spun, bringing up the .38.

He saw the long, double gun barrels rising toward his crotch and knew he was done for if the shotgun went off.

He recognized the wiry figure, even drenched in blood.

"Mack, don't shoot," he shouted.

"Payne? Izzat you?"

Both gun muzzles fell away.

"You're hurt."

"No."

"All this blood . . ."

"The mare. I tried to tend her and she coughed up a gallon of blood on me. She was hurting, Payne, I'm sorry. I had to put her outta her misery."

"It's okay. What . . . caused it?"

"Could of been that little monster."

The little hairs stood up on Mark's back from his buttocks to his scalp. "What . . . monster?"

Dodson wiped his hand across his face.

"The one that broke into Lisa's cage and kilt her too."

"The lion? It killed the lioness?"

"Yeah."

"Where is it now?"

"Still in the cage."

"No, Mack, not Lisa. I mean the monster."

"That's what I'm talking about. It's still in the cage with her. I done killed it a minute ago."

"How . . ." said a distraught Mark.

"With the shotgun . . ."

But Payne was gone, sprinting toward the lion's cage. As he ran, his mind raced. All the other animals were in an uproar. The walled enclosure of the hyena pit was clouded in dust stirred up by the agitated animals. The small cats paced in their small pens. Birds and night mammals raised a raucous uproar.

He found the cage. Inside lay two carcasses, both ripped and bloody, neither recognizable.

The trio caught up. They stared inside as Mark

prowled around the perimeter of the cage, pulling on the wire, rattling the bars, searching the seams and corners.

"Mack, you have any—"

"I got no goddamn idear how that little bastard got in. All I can think of is it squeezed through one a these squares."

Mark inspected the hogwire. He couldn't get his hand through.

"God almighty. Where's the mare?"

"I told you, she's dead, Mark. You don't want to—"

"The mare, Mack, where's the goddamned mare?"

"The corral just ahead."

Mark vaulted the split-cedar rails and ran to the ghostly swollen figure lying in the dark spot in the center of the corral. By the time the others had climbed in, he had his pistol out. He started firing into the mare's belly and didn't stop until the hammer fell on spent cartridges.

The words of the three-fingered man came back to him. He had said he wasn't trying to hurt Beth. Yes, he *was* trying to kill her, but not because he wanted to hurt her.

The sudden realization of what Spellers had meant choked Mark where he stood.

"What the hell?" whispered Dodson.

"Mark . . ."

Mark wheeled on them, fumbling with the pistol, shucking brass casings to the ground, fishing in his pockets for more shells. His expression of agony, visible enough in the faint light of the security lamp, held their tongues.

He snapped the cylinder shut and looked up. He wore a drawn, fearful expression, as if he'd just been told somebody had died. He stuck the pistol into his waistband and vaulted the fence again.

PJ was right behind.

He shouted at her to stay.

She shouted back and climbed into the Camaro as it roared away.

2

In the darkness a spot appeared. The spot grew, black on black—red on white, if light were to show—first slowly; just a gentle, seeping spot, then more rapidly, a flow drenching the sheet. A two-inch thorn pierced the spot. Then three more thorns.

It had taken the duty resident only moments to pronounce her. "Page Doctor Morton," he had ordered. Then he wrote in the time, 4:45 A.M., and the cause, cardiac arrest, for lack of specifics on either. It didn't matter to this poor body whose soul had departed long before her physical death in the night.

The code page for Doctor Morton brought a pair of orderlies wheeling a covered cart stenciled, CLEAN LINEN. The side of the cart was a hinged door that folded up on top of the box, revealing a stainless-steel slab exactly at bed height. The orderlies rolled the folded corpse, barely seventy-five pounds. The maneuver simultaneously wrapped it in the sheet and rolled it onto the slab. They dropped the door and pushed the cart toward the express elevator that would take them to the basement. And the living patients who saw the cart would not be alarmed by the sight of a corpse; would not fret about a surgical error or missed diagnosis in their own cases. All could still delude themselves that everybody left this fine hospital by the front door.

Inside the elevator, the pair stood glumly counting the descending floor numbers. The death hardly bothered them—they'd rolled hundreds of corpses into erstwhile linen carts. But as they neared the end of their shift, fatigue had dulled even their senses of humor.

"Knock it off," one ordered the other.

"Knock what off."

"Rapping on the box, jerkoff. I ain't in the mood for none of your morbid jokes."

The other raised his hands. "I haven't touched the box." He cocked his head. "Now I'm hearing it. You're doing that, right?"

The one raised his hands, too.

The other put his head near the linen box.

There came a scratching and rattling from inside, then the sound of tearing cloth.

The one shuddered and reached for the elevator alarm. "She's 'sposed to be dead. If she ain't, there's gonna be one resident with his ass in a sling today."

The other lifted the folding door. "Yeah, this is grounds for a disciplinary board. . . ."

The one stiffened as the other shrieked.

The shriek ended in a gurgle as the other's throat was ripped away, leaving a ragged, gaping, raw hole from which blood and steamy air spurted. The head, no longer supported, fell over onto the orderly's back before he hit the floor.

The unharmed orderly screamed and hit all the buttons on the panel, pounding them with his fists.

The hinged door to the linen cart flew open, loosing a torrent of blood from inside.

The orderly tried to climb up the wall into the corner, but he slipped in the lubricant of the other's gore and fell to the floor.

PJ sat immobile inside the Camaro as the lights of the town raced by. Mark had just finished his summation of what he thought was happening.

"Spellers knew. Somehow he figured out this beast could fertilize animals of other species. He was trying to save Beth from suffering."

"It can't be," she said. "It just can't be true."

"It has to be. That little monster didn't break into the lion's cage. It tore its way out of her belly and killed her, but it couldn't escape the cage."

"The pony?"

"She was dead, but I swear her belly was alive when I emptied my pistol into her. We can find out later by cutting into her."

"Surely . . . not Beth."

He took his eyes from the blurring strip of asphalt disappearing beneath the front of the red car. His expression told her yes, Beth too.

"What will you do if it is true? If she is . . . bearing a beast?"

"I . . . I'm not sure. Maybe we can have her x-rayed to be sure. Maybe a C-section . . . I don't know. I haven't thought it out."

* * *

They found pandemonium at the hospital. At the emergency entrance he saw two police vehicles, lights flashing. He recognized Beard's Ranger pickup.

He could see a knot of people through the glass doors.

"Stay inside the car, PJ."

"You know better than that."

He stopped behind the Ranger. "Listen, you get behind the wheel and be ready to drive away in a hurry in case something goes wrong. If necessary, I'll meet you out front."

"What could go wrong? You haven't done anything."

"That's Beard in there. I've been too stupid before, walking into trouble. Not this time. You be my getaway driver or . . ."

"Or what?"

"Or . . . hell, I don't know . . . the marriage is off."

It was an incongruous time to laugh, but they both did. "I'll wait. But if you're not out in a minute, I'm coming in."

Inside, the knot was gathered around the elevator door. Several onlookers turned away, ghostly pale. One ran off gagging.

Mark knifed into the crowd to get a look. A glance was too much.

The elevator doors had been pried open. They were propped open with an iron bar. The floor of the car had stopped a couple feet below the hospital floor.

Two corpses, possibly men, lay shredded on the

floor of the car. A bundle of bloody linen lay in a cart on a slab that was nearly at floor level. A figure worked behind the cart.

"Who was the one in the morgue wagon?" asked a hushed voice.

"Mrs. Howell. Beth Howell."

"Poor soul. The one the brother tried to kill."

Mark stiffened. His hand went to his gun. It wasn't the accusation of the nurse that bothered him. It wasn't even grief.

It was the realization that another beast was now on the loose.

He ducked down to peer into the mess of shredded sheets. Then he peered over the edge and saw that the floor of the car was below the opening into the elevator shaft. A series of parallel scratches ran through the drying blood and over the edge. The thing had dropped down the shaft.

"Anybody here see anything strange?"

Mark recognized the raspy voice and ducked away.

"Any strangers?" came the wheezing, labored whisper from behind the linen cart.

First appeared a Stetson. Then the tired, angry face of Sheriff Jacob Beard. The *surprised*, tired, angry face of Sheriff Jacob Beard.

"Hold it right there, Payne. You're under arrest."

"There he is," yelped a nurse. "The killer."

"He's got a gun," shouted somebody else.

Mark saw Beard's cannon bore coming over the box.

He threw up his palms. "Don't shoot, Sheriff."

The .44 bore kept coming. Mark might even have

called the look in Beard's eyes a gleam. He was telegraphing. He was going to shoot. No Miranda rights here. No questions, no confession, no pinko defense lawyers, no bail, no trial, no jury, no nothing. Just an execution of Beard's verdict. For all the mysteries and deaths, most especially Britton's, the .44 erupted in Beard's fist just as Mark dived left.

Hot gasses burned the peach fuzz off his neck behind the ear. Bits of lead, melted shavings rasped off the slug by the lands and grooves of the bore, peppered his neck. His right ear rang, filling up with liquid, leaving him deaf on that side.

But the slug missed his head. It tore into a concrete pillar in the wall across from the elevator, ricocheting upward into a bank of the ceiling lights, showering the screaming, scattering crowd below with a rainfall of glass and increasing the clamor.

Mark rolled left, in part spun by the shot past his right ear. He hit the floor and came up on all fours. He started to lunge for a doorway to his left.

"Freeze, Payne," roared the sheriff.

Mark looked at the elevator door. Six feet away, Beard, his right arm awkwardly bent, held the pistol unsteadily at the center of his face. Behind the cavernous bore were hate-filled, murderous eyes.

"I got you dead to rights now, you bastard."

"Sheriff, I didn't have anything to do with this."

"Tell it to all the other bastards you meet in hell."

"You shoot me now, and you'll be a murderer, Sheriff."

Beard hesitated an instant. As if to confirm, several

gasps rose up from the potential witnesses lying everywhere on the floor. Beard flinched.

But Mark saw the eyes telegraphing again. *It had to be now.*

Beard deliberately cocked the .44's hammer.

Mark lunged left—toward the door marked EMERGENCY EXIT. He'd either make it or he wouldn't. Beard would kill him anyhow if he stood still for it. Maybe the arm being bent the wrong way would throw off his aim.

As he took off, he thought he heard a man's scream rising from the elevator shaft, either above or below. He couldn't be sure for the deafness already in his ears and the second explosion of the .44. The second bullet sang off the floor and down the hall. Mark hit the door and rolled. He came up and nearly dived down the flight of stairs before him, catching himself with the safety rail. His pubic bone hurt where the barrel of the .38 caught him as he hit the floor. But he was alive and running down the stairs when he heard a man's scream from below. Definitely a scream. He pulled the pistol from his waistband.

Charles Russell hadn't heard about all the trouble in ER. All he knew was the elevator alarm had gone off, rousting him from a perfectly good nap among the blanket piles at the back of his maintenance office. The phone added its ring to the nagging alarm, so he couldn't ignore the ruckus. An excited voice gave him instructions over the phone to fix the elevator.

"Of course I'll fix it, you fool. It's my job."

Charlie fixed his coffee first. And had a smoke. *God-*

dammit, if they don't like it, they can fix it theirselfs, he thought. *'Cept they don't know how.* He lit a second smoke and decided to shut off that damned alarm.

Outside his basement office, he tried a master key in the elevator panel. The doors slid open. Maybe the pulleys or cables had gotten cockeyed in the pit below the elevator stop. He reached inside and hit the shaft lights. He was startled by the strings of blood dripping from above.

"Holy mackerel."

He leaned into the shaft and gawked up at the dim light coming from the next floor up. A pair of doors were open.

He was startled a second time by a bang from above. It sounded like a shot. He opened his mouth to *halloo,* but he was startled again—this time by the raking of claws down his thigh—and his shout came out a scream.

He leapt back from the shaft door. Another bang came from above. He expected his attacker to show itself. Nothing. He backed away. Toward the stairwell door. He heard the scratching of claws, like a giant rat's.

Charles was suddenly lame; his shoe filled with blood and overflowing. He desperately dragged himself to the stairwell door.

A scream rose in his throat as the scratching came from behind. He hit the bar and turned to shut the door. But his leg wouldn't move fast enough and he closed the door on his ankle. With both hands he heaved on his leg, freeing it and stumbling backward.

The door swung back. It would close, keeping the

giant rat inside. No rat, no matter how giant, could push a panic bar open.

But the door didn't close.

It rattled with the impact of the claws and flew open.

Charles saw it, and it was no rat.

It was . . . he didn't know what. He pulled the claw hammer from his tool belt, backpedaling all the time.

His leg buckled, and he hit the exit with his butt, falling partly into the parking garage on his back.

He swung the hammer and screamed as he struck himself, shattering his kneecap. Horrible as that was, it was nothing compared with the pain that came next. It was as if a chain saw was climbing up his good leg, tearing up his crotch, through his belly.

He screamed until the chain saw reached his throat.

PJ heard the first shot before her minute had expired. She backed the Camaro up to see inside the emergency room. People inside were diving and crawling and creeping on their bellies. She saw Mark, saw a gun at the end of an arm, saw Mark dive out of the hallway.

A heavy lump of ice filled her stomach. He said to meet him out front, so she took off; the rear tires breaking away and squealing.

Even before she reached the lighted front entrance, she knew he wouldn't be there. Not now or later. He'd be cut off by the pursuit from the ER. The stairwell—it must lead to a basement, maybe a back door.

As she flashed past the front, she saw uniformed security men, pistols drawn, run into the lobby and crouch behind the flimsy furniture.

If he had a chance at all it would be out back.

Mark took three steps at a time on the way down the stairwell. *Rushing is crazy*, he thought. He ought not be in such a hurry to confront the beast that must now be there. Nevertheless, he couldn't slow down.

The screaming had stopped—was cut off.

One more landing and—he froze, gun pointed down at a quivering body, its blood still pooling out. Another victim of the same animal, whatever it was, the man torn up as the others had been. A tingle rose on the back of his neck; a tickle slid down the right side of his neck.

He started down, pistol covering the door propped open by the body. From outside he heard scratching on the pavement. He *thought* he heard it. His right ear was filled with the roaring of surf. He cocked his left ear. There. Definitely claws on the concrete, but heavy ones.

He stepped over the man—the corpse with the bubbling throat—and waved his .38 into the lighted garage. He saw the wet tracks leading toward the exit and ran in that direction. It couldn't be let loose. He knew he must kill it. He knew the consequences if he did not.

PJ restrained her foot, trying to keep the Camaro under control.

Around the most distant corner from the ER she flew. The signs warned her not to drive here because only official and service vehicles were permitted. Ahead was a delivery entrance. She would pull in there and . . . What? She didn't know what.

She started her turn.

A black shadow dashed from the garage entrance.

She hit her brakes, barely stopping before she hit it.

"Damned dog."

It stood up in the lights. It was no damned dog. She knew what it was. It snarled, baring its fangs. She hit the accelerator. The Camaro leapt. The beast leapt.

PJ came face to face with the beast as it hit the windshield spread-eagle. It bounced up onto the roof. She heard the claws scratching as if trying to dig in. She hit the brakes again and spun the wheel.

Its claws raked around, seeking a purchase, and it was on the windshield again looking in, trying to dig in through the glass. Enraged, it began swatting in whirling, roundhouse blows that ended in sharp raps as the claws pecked away at the windshield.

A star appeared beneath the rearview mirror. The beast went to work on that spot, enlarging the chip. It grew into a tiny spider web. Like a terrier after a rat, the thing dug furiously. PJ felt chips of glass raining in—A spike came through.

Then the beast was pulling out the edges of a hole the size of a fist.

She screamed and launched the growling Camaro ahead and hit the brakes. The thing tumbled off the hood, out of sight, taking with it a chunk of glass. The hole in the windshield was now the size of a bowling ball.

She hit reverse and backed off, tires smoking. There. It was coming again. It leapt. She hit the brakes. Its timing off, it crashed heavily into the grill. She hit reverse again. Two shots from inside the garage kicked up sparks between the Camaro and the beast. And it was gone, a black shadow melting into the night.

She started to spin the Camaro away from the gunman when she saw it was Mark. He ran past her after the shadow.

"Don't do it, Mark. It's too dangerous." She was doing everything to control herself, to keep from disintegrating into hysteria.

He was leaning into the darkness.

"Don't be stupid, Mark. The police are everywhere. They'll have heard the shots," she shouted. She knew she was hysterical and didn't care that he knew. "I'm afraid. Don't leave me, Mark. Please, Mark." She was begging.

He ran to the Camaro. She climbed over the console. The Z28 leapt once again and shot away from the hospital, a stiff breeze blowing through the hole in the windshield.

"Are you all right, PJ?" he finally asked when he was certain they weren't being followed. "Darling."

In answer she said, "My God, you've been shot."

He adjusted the mirror and saw the crescent cut into the top of his right ear and the blood painting his neck.

"It's nothing."

She burst into tears.

He held her hand, letting her cry herself out, letting her squeeze his arm and wet his sleeve with tears. He might have cried himself if it were not for the fears that surmounted his grief.

"Poor, poor Beth," she finally said.

"Beth," he whispered, as if calling to her.

"That terrible animal. . . . Mark, it came after me . . . I thought it would get in. It was so . . . Mark, it had a human quality to it. Yet it wasn't a beast and it wasn't a man."

"It's part human, Peej. It's the ultimate monster, a . . . a beast with the mind of a man."

"What can we do about it?"

He told her. He wasn't so sure anything would work—so he didn't really know what to do, but he told her a plan anyhow. First he would get some things from her apartment. He didn't dare go to his own house. Half his things were at her place anyhow. Then he'd ditch the Camaro for something less conspicuous. Then he'd go hunting for beasts.

"Beasts? Plural?"

"Plural. Every ranch and farm raided by that original monster."

"But why?"

"Even Howell didn't figure out the clues in his log. But we had the chance to observe, to count the incidents. We have to assume every instance was an attack on males and a bestial rape of females. All the males were killed, remember. But not all the females. They sometimes survived. And sometimes the ranchers destroyed their cows. The Shetland mare survived. Dodson's lioness survived. There must have been others. I have to get to them."

"The authorities have to know, Mark. You'll need help. These things . . . my God . . . If one beast was capable . . . you don't think . . ."

"That's *exactly* what I think. Any of this thing's offspring will be more vicious than the last generation. That's the bug my brother-in-law couldn't seem to work out of his calculations. What he didn't know was, he'd invented something capable of breaking the natural barriers between species. These beasts are able to mate with . . . maybe any female. Each birth is going to take place in a third to half the normal gestation time. Each animal will mature at an accelerated rate. Each beast will be more savage than its parent."

She clutched his arm. "And each one is virtually a species of its own. In several generations . . . there won't be any order—"

"That's right. There will be no distinction between the species. These things will be attacking each other and the normal animals—killing males, raping females, turning out more generations of monsters."

"You've got to have help."

"I've got you."

"Get serious. You need the authorities. Shouldn't you notify somebody in government? Federal government?"

"I have the uneasy feeling that this is the kind of thing the government has been involved in from the start. Remember those invisible people who made things happen? Remember the disappearing bodies? I think the invisible hand has been government. And I wouldn't be a bit surprised if government—part of it, anyhow—is already mobilized over this latest little beast."

At PJ's apartment, Mark had hushed her protests. He rushed her inside and gave her instructions as she followed him around, helping to collect clothes, flight gear, and some provisions.

"You can't come."

"Baloney, Mark. You can't play hero all by yourself. You have to get help."

"You're not listening. I'm not trying to save the world. I'm also not going to jail—what I mean is, I'll never make it to jail. I saw the look in Beard's eyes. I'd be killed trying to escape."

"Turn yourself over to the FBI."

"Good. Yeah, I'll do that . . . 'Listen, sir, if you can forget for a moment that I've been accused of a couple-three murders, I want to tell you about this fantastic monster that is threatening to destroy the planet.' "

PJ had no response to that. He held a finger to his lips and led her outside. When they were clear of the building, he resumed.

"Listen," he said. "I'm no savior of mankind but I do know there's no use in wasting time trying to clear myself."

"But—"

"Later." He put a hand to her lips. "Right now we need an authority to set things in motion. I made a friend in the sanitarium in Marble Falls. A doctor. His name was Matt Junker. You get him out to Dodson's—then when he's seen the two beasts we killed out there tonight, have him talk to somebody—you just leave that to Junker."

"What about you?"

"I'm going hunting."

"You can't find that beast. Not alone."

"I won't be trying tonight. First I'm going looking at each of the ranches and farms when we wanted to search for the first beast. I'm going to see if I can find some . . . damaged livestock and . . . destroy it before we have an army of beasts being born around here."

"What if you have one of your . . . spells?"

"I have to assume I won't."

She was silent for a moment. Finally, she said, "How can I get in touch with you?"

"You can't. I'll call you and uh, try to sell you, uh, a subscription to *Army Times*. You just refuse to talk. Then leave and go to the pay phone at the Zippy store down the block. I'll get the number tonight and call you there in five minutes after you hang up."

"Mark, I don't know about all this cloak and dagger stuff—"

"PJ, we can second-guess ourselves later. I've got to get moving before light and get rid of this car. It'll be picked up in a heartbeat."

"Where—"

He silenced her with a kiss and was gone.

The double doors swung open and lay flat against the rear of the quonset and two planks dropped into place. The starter inside whined angrily but finally the reluctant engine caught, and *Shitbird* idled out into the night. In a minute, the red Camaro, paint chipped and peeling around the bullet holes, windshield smashed as if a cannon ball had gone through, sat over the drip pan in Poole's office.

Mark piled the last of his gear, flight bag, gallon of water, and a case of field rations. The ramp guard hadn't come by to challenge him. Maybe things were changing for the better. He had little confidence that any part of his scheme would succeed, regardless of what he had told PJ. He was no sleuth, no hunter, no agent—let alone a savior. Junker would probably laugh off PJ's plea for help. An irate chicken farmer would probably pump him full of buckshot first time he tried to check out a barn. The army would arrest him for AWOL and charge him with murder. He'd spend the rest of his life in Leavenworth as a convicted killer and erstwhile chicken thief. In disgrace. Without the woman he loved, the woman he was continually dragging into this mess. He'd . . .

He'd have to stop feeling sorry for himself and get on with trying to put an end to this nightmare. Somebody had to at least try to find and kill that beast . . . those beasts. He shook his head. It ached. His ear had begun to throb and the impaired hearing on the right side kept trying to reel him off balance.

She had warned him about one of the spells. He felt one coming on. Gradually. But it was coming. He had to move.

He pushed the double doors shut and planted himself behind the wheel of *Shitbird*.

The injured eardrum, the idling jeep, the vibrating

hood latch. They prevented him from hearing the footfalls rushing across the gravel.

Before he could floor the clutch pedal and shift into gear, it was suddenly daylight inside his head.

3

The wiry man knelt in the gore next to the mare. He could hardly have cared about getting more messy—it wasn't possible.

His squat wife stood behind him; arms wrapped around her own torso.

The sky had barely lightened, bathing the scene in ghostly blue.

Dodson unfolded his Buck knife and touched the swollen belly of the Shetland. The blade parted the flesh and released a hiss of gas from a pocket not yet punctured by Payne's slugs. Dodson steeled himself and drew a black line from the ribs to the flank, releasing a flood of blood and placental fluids and an indistinct miscarriage of a form that slithered out onto his knees.

Dodson recoiled. "The thing looks . . . like . . . a pony with fangs and claws."

Behind him, he heard his wife's breath explode with a pop. And she fell over his back into the carnage.

"Rhonda girl, for chrissakes, don't faint on me now."

Struggling to pull her out of the mess, he never

heard the sound behind him, never felt his brain ripple like a dropped bowl of gelatin, never knew that someone else had come into the corral to join them.

The rising sun shed little light on the thing that had delivered itself onto the planet.

An observer from a distance might have mistaken it for a medium-size dog. In fact, it had stopped along the roadway outside town to tear at the carcass of that species of broken-shelled armadillo that frequents such resting places. A stray dog, mostly golden retriever, arrived on the scene to dispute ownership of the roadside meal and had become a meal itself.

The beast's muzzle was something like a dog's, and there was the size and thin, black fur. But those were about the only similarities. It was many things, but it wasn't a dog.

Like a shrew it had an enormously accelerated metabolism. It needed food constantly—protein-rich food. And the energy obtained from its flesh and blood diet wouldn't be dissipated like a shrew's in the search for more food, but in growth.

Like many animals, it had a fast growth rate. Unlike most, the rate was not constant. From conception, the cell division rate was normal. But as the embryo grew, the growth rate increased. Not only was the beast growing now, but its rate had increased so that it was driven by the need for more food, driven beyond even its normal ferocity. When they autopsied Beth Howell's body, they would discover that it lacked many vital organs. A careful examination of the other dead would reveal that the bodies had been more than slashed and mutilated—they had been largely consumed. Physically, the beast was an uncontrollable appetite growing in size and ferocity by the hour.

It had hands and feet reminiscent of human extremities, and a vaguely human form. The eyes seemed more human than animal. But it was all wrong—the hands and feet tipped with claws, the mouth filled with fangs. The form was a throwback beyond prehistory: neither man nor ape. And the eyes were full of hatred.

Those things, observation and deduction would show. Never studied would be the mind of the beast. Though only alive for hours, this animal had a lifetime—several lifetimes—of memory, genetic memory of its ancestors. It was memory passed along in the strings of proteins and acids in the genes comprised of part of every species in its makeup. In the surface memory, this beast recalled the sights, sounds, smells and tastes of all that went on since it had torn from the woman's abdomen. But on another level it knew the rage of a creature, confined in a cage poked and probed at by men; the rage of killing one of the men in triumph, of attacking a woman—the same woman it left behind on this night. Buried deeper in its mind was the memory of corrals and pens and forests and rivers and close-ups of the earth's surface. Each of these sensations competed with the others for a moment of consciousness and comprehension even as the animal tried to comprehend its immediate environment and its current experience.

Faced with the overloaded memory it could not control, with genetic instructions from multiple species, the beast found mountains of contradictory sensations and competing feelings. And the only outcome was something that approached rage.

It had been moving in the direction this emotion told it to go since it awoke.

The instant she hit the parking lot at Dodson's, PJ knew things had gone wrong. The ambulance and volunteer fire truck established that. As did all the police cars, with flashing lights. An instant later, as if to confirm, she sat in her Tempo, surrounded by an angry, uniformed mob. The ring of men bristled with guns of every description and caliber from the law enforcement arsenal—all pointing at her.

She sat immobile, her hands gripping the steering wheel. Until a big paw snatched open her door, latched onto her collar and not a little blond hair, and dragged her from inside.

Beard threw her against the Tempo's side.

When she protested the manhandling, he pulled her away from the car and threw her against it again, knocking the wind out of her.

Another lawman took the keys and searched the trunk. Beard holstered his pistol and searched PJ. His hands probed and poked her entire body without the least regard for her sex.

PJ was scared. This was no lecherous patdown. This was the egalitarian search of an angry policeman who would have been as thorough and fierce with any man. She remembered what Mark had said about being killed trying to escape.

"What's wrong, Sheriff?"

He yanked her right arm behind her back. She felt a metal ring snap onto her wrist.

"That hurts." Her left arm joined the right in the handcuffs.

The pistols were lowered. Beard gripped her arm and propelled her toward his truck. "Where the hell's Payne?" he growled.

Now angry as well as humiliated, PJ said, "Don't I get my rights."

"You bet your ass you get your rights. You can have your rights right up your ass, if you want. You're under arrest. Suspicion of murder and accessory to murder of the Dodsons—"

"That can't be—"

"You have the right to remain silent—"

"Sheriff, I called and said I'd meet you here. Why would I—"

"You have the right to have an attorney present during questioning." His grip grew tighter on her arm.

The pain in her arm wasn't what was bothering her. Now she wouldn't be helping Mark—couldn't help him.

"Sheriff, be reasonable," she pleaded.

"—If you give up any of these rights, anything you say can and will be used on you. . . ."

The explosion of daylight inside Mark's head slowly became reality. It was well into the afternoon before he regained consciousness. Since the moment he was struck on the head, he had slumped into the deeper unconscious characteristic of the adrenaline letdown he'd experienced spasmodically since basic training.

With the daylight came the sound of the radio. It was a most realistic dream: the news reporter describing the scene of bloody crimes at the hospital, where at least three men and a woman were killed. He reported their names. At the sound of Beth's name, dream and reality melded. He opened his eyes and looked at the sky. Too bright. He squinted, feeling the sunlight intensify the throbbing headache. He thought he might vomit, so intense was the pain.

But the radio reporter had hardly begun. He told of the possibly related case, as yet unconfirmed by Coryell County Sheriff Jacob Z. Beard—a double murder at the roadside zoo of Mack Dodson.

Mark tried to spring erect. No use. He lay on his bound hands. His boots seemed glued together. He finally forced open his eyes. He was lying face-up in the rear seat of *Shitbird*, looking at the sky. He saw his ankles were tied. Tightly. He could find no feeling in them no matter how he concentrated. He realized his hands were numb as well. And he was thirsty. And ill. He felt the bile rising and barely had time to turn his head before he threw up on the floor of the jeep.

"You're awake."

Mark searched for the voice's owner, a man. He couldn't see for the tears in his eyes. He did smell the rank sweetness of body-oxidizing liquor, and he retched again.

Shitbird cranked to life. He felt it backing; then he felt the shade. In the distance he heard the radio reporter droning on, describing the scenes of murder.

He opened his eyes and saw the tree above him blocking out the sun and sky. Still he couldn't see his captor. A cloth came out of nowhere and fell across his face. He knew he would be smothered now.

But the wet cloth was gently held. It wiped his face, refreshing him.

"Want a drink of water?"

Mark tried to speak, but only a hiss issued from his throat.

A hand held his head up. Another hand spilled water from a canvas desert bag into his mouth and down his face. He remembered the taste of water stored in canvas, cooled by evaporation of the seepage. It was a memory from his childhood when every family traveled with a water bag tied to the grill or draped over a side mirror. The memory refreshed him as much as the water.

He shook his head and grunted when he had his fill. The hand lowered his head. Gently.

"I'm going to untie your feet. Don't struggle or kick because I'll tie you up again. You're going to have to listen."

Listen he did. Mark heard the radio voice report the arrest of a woman suspected to be an accomplice at the hospital in at least one of the murders. The woman was one Pamela Jane Larson of Killeen.

A face leaned into the backseat and hands worked on the ropes. It was a tall man, a gaunt face. It was one of the phony insurance men he'd seen in the sheriff's office the day Beard arrested him for trying to smother Beth.

The radio reported that officials were broadcasting an alert to law-enforcement officers nationwide about a suspect, one Mark J. Payne, thirty-three, an army captain whom officials at the fort also wanted to question for his unauthorized absence. Mark heard his description being reported in detail. The weight was wrong. Since he met PJ, he'd dropped nearly ten pounds.

The radio reporter's voice was snapped off just as it rose to a new pitch of excitement to tell about a suspected anthrax outbreak caused by infected hogs imported from Mexico.

"I'm going to sit you up and untie your hands. I warn you, your feet and hands aren't going to function very well for a while. In fact, they're probably going to sting as the circulation is restored. It wouldn't be wise to try anything stupid. Besides, I have a pistol. I won't hesitate to use it."

"What the hell is going on?"

"That's what I'm going to tell you. For starters, my name is Paul Winston."

"Mark Payne."

"I know. I know more about you than you do. So you just listen to what I tell you."

Winston told him everything. He revealed the stories of the drug experiment gone awry in the officer candidate platoon in basic training, Howell's monster set loose in the fire at the clinic, the helicopter crash, the fate of Howell and Spellers and Parish and Buchanan, his theft of the research log from PJ's apart-

ment. He dwelt on the story of The Corporation and
its domestic mission of intelligence gathering. He
speculated on the certainty that Washington was now
renewing the case, trying to cancel Winston's insurance policy—Howell's research journal and copies of
corporate documents ready for mailing to selected
members of the press and Congress. He told the bewildered captain that their lives were in danger, that
PJ was probably safer in the hands of the police than
not.

Mark sat and listened, for the moment unmindful
of the stinging in his wrists and ankles.

It was an hour before he even thought to speak, to
ask a question. "This corporation? You think they
killed Dodson and his wife?" Mark said, the circulation finally restored to his hands and feet.

"No question."

"Why kill the Dodsons?"

"The dead animals out there. You know anything
about them?"

"Yes. A lion and a horse—a Shetland mare. They
were pregnant, each with one of those . . . things."

"Then that's the reason the Dodsons were killed.
Evidence. The fetuses, or whatever, won't be found.
Nobody who's seen those things can be left alive.
This story can't come out into the open, believe me.
It would do untold damage to a lot of very important
people in important places."

"Then PJ—"

"She's in danger, yes. That's why it's better she's
been arrested. At least she'll be kept under guard."

"What kind of a godforsaken element of society do

your people come from? What kind of people could do these sorts of things in this country?"

"Think of them as patriots—"

"Bullshit."

"Let me finish. Think of them as patriots, zealous patriots, no longer able to tell right from wrong. Think of them as bureaucrats buried so deeply inside the bureaucracy, they are no longer inefficient. Instead, they are murderously effective. Invisible. Answerable to nobody or nothing except that feeling of mutated patriotism. They have enormous amounts of information about the criminal activities, legal and illegal, national and international, friendly and enemy, political, religious, business—you name it. They see that all the rules are only shams. They see that to follow the rules is to surrender to those who believe in no gods and accept no regulation. They see that ruthlessness and cruelty are facts of life in the world and that things like honor and trust are synonyms for weakness and incompetence. So . . . All the rules of righteous behavior are rewritten. All the parameters are defined in terms of self-interest. First it's national self-interest—that's the term you come up with when nationalism is redefined. Then it's personal self-interest. After all, if you allow yourself to be sacrificed to the interests of the nation, you can no longer help the cause. That's what happens when you redefine patriotism.

"In Washington there's a term: Potomac Fever. It's what happens to journalists and politicians—and military people, for that matter—when they have spent a few years in the district. Pretty soon, everything outside the capitol loses its importance. People everywhere outside D.C. become hicks and buffoons. Only the insiders know what's going on. Only they are well enough informed to decide what's good for the rest of the country. Well, just think of this as an especially virulent strain of Potomac Fever."

"I think of Nazis."

"I suppose that *is* what happens when a nation's entire government is infected."

"Well, what about you? How come you think you're cured . . . ?"

"*If* I'm cured, you mean? Well, I'm simply one of those who signed on to do a job of looking in on other people who might be . . . dangerous to the country. I'm not making excuses for myself. I knew what was going on. I know domestic spying is illegal. I kept saying I'd never be a participant in the killings. I'd let corporate auditors clean up the dirty business. If I should ever come to face a modern-day version of the Nuremberg trials, I had decided long ago to claim the Nuremberg defense—I knew nothing except my orders, which never included killing anyone. My conscience was clean. It was clean until the night I attempted to kill you and your sister. It was the night I tried to burn you both inside that clinic. Then I knew what I was capable of, what I had become.

"But you saved me when you dragged yourself and your sister from the flames. You saved me from being a murderer. And even though I was the supervisor of Parish when he sabotaged that helicopter, I had nothing to do with that—truly. By then I had already decided. I went for the logbook, for an insurance policy.

I retired myself; ran away. But even that wasn't good enough to salve the conscience. So . . . I'm back . . . and here we are."

"And now what?"

"Well, what were you going to do when you took this . . . jeep?"

"I was on my way into the countryside to find other barns and corrals where livestock might have been impregnated. I was going to carry on my own extermination campaign until I got caught myself."

"No need now."

Mark cocked his head in question.

"The anthrax outbreak? You heard that bit on the radio?"

"What's anthrax got to do with anything?"

"It's got everything to do with everything. What happens when anthrax breaks out?"

"Ranchers go up the walls. Government steps in and destroys all the herds. . . ."

Winston smirked.

"Christ," whispered Mark.

"Somebody representing Agriculture will take care of all the little beasts ripening in the bellies of sheep, goats, cattle, horses—"

"Horses don't get anthrax."

"They get beasts, don't they? So they shoot everything, including the horses, pay off the farmers and ranchers, and disappear."

Mark stretched his neck and worked his hands. "So what do we do?"

"We look for your escaped beast by listening to the radio. It's maturing every minute. If it reaches sexual maturity, it could sew its seeds of damnation all over the region. Can you imagine a planet infested with those devils."

Mark remembered the torn body of Beth.

"How? Where do we start?"

"A helicopter would be a start. Any ideas on how you can get one?"

"When do you want it?"

"We'll wait."

"For what?" Mark fingered his tender ear, feeling the crescent.

"We sit tight. We'll hear what happens. If the anthrax scare subsides, fine. We'll listen for news on the manhunt for you. We'll listen for word of any bizarre killings that can tip us off about the beast's location."

"And then?"

"Then do it. Then steal the chopper and go after the beast."

"What do we do when this is over?"

Winston smirked tiredly.

Mark said, "Yeah, right. That rap on the head must have made me stupid. Who says it will be over, right?"

By the time her lawyer came for her, PJ was frantic and near tears. She knew Mark would be calling and receiving no answer. She had no idea whether he had begun tracking that animal or whether the animals who killed the Dodsons would be tracking him. Or whether the police were closing in. Maybe he was already dead.

Then she was free.

"You raised bail?" she asked the lawyer incredulously.

"A hundred thousand? Are you kidding?"

"So you had it reduced?"

"Naw," said the woman with the gray complexion and long face. "The judge dropped bail at the request of the county attorney. You're free. Not enough evidence to hold."

"But why?" asked PJ.

The woman shrugged. "You're supposed to report to your army unit tomorrow. That's all. Otherwise, you're perfectly free."

"No charges at all?"

"None."

At home, the second thing she did was climb into the shower and begin scrubbing the jailhouse itch from her skin. The first was to move the phone as close to the bathroom as the extension cord would allow. She prayed for it to ring. Twice while showering she turned off the water because she thought she heard it. But the ringing was either in her ears or in the water pipes.

She missed Mark so bad it hurt.

4

The shadows had lengthened, exaggerating the frenetic mating ritual of the two rabbits darting about below the rising slope of Owl Creek Mountain. They had barely begun copulating when they became carcasses, flying through the air as if they'd set off a furious, growling land mine.

The building evening breeze sailed tufts of down across the landscape amid the blasts of erupting howitzers a half-mile away and the crackling of bones in the beast's mouth.

Near dusk, three soldiers found the scattered fluff. Their job was to guard the Cold Springs Road access to the artillery impact area. But one private first class asked the corporal in charge for permission to take a walk, since the evening was bringing cooler air. He said he wanted to "scope out the place them dudes fried theirselves under their quarter-ton." He said he might run across the head or the ghost of that "second looey who got hisself chopped up by the Huey. They been seeing the ghost of a headless second looey at night around here looking for his noggin."

The corporal said fucking-A, he'd go along on a ghost hunt.

The third soldier, a tough-talking private, insisted she would not be left behind with the shit-detail.

They argued awhile, and the privates finally persuaded the corporal they could all go. One would carry the backpack with radio so they could answer calls as if they were on site. They could all be back by dark, the private first class assured him. In their absence, they could drag a log across the road. "Nobody but a dumbass would go into the impact area with all the signs and a log in the road."

"They's where the chopper crashed," said the private, pointing to a blackened spot across the wash. The last of the sun was sinking.

"Fuck," whispered the woman. "What coulda done this? No bones or nothin' but this lucky rabbit's foot." She shuddered.

The man checked the sky. "Hawk," he said with a Mutual of Omaha air of authority. "And here's where them dudes went off the road and turned themselves into crispy critters."

"This place gives me the creeps," said the corporal. "Let's get our asses back to the guard post before we get in a jam with the topper or somethin'."

"Hey, they's something in them bushes," said the private. He picked up a stone and tossed it into the quaking leaves. "Maybe it's the second looey come back for his head."

The beast was greatly agitated.

It had doubled its size in only three days as it consumed its own weight in hot or cold flesh daily. But the rabbits had not been so satisfying, being mostly bones and fur.

And this place had been the most disturbing of all the others it had visited, led on by some especial sense that went beyond instinct to Hubbard Lake, to Preachers Creek, to the Finney farm. Like a rabbit that had disappeared into the air in the talons of a hawk, there the trail of its ancestor ran out.

Then a stone rebounded off its skull.

"I'm tired of this waiting, Winston. I'm going to do something."

"Do what?"

Mark raked his nails over his three-day beard. "I don't know what. Anything is better than this."

"You'll get your chance."

"How do you know?"

"I don't, really. All I know is I've made a career of waiting for things to happen. And they eventually do."

"How could you do that sort of thing day in and day out?"

"You learn to wait. You wait. You make a move. You wait for a result. Believe me, this one will be hell busting loose."

"Maybe I should go pick off that helicopter now and have it standing by when we need it."

"Look, it's one thing to have the police looking nationwide for a fugitive. As time goes by, they assume more distance between them and the fugitive. It actually becomes safer. But if I let you steal that chopper now, they'll narrow the range down to the distance the thing can fly. They'll search every piece of dirt within the circle. They'll launch every chopper on this fort—how many? A hundred? Two hundred? So where you going to hide it?"

Mark had no answer.

"We'll get our break," Winston continued. "Don't you worry. Every hour we get a report on the anthrax teams, so we know what The Corporation's doing. We get a periodic word on your woman—we know she's still safely in jail. Reporters are crawling all over this region, getting colorful interviews at every two-bit farm and ranch. If something breaks loose, we'll know within an hour. And you can go steal your chopper. Don't forget, there's always the chance they'll kill that beast. If that happens, we don't have to do anything."

"What about us? We can't stay out here forever."

"If the story of these beasts gets out, my life insurance policy"—he patted the research journal by his side—"will be worth very little. In that case, I don't know what we'll do. The rest of The Corporation's story is explosive, but the best thing for us is the threat of a well-placed set of newsmen putting out exactly the same story of a domestic nightmare caused by a secret, quasigovernment agency. It's that threat that will set us free in another part of the country with other identities and other lives to live. A story blown wide open . . . openness . . . . It's the only threat The Corporation fears."

* * *

Mark lay coiled in the back of *Shitbird* when the radio issued the report an hour later. He shot up as Winston raised the volume on the portable set.

"And now this Red-Hot update on the hospital slaughters. Coryell County Attorney Thomas Brudenell announced the release today of army Warrant Officer Pamela Jane Larson from the county lockup. Larson had been arrested Tuesday on charges she helped in the escape of Captain Mark Payne, a suspect in the hospital deaths. Brudenell said the evidence against Larson as an accomplice after the fact was not sufficient to sustain an indictment. Brudenell declined to say whether the Fort Hood woman was questioned in the deaths of three men and a woman whose bodies were found mutilated in the elevator and stairwell at the hospital.

"Payne, who escaped from the hospital after a shootout with the sheriff's officers, is still being sought in a nationwide manhunt that saw the FBI invited into the picture today. Authorities—Hold on, we have an update . . . no? No, we have a bulletin just in. Red-Hot Radio nine-fifty News Director Howard Russell has the report."

A somber voice full of sorrow came on to dampen the gossipy tone the news reader had set.

"Thank you, Jason. This report just in of yet another triple murder. Details of the crime still sketchy. In fact, police and military authorities have just arrived at the scene of this tragedy which took the lives of three. At least one of the victims is a woman."

Howard's voice brightened a touch.

"Red-Hot Radio nine-fifty Reporter Karen Wilson is roving near the scene and is ready to deliver her report live. Karen?"

"Thank you, Howard. Authorities are puzzled by this hideous crime. They are putting together the pieces at this scene of human carnage. Three bodies lie in the dust so horribly mutilated one can barely tell whether they were men or women. One of them is definitely a woman, a source tells me. He is saying privately that the woman has been raped."

"Uh, Karen, can you tell us the location of this tragedy?"

"Yes, Howard. Ironically, the scene is almost exactly the site of an earlier catastrophe. About three months ago a jeep overturned in a gully near Cold Springs. And the same day a helicopter crashed. Just to add more irony to today's news, the pilots in that helicopter crash were the same Warrant Officer Larson and Captain Payne allegedly involved in the hospital deaths just days ago."

"Looks like you're going to get your action, Mark."

"It's the beast, isn't it?" Mark was staring at the radio as if it could show him the blood and the bodies.

"No question."

"The rape—that means it's matured sexually."

"It's lucky the woman died. If that thing impregnates other animals we won't be worrying about one or two beasts. We'll be dealing with an exponential population explosion. In a couple generations—"

"I'll get the helicopter tonight." Mark began arranging his flight gear for the tenth time today.

"I'll get Larson."

Mark looked over his shoulder at Winston. "No."

"Yes."

He spun on Winston. "I won't let her be involved."

"She's not in jail anymore. She'd be safer with us. The sheriff almost certainly released her so she'd lead them to you. Meaning they're out of leads and ideas about where to search for you. It's a last gasp because the trail is cold."

"Fine. I agree. I'm glad you see it my way. That's a good argument for not dragging her into this. The sheriff will keep an eye on her for us, and she won't be burdened with knowing where I am, won't be involved, won't be suspected."

"I said the sheriff will keep an eye on her. But that won't stop one of The Corporation people from stepping in to dim her lights when all hell breaks loose out here. As soon as she's left unguarded for even a second . . . maybe even already . . ."

Mark was silent, mulling over Winston's logic.

"Another reason is your blackouts," the agent added. "I don't want to be flying alone with you after some of the things you told me in the past couple days. I want a copilot along to fly if you get dizzy."

Mark was persuaded. "Let's go. I'll make the phone call just after dark. Then you drop me off outside the flight line and pick her up." He dug inside his duffel bag. "Here," he said, throwing a crumpled flight suit to Winston.

After he tried it on, he pulled at the too-short sleeve cuffs and wrinkled his nose.

"Where you're going," said Mark, "nobody will notice how rank you smell or how stupid you look in short sleeves and high-water cuffs."

PJ's heart hadn't stopped pounding since the phone call. The caller tried to sell her a subscription to the military gossip rag known as *Army Times*. But she knew his voice. It required all the self-discipline she could muster to hold back the *I-love-you-I-love-you-I-love-you-I-love-yous* she wanted to blurt.

"I'm not interested."

"But, ma'am—"

She hung up.

In minutes she was standing inside the wings of a phone booth, watching customers flow into and out of the Zippy Mart. She pressed the phone to her ear with one hand and held down the hook with the other and talked aimlessly. It seemed the properly surreptitious thing to do. And it had been, she discovered, when a pair of teen girls began hanging out next to her, leaning on the brick wall, puffing cigarettes as coolly as they could, hinting at first at how they needed the phone, then complaining about people who never got off, then—as they stalked away— loudly cursing out the shitass jerkoffs who couldn't get off the phone so somebody could make an emergency call to a boyfriend.

PJ felt a momentary charge of embarrassment. What if the call was really a phone sale attempt from *Army Times*? How long had she been here? What if . . . ?

The phone ring scared her out of her wits.

"Hello," she said tentatively. "Mark?"

"PJ."

"I-love-you-I-love-you-I-love-you, darling."

"I miss you, love."

"When will I see you?"

"Soon. Now listen. Don't say anything—any names or places. Just answer the questions, PJ."

"Okay."

"I want you to meet a man at the place I first stood you up. Do you remember the place?"

"Yes, I remember. What man? How will I know him?"

"He's a friend. He'll have something of mine for identification. He'll give you a note telling you to do some shopping for supplies and asking you to deliver them to the place where I let off Poole that night he took me flying drunk."

"Yes, I know the place, darling. What kind of supplies?"

"It's all in the note. Wear that special outfit you had on the first time I met you—and bring all the accessories."

"The day you took one look at me and puked?"

"The same. You made such an impression on me."

"And you on me. . . . I love you, Mark."

"I love you, darling."

She pulled the Ford into the parking lot of the West Club, her heartbeat quickening its tempo. It was a little after midnight, and she expected to see a thinning crowd inside. She hoped nobody from the Vultures would engage her in a conversation about the life of a jailbird.

Inside, the crowd was anything but thinning. She carried her flight bag behind her, hanging her head as if ashamed, and moved toward the edge of the crush near a corner that smelled of urine. Before her eyes could even adjust, a tall figure stepped up to her.

"You recognize this?" he asked.

She looked at Mark's helmet bag, his name tape, and Vulture patch sewn on below the handles, the man wearing his flight suit.

"Yes," she said, voice trembling. "Who are you?"

"Come with me, PJ. Please, we have to hurry."

He took her hand firmly and led her through the crowd. They were nearing the rear door to the party patio when PJ heard the unmistakable voice of Maggie Anzola calling her name.

Her leader tugged insistently, and they were out the door and into the shadows by the wall of the club.

A hand pressed her down like one of the squatting shrubs. A finger tapped her lips.

"PJ. Peeej."

PJ could see the outline of Maggie's breasts in the eerie light cast by colored bulbs among the live oaks. The trees formed a huge umbrella over the patio.

Bootsteps clumped across the concrete and a dark figure in a baseball cap ran up to Maggie.

"Did you see a woman named Larson out here?" he whispered hoarsely.

"Why you whispering?"

"Did you see Larson come out?"

"Who the fuck wants to know?"

"Lady, this is a police matter—"

"Yeah? You got a badge? You want I should call some of my friends out here to check your ass out?"

The dark figure whispered an oath under his breath and ran toward the patio gate. He looked outside, then lifted a box out of his pocket and whispered urgently into it. Then he was gone.

Maggie cursed and went back inside the club.

The stranger found PJ's hand and pulled her erect. He led her along the building to a hedge. He ducked out of sight. She crouched. He crawled through a hole under the hedge. She heard the noise of many booted feet rushing around the club and hesitated. A hand came through the hole and jerked her forearm.

They crawled on their bellies toward a giant weeping willow that bowed to the earth. Once past it, the man stopped and they stood up, the foliage ball between them and the club, and ran to the post housing area adjacent to the officers' club.

He insisted they run, and she needed no urging. They turned west, and ten minutes later crossed the access road to Robert Gray Army Airfield, crouching low. Fifty feet into the grass and shrubs he halted, and they lay catching their breaths and watching the frantic sweeping of headlights and spotlights through the streets of the housing area.

This is serious, she realized. *This is no game.*

When the frenetic pace of the light sweep slackened, he said, "Let's go."

"Where?" she whispered.

"No need to whisper," he said. "I'll show you."

They headed west. She remembered the map of the area as they homed on the lightened sky above Copperas Cove. About two miles away was Rattlesnake Hill, nearly dead off the end of the runway, she recalled. That seemed to be the direction they were taking, stumbling, plodding along in the rugged footing.

Once, behind them, a helicopter joined the search, its searchlights scanning the housing area. But he kept them moving until the mass of Rattlesnake Hill moved blackly up into the glowing lights from the Cove.

"What about the supplies?" asked PJ once, her only attempt at conversation while they were on foot.

"That was just in case anybody was listening in on the phone."

5

For nearly two hours Mark lay on his belly waiting for the lights to go off in the Vultures operations shack. Now and then he would shift the research log that ill-served as his pillow. Winston had left the log with him. It was now his insurance policy as well as the former agent's.

Little comfort, though, considering what faced him now. The walking guard—guards plural. Every fifteen minutes a pair appeared out of the shadows from the far end of the ramp. It took half an hour to walk the post, so that meant two pair were out.

At midnight, four new guards stomped and grumbled out of operations to relieve the first set. A lone man he couldn't identify was probably a sergeant of the guard. That made nine men. If there was a third shift, that would make thirteen men. All armed, all on the alert. All probably looking for him.

Stealing a helicopter would not be so easy after all. He remembered the Camaro he'd left in Poole's office. That was the flub. They knew he might come back for it. At least they knew he had the wherewithal to break into operations. He'd done it twice already—once to steal a helicopter and once to steal *Shitbird*.

No way was he going to get a helicopter again. And there was even less chance he'd get in and out with the Camaro. And even if he did, how would he get all the way past Killeen and Copperas Cove to Cold Springs where he could do any good? Answer: He wouldn't. Not in that red-flag car. And even if he could get away with it, he'd be confined to the roads in looking for that beast—the same road the police were confined to. He needed a helicopter.

What were his chances of getting across the seven miles to the main heliport at Hood Field—seven miles as the helicopter flies? Exactly none. He didn't even know where logbooks and keys were stored over there.

The only helicopter ride he'd be getting tonight would be after the police shot him full of holes and *Lifesaver* carried him to the emergency room—make that the morgue—at Darnall. . . . *Lifesaver*. That was his ride.

Finally it was 3 A.M. Time to move. Mark had lain in the shadow beneath the tower watching *Lifesaver* for hours. He lay on the airstrip side where he could keep an eye on the ambulance helicopter. He lay planning, visualizing success. And while he planned, he wanted to be ready, to be within striking distance in case an actual emergency caused *Lifesaver* to launch. He had decided. Yes, he'd commandeer the craft even if it meant somebody might die waiting for *Lifesaver*. What he had to do involved that beast and a

hell of a lot more danger to a lot more people. He
could do it.

The Corporation crossed his mind. The thought
came with a flash of anger—hatred, really—for what
it had reduced him to.

At 3 A.M. it became academic. He wouldn't have to
pirate the craft in the middle of a rescue. Next problem.

He had tried to picture the ready room where the
crew bunked in the basement of base operations.
He'd only been in there once to take a shower after a
workout. He decided against creeping around the
sleeping men in the dark to look for ignition and door
keys. They would be alert to odd sounds, on edge,
always waiting for the surge of fear brought on by
the ghastly alert buzzer. They'd be ready to leap out
of their bunks. They'd be fully awake in an instant.
They'd jump an intruder and beat the living—

Forget that. Forget failure. Time to go.

He brushed himself off and strode into the base
operations building, trying against all appearances to
look self-assured. Pilots, even army pilots, did not
mosey around base ops looking like scum with four-
day beards—not if they were sober.

He patted his pistol and hoped to God he wouldn't
need it. Nobody was visible from behind the chest-
high counter. This was the hour of letdown, just before shift's end. And in the basement, he knew, each
crew member slept his deepest, experiencing a similar letdown, the subconscious realization that he
would make it through the night without that call to
gory accidents.

Mark turned right and padded as quietly as his boots would allow—not quietly at all, it seemed—toward the pay phone.

He knew that once that alarm went off the crew would scramble to life automatically. Literally automatically. They'd take not a single step or execute a single motion outside the precise scenario rehearsed daily. They'd expect the routine to hold true, as it had for thousands of real and practice alerts in the past. Once inside the craft and on the way to the accident scene, their human metabolism would catch up with the programmed automaton each had been. Then they'd begin preparing for the unexpected always found at a disaster site. But until then, they'd not be ready for anything unexpected.

And Mark intended to give them anything *but* the expected. Holding the receiver to his left ear, the good one, he hesitated. Stealing a life-saving helicopter. What was he about to *do*?

His answer came in a flash of hatred: He was about to bring down The Corporation.

He dropped a quarter into the slot of the pay phone and tapped out the emergency number. From down the hall he heard a phone ring, a chair squeak. Odd, he'd never noticed that the ring in the receiver and the ring of the phone were not synchronized.

"Gray flight ops, Anderson," said a just-awakened voice.

"Lootenant Sammons, Department of Public Safety," Mark drawled, cupping his voice so it wouldn't reverberate down the hall.

"Yes, sir?" The voice sharpened, anticipating trouble.

"Mr. Anderson, we got us a fower-car fatal involving fower sojers, two fatals, two critical ten mile south of Killeen on Florence Road. I wunner if yew might git us yer ammulance bird on down year?"

"Yes, sir. Can you give me some more details of the nature of the injuries?"

"I'd be proud to, sir, but I'd 'preciate it you could just git that bird in the air. . . ."

Mark leapt when the buzzer went off.

"Lieutenant, the *Lifesaver* is launched—maybe you can hear the alarm in the background? Now I need some information so they'll know how to respond on the site. I need condition, nature of injuries—"

"Jeezus criminy sakes, the car just blew up. Yew just hode on and ah'll be right back."

He dropped the phone. He hoped the man behind the counter wouldn't begin wondering how the patrolman could find a phone so conveniently near an accident or how he could hear the buzzer in his own earpiece. With the incessant racket of that insistent buzzer obscuring clear thought as well as sound, Mark knew he'd have the minute he needed.

He ran for the side door at the end of the hall, locked from the outside but equipped with a panic bar. He stepped into the night and began running around the building, keeping to the shadows.

The *Lifesaver* crew was good. Already the crew chief was swinging the blade, already a pilot had hit the starter. The crew chief pulled the tiedown hook out of its hole in the blade tip, and the blade just kept coasting, faster and faster as the turbine picked it up.

Mark approached at a dead run. Inside, the pilots were occupied with switches and dials, having divided the start-up duties, and set everything that could be preset.

He caught the crew chief kneeling in the cabin trying to mate his helmet plug with the aircraft's long extension cord. He literally caught the man around the collar, both hands gripping, both feet braced on the craft's skids, and jerked him backward out of the cabin onto his back. The enlisted man was bigger, but Mark had all the advantages of surprise and alertness. He drove a knee downward into the solar plexus and planted a left hook under the helmet's ear cup, into the neck. He followed with a quick combination of left and right, to be sure. He scraped a knuckle in the process but hardly noticed. He was too busy peeling the helmet off and squeezing it onto his own head. For such a large man, the guy really had a small head. He felt the fresh scab ripping off his right ear and it hurt, as if somebody were holding a flame to the spot. But there was no time for agonizing.

Next was the aircraft commander riding in the left seat. He pulled down the crew chief's visor in order to hide his face and then opened the door. He shouted incoherently at the surprised man while reaching up to separate the pilot's helmet from the intercom system. The man shouted back. Mark pointed at the figure lying on the ground. The pilot, a captain, unbuckled and dismounted.

Mark shut the pilot's door and drew the pistol from

his pocket. He looked back at the copilot, who would be able to see all the rest. Mark counted on being too fast for a reaction. He reversed the pistol and swung it by the barrel at the kneeling captain's neck.

Before that body had crumpled over the other, he reversed the pistol again and leapt into the Huey cabin. He stuck the barrel into the crook of the other pilot's neck and shoulder, and pointed. The man's mouth and eyes were wide. He was paralyzed. Mark cringed and slapped the side of his helmet with the barrel. That worked. The startled pilot ripped open the quick release of his lap belt and shoulder harness and started backing out the door. Mark jumped from the cabin and met him. He signaled him to walk around the front of the Huey.

He became aware that he was being watched. Inside ops he saw a harried figure gesturing and talking into a telephone inside. He glanced up at the tower and saw two dim figures scurrying around behind the green glass.

He booted the pilot in the pants. Instead of running, the man turned around, waving his palms in front of his chest and begging for his life to be spared.

Mark waved at him to run. The man put his palms together in supplication. Mark fired the pistol at his feet. The pilot got the message and took off. Mark ran to the shadow of the building and retrieved the research journal. He barely got back to the craft before the captain. The figure staggered as he pulled the door open and stepped up on the toe of the skid.

As usual, things weren't happening according to the best-laid plans. He grabbed the captain's belt and yanked backward. The pilot splayed out as he hit the ground. He lay still, finally.

Mark began to worry about reinforcements. No doubt the cavalry was on the way. The guards from the parking ramp—the police—would be swarming the place in minutes.

He tossed the research log and pistol inside and began pulling pitch without concerning himself with buckling up or pre-takeoff checks and similar formalities. The aircraft lifted back on its heels. But then it rocked violently left. Had the skid caught?

No. The dazed captain, insistent on going up with his ship, was standing on the left skid, trying to throw a knee into the cabin.

Mark saw movement from the operations building. Three more men, possibly from the tower, or fire station, or ops. No matter. A crowd was forming. Soon another foolhardy soul might try to climb in. He couldn't afford a half-conscious hero hanging on his neck or taking his gun away.

He yanked the Huey to a hover with the collective. The craft drifted left with the unbalanced condition of the man climbing on the skid. He let it drift closer to the building. The crowd of three saw it coming and scattered.

When the blades were in the shadows and the trio had all flattened as they hit the ground, he laid the cyclic to the right. The craft rocked gently right. And the would-be hanger-on, fingernails scratching for a purchase on the pimpled metal cabin floor, was launched into an arc that ended in a back flop on the ground.

Mark slammed the right pedal, turning the sideways glide into a takeoff run at an altitude of barely two feet. In seconds, he was passing through eighty knots. He drew the cyclic back between his thighs and *Lifesaver* leapt into the night. He turned off the lights and transponder and vanished into a sea of blackness.

From the base of Rattlesnake Hill, the pair walked another mile southwest toward Seven Mile Mountain. At the base of Rattlesnake Point, a half-mile-long finger of the mountain, they started widening the circle. After ten minutes and three tries, they found the juniper stand that hid *Shitbird*. The chopped jeep took the gentle east slope of the mountain easily and was soon on the way south, riding the ridge.

More than two hours had elapsed since PJ's arrival at the club. She drank in the breeze, cool and cleansing after her confinement in a cell and the harrowing experience at West Club. She thought about starting up a conversation once or twice with the stranger, and in fact, asked him his name.

"Winston," he said. "Paul Winston."

"I'm PJ Larson," she offered.

"I know."

And the attempt died there. Until they reached Radar Hill at the southern tip of the ridge, when he initiated a necessary exchange.

"Where do we go from here?"

PJ saw the black hulk, its flashing red beacon ward-ing off aircraft approaching or departing the south end of Gray.

She pointed to the southeast. "Manere Mountain is the top of that hill about two miles away, Mr. Winston. Didn't Mark tell you?"

"Call me Paul. Yes, of course. But I mean what's the best way up?"

"Call me PJ." They were at the base of Radar Hill and she said, "Turn left."

As he started left, a pair of speeding lights swept the road and he hit the brakes. A car followed the speeding lights on by. A police car. Bubble-gum machines started flashing. Tires squealed. The headlights reversed direction and pointed right at the *Shitbird.*

Shitbird roared in its distinctive little voice and took off.

"Paul, what are you doing?"

A rhetorical question. For he was obviously driving right at the sparkling grill between the police car's headlights.

The officer behind the wheel had already begun reporting the stolen jeep, recognizing it from its description at roll call the past three nights. He reported he would be in pursuit. And he would have. Fugitives *always* ran. Except this fugitive. He was heading toward him. He stepped on the brake pedal and dived right, across the seat, groping for a bracing position on the floorboard, waiting for the impact.

It didn't come right away.

When it did, it was a gentle thump as his squad car

idled off Ivy Mountain Road, nosing into the ditch.
He sat up in time to see the jeep bouncing across the
field, weaving among the black juniper shrubs. He
called for backup, reporting that he was in pursuit of
Payne, the fugitive army captain. The dispatcher told
him to get in line, that half the law-enforcement force
in the region was already getting ready to board helicopters to chase Payne down—that the stolen helicopter report to which he'd been responding had definitely been laid to Payne.

The officer, Andrew Bowen, wasn't particularly
concerned about whether Payne was flying or driving. He just knew he had a pursuit on his hands. He
jockeyed his car back and forth until it cleared the
ditch. And he took off, bouncing after the jeep.

Mark headed the craft toward the impact area. This
was déjà vu. He'd done the same thing the night
Poole had stolen the helicopter and passed out dead
drunk.

The impact area was so very dark. Or was the
blackness coming from inside his own head? Was the
rushing noise coming from the helicopter? Or the air?
Or from the state of half-consciousness he felt? Was
the pain from anxiety? Or the tight helmet? Or the
numbness before he blacked out?

He began singing to himself. He shook his head
violently. It didn't help; on the contrary, it merely
brought on a mild case of vertigo and made his ear
hurt worse. The trickle on his neck told him it was
bleeding again. He leaned close to the window, then
cupped his hand into the one-hundred-mile-an-hour

wind and deflected the cool chop into his face. That helped a little.

He dropped into the valley of the Cowhouse. The thrill of flying low level at night stimulated his adrenaline, revitalizing him. He knew he could make it as long as he could keep himself at the edge of excitement.

As he dropped below the inquiring eye of radar and headed west, retracing the path he had taken the night he saved himself from Poole's death wish, he wondered how long he could sustain the necessary edge of excitement that kept him awake. He wondered about running out of adrenaline. He wondered when he'd be gone. And if he'd ever awaken.

Multiple long shadows of the beast crept across the moonscape, each flare above hanging from a parachute, casting a slightly different shadow from the other half dozen now illuminated. One would pop. One would burn out. Like candles. Offerings.

The monster headed past the line of blackened metal hulks toward the shrapnel-battered dirt pile that was Smith Mountain.

"Paul," PJ whispered. "What are you doing?"

He'd parked *Shitbird* and killed the engine. She'd turned and listened to the rear with him. From behind came the irregular rushing and protesting of a sedan negotiating the rough terrain. She could see headlights occasionally leaping up at the sky.

"Stay here," he said. "He's following our track."

"No," she protested. But he was already gone.

*   *   *

Andrew Bowen wished he had his own pickup. He'd never catch up to a jeep in the sedan. It would have been better to stay on the road and pick a spot from which he could see the farthest and watch. Matter of fact, he'd already decided to turn back to Ivy Mountain Road at the first dirt road he encountered. The jeep had probably already turned back that way and disappeared for good.

When he saw the log across the jeep track, he knew it was truly hopeless. They'd be in Austin before he'd ever get out of here. As he stepped out to throw the log to the side, it never occurred to him that the jeep hadn't left any tread marks on the log as it climbed over. Only after he'd wrestled it off to the side did he realize that there were no marks at all on the log; that it must have been thrown across the path by hand after the jeep had passed.

He reached for his pistol.

At that moment, Officer Bowen experienced the shortest, yet most excruciating, headache of his life.

When he returned, PJ asked, "Paul, what happened?"

"He got stuck and tried to bull his way out of a rut. I think he knocked a hole in the oil pan because the car died a smoky death. Then he just started cussing and walking back toward the road. I won't start up the engine now. He might hear and come back on foot. And we might as well not try to get up that mountain, either. It will just give away our destination. About ten minutes before Payne is due we'll give it a try."

Mark found an ideal spot on the Lampasas River, a bend with a flat beach and hardwoods forming an eastern wall. If something should happen to keep him there, the early-morning shadows would hide the Huey for a couple of hours. He sat down and shut off the fuel after less than the specified two-minute cooling period. He calculated thirty minutes' fuel expended, leaving about two hours more.

He'd been listening to AM radio on the ADF band. Already he was big news—the daring, armed helicopter thief who eluded a dozen armed guards on the helicopter parking ramp to steal the unguarded *Lifesaver*. Already there was a statement from the on-duty spokesman at the Pentagon—even if it was only "no comment."

After Mark landed, he got mostly static on the ADF. And after ten minutes, he grew sleepy, then worried he might be wasting valuable battery current. So he shut off the battery switch and peeled the helmet off his head. Glued to his head by blood, it peeled yet another scab off the ear and warmed up the flow down his neck.

After all the excitement, the sounds of the helicopter and the rushing static of the radio, the silence was staggering. He felt weak and drained. A little more than an hour left till launch. Too little time to sleep, too much time to sit idle.

So tired.

He thought about the red crosses, giant ID badges

on each cargo door and one on the nose. He had to do something about them.

Stupid of the crew chief to leave a toolbox on board, he thought. *Somebody might steal the tools.*

All it took was the removal of a couple of doorstops and latches. The doors then slid off to the rear. He dragged them into the tree line.

The cross on the nose compartment door was a different matter. He needed a different approach. He smeared on globs of mud. It would dry brown, camouflaged. Too quick and easy. He still had fifty minutes to kill.

Fifty minutes and so tired. So . . . dizzy.

He tried walking briskly up and down the beach.

That seemed to help. It got his blood moving. If he could only keep it up for fifty minutes. What was the distance he could run in that time? Five miles?

He started jogging up and down the beach.

He imagined what somebody standing in the tree line would be saying if they could see this escapade. What would they think? Some kind of new training system?

Something else.

He tried focusing on his anger, dormant since he'd been so preoccupied with stealing helicopters and evading radar and the police.

The Corporation. The bastards had killed his sister as surely as if they'd cut her open themselves. They'd turned him into a criminal. They had put PJ in harm's way. He felt his vitality returning with his hatred.

Fueled by this renewal of hatred, he jogged fifty yards up the beach and back.

Fifty up, fifty back.

Up and back.

Up and back.

6

PJ slumped in the seat, watching the sky. Now and then a helicopter would fly by on an approach to Gray. Every one stirred her anxiety. *Is it Mark? No. Not one is.* She looked over at Mark's friend, her defender and watchman for the night. Who was the benevolent stranger? Why had he stepped in to aid her lover?

He lay as if dozing, but she could see the glint of the sky off his right eyeball through the slit eyelid. After a time she realized that juniper outlines had begun to acquire faint details. She checked her watch. Four-fifty. She started to ask, but he had already begun pumping the gas.

Shitbird kicked to life.

"I'm just going to slip up to the base of the hill. We'll wait until we see him landing and then make a dash to the top."

After ten minutes, she wished they had started moving earlier. Already the dim outline of Manere Mountain had begun taking shape and they were still half a mile away. At least that far. Mark would land and not find them. He'd give himself away because of her lousy navigation, because she hadn't insisted they move on last night, because . . .

"Halt."

White lettering on a black helmet took shape out of the junipers. The two letters were M and P. MP. The face that appeared beneath the helmet was a girl to match the frail command. But the set jaw demonstrated her resolve to make this arrest. And the shotgun she carried at waist level—pointed at PJ's belly—was meant to back up the resolve.

It was over.

"What's the matter, officer?" PJ said weakly as *Shitbird* coasted to a stop. It was such a feeble attempt. The MP's lip turned up in a sneer. She'd heard it all before. PJ braced herself for the smart remark.

But the woman's sneering face imploded into the red, bleeding welt that appeared on the cheekbone beside her nose. The head snapped back, throwing the helmet off. PJ became aware of a snort, a popping sound that had preceded the welt. The MP fell flat on her back; the dropped shotgun lay across her thighs.

PJ looked at her driver. He slid a pistol under his thigh, freeing his hand to shift. He gunned the jeep. PJ, stunned, flew back against the seat.

"My God, Paul, you killed that woman."

He darted through a break in a juniper wall and shot an incredulous glance at her. "It was her or us, PJ. What else could I do?"

"Did you have to kill her?"

"You weren't exactly talking her into a fucking warning ticket."

They both ducked automatically as blind gunfire sounded from behind.

"But you might have wounded her or something."

"Did you see where that shotgun was pointing?"

Shitbird was bouncing wildly, spitting gravel, flying over mounds of earth. PJ held on literally for her life.

"But . . ."

"PJ, do you want out of this? I'll let you off if it's going to be against your principles."

She had no answer.

"What's it going to be?" He let up on the gas ever so slightly.

"I'm . . . in this to the end," she said.

"Fine." He slammed the accelerator down. "Keep your eyes open for more cops. And that damned lover boy of yours with the helicopter he was supposed to steal." He dodged a limestone boulder. "Where the hell is he?"

Good question, said PJ to herself. She was getting scared of being with this Winston character. Where the hell was Mark?

Mark lay in paradise, nude on the beach, his wife, Pamela Jane Payne, lay nude beside him. He couldn't remember the wedding ceremony exactly, but he kept worrying about how her new name sounded. PJ Payne. Pam Payne. Pamela Payne. Pamela Jane Payne. All too lyrical. He told her she could keep her maiden name if she wanted.

"Bullshit," she retorted with an uncharacteristic word and tone.

He insisted.

They argued.

So, though he lay in paradise, he was upset. He gripped fistfuls of sand in anger.

And dammit, the sun was too hot too.

"He's an hour late. Where the hell *is* he?"

"How should I know?" said PJ. "I'm . . . more worried than you, but I don't know any more than you do." She made no effort to hide her disgust with this man Winston. Why would Mark align himself with somebody so cruel? How?

They lay on their bellies atop Manere Mountain, peering over the edge at the activity to the west. There were ambulances, police cars, patrols of men on foot. The sun had grown hot on their backs.

"It was a mistake to bring that jeep up here."

"Why?" asked PJ.

"It's just a matter of time until one of those helos flies over and spots it." He pulled his pistol and unscrewed the silencer. "Won't need this." He laid out his arsenal, an inventory of three clips and a dozen loose rounds. "We won't be able to hold out for long."

"Do you want to try driving it down into the bushes—push it over the side?"

"No, they'd see us for sure." He pocketed his pistol and clips. "Best thing for us to do is drop over the edge into the foliage. If they spot the jeep, they might write it off as abandoned and search the base of the hill. That will buy us a little time. Where the hell . . . ?"

A helicopter took off from the site where the MP had died. It climbed toward the top of Manere Mountain as if on a string.

"Here comes trouble," he said.

They dropped over the edge and braced their feet in the bushes to keep from sliding down the steep slope.

PJ prayed for a miracle.

He lay facedown in the sand where he had fallen— at the most distant point from the Huey on his jogging circuit. For more than half an hour the sun had soaked into his Nomex flight suit.

Hell with this. He'd had enough of baking on the beach. He had to find PJ and settle this. Newlyweds shouldn't be arguing.

But he couldn't move. A netting had been thrown over him. None of his muscles would respond. Oh well, he decided, he'd just have to die and rot. She'd feel sorry when she found him pecked to Swiss steak by the vultures.

When the first vulture's shadow passed over him, Mark changed his mind about making her feel sorry. When he heard it hopping across the sand, its claws scratching faintly on the beach, he found the strength to move. When the dull talons bit into his back and the bird nipped at his ear, Mark exploded to life.

There was no vulture. His heart still pounded. And the ear truly throbbed as if something had taken a bite from it. But there was no vulture.

So real.

So . . . *late.*

Christ, he was late. How late, he didn't know. But the sun had climbed high enough so only half the

Huey was still shaded. They were probably up on that hill worried to death he wouldn't come in time.

He fumbled with switches and buttons, barely remembering the starting sequence. It took an eternity for the turbine to fire, a lifetime for the blades to climb to operating RPM.

Soon after he cleared the trees he saw a rising column of smoke from the base of Manere Mountain less than ten miles away. And he knew PJ and Winston were more than worried.

The Huey had turned north toward Gray before it passed over Manere. Then it snapped into a tight circle and came around to the left.

"They've spotted the jeep," said PJ.

"No shit."

The helicopter flew around the hilltop in a tight circle, the people close enough to be seen gesturing.

"You've been spotting from a chopper before. How easy is it to see people on the ground?"

"With these flight suits, we'd be hard to see even if there wasn't the foliage and the shade on this side of the hill."

"Then we'll assume they haven't seen us. They'll land in a minute or so if they don't find us here."

"Why would they land?"

"Either because they're smart enough to realize we're hiding nearby or because they're so stupid they don't realize it. I'll bet on the last. They'll be looking to plant the flag on this hill or some dumb trick like that." He looked at her sarcastically. "That's how the amateurs operate."

She shuddered at the evil look that crossed his face —the evil was in the eyes. Snake eyes, dark and hard.

"Which way would you land on this pinhead of a hill?"

She collected herself. "Uh, Gray is landing north. They'll come in from the south."

He grimaced sarcastically.

"That's the south." She pointed. "Maybe from the southeast to avoid the pole."

"Which pilot will probably be at the controls?"

"Uh, counterclockwise orbits. Left seat flying. Definitely. What are you going to do?"

"I'm going to try to discourage them from landing. When you hear me yell, run for the jeep. We'll have to try to break out cross-country. You watch the cops over there. They've already gotten the word on the radio, you can bet on that. Try to get a fix on the routes they take to get up here. You'll have to be the guide to get us out once we tear down this damned slope."

The Huey widened its orbit far to the south and climbed, setting up for a pinnacle approach. It came around and started letting down steep and slow, blades snapping the air like machine-gun fire.

She looked at him and decided he wasn't afraid. He was determined. Murderously determined.

"What are you going to do?" she asked.

"I told you. Just watch the posse."

When the Huey was fifty feet from its landing spot, he scrambled over the ledge.

Against orders, PJ watched him instead of the men below. He ran out to the southern edge of the rim and dropped to one knee, the pistol raised in his right hand and supported by his left.

At twenty-five feet the pilot tried to abort, dropping the nose down and right. The Huey had room to slide past the hill, regain airspeed, and climb out safely.

Except the kneeling figure's right hand recoiled three quick times.

The nose of the craft tucked.

The Huey hit the hillside and rolled, bucking over onto its top, the blades slapping into the dirt. The fuselage came apart, breaking like an egg, letting its cargo of broken people spill out. It rolled in chunks down the slope. A trail of black smoke began flowing in a river down the side of Manere. Then orange flames and the seeping cloud of smoke enveloped the crash site.

Just like that, the deafening, whopping, popping roar of the landing helicopter was silenced, leaving the rush of an angry fire.

PJ heard him yell. But she was frozen. She hadn't seen the actual crash. But she saw the shooting, even the tight group of three asterisklike marks on the windshield. She saw the nose tuck. And she saw the rising column of smoke and flame.

Suddenly she scrambled over the rim and ran toward *Shitbird*. The sound of gunfire from below and the snapping of rocks followed her. All at once, a dozen men were running out of the trees to the slope on the west side. In pairs they stopped to fire. This was for real. This was war.

"Winston, they're over here shooting," she yelled.

"No shit." He ran to the edge and fired off three rounds. A cry came up from below.

"Get into the jeep," he shouted. "We're going down before they surround it. We'll take the east side. Maybe the smoke will give us a shield."

"No," she said.

He wheeled, the pistol leveled at a spot between her breasts. "Then this is it for you?"

"Winston . . . no. . . ." She pointed over his shoulder to a growing speck above the horizon. "I mean it's Mark. I'm sure of it."

He blinked. Hard eyes. Then he lowered the pistol and looked over his shoulder.

She shuddered. He was about to kill her—she had seen it in his snake eyes. Just then he was going to finish her as wantonly as he had done in the woman cop, and the pilot, and the man below . . . and probably the policeman last night.

Her skin prickled. Was he going to shoot down Mark's helicopter as well? *Who is this Paul Winston?* she asked herself again. If he pointed the pistol at this helicopter, she would jump him; whether it was Mark or not. She wouldn't be party to another killing. If she had the wherewithal, she would jump him. If she had a gun, she . . .

She found she was becoming quite the cold-blooded woman herself.

They ran to *Shitbird* and pulled on flight helmets. For a second he laid the pistol on the fender. She thought about grabbing it and . . . and then what?

She pulled her helmet on and dropped the dark visor. He did the same.

They crouched beside the jeep and waited.

Mark closed on Manere Mountain at one hundred twenty knots. The ship hummed along as smoothly as if it would do another thirty. He might need that reserve later, but for now he was planning to set the Huey down at that speed in such a small space—part of it taken up by the pole.

He saw the ants swarming up the side and knew Winston and PJ had been discovered. The smoke was without doubt from a crash. He'd seen that sight twice before. Crashworthy fuel tanks—what bullshit.

The men could easily shoot him down as he approached. But, he reasoned, they wouldn't know who he was, at least not for a few seconds. They wouldn't be able to see the red cross on the nose. He wasn't so worried about getting spotted as about PJ. He was getting a bit less selfish in his old age. He found he liked that about himself. Too bad he had to discover it so late in life.

He dragged back on the cyclic, raising its nose. Simultaneously, he dropped the collective to the bottom, cutting pitch and power so the Huey wouldn't balloon. Right pedal kept the nose straight.

He couldn't see out to the hilltop anymore. The windshield opened up into a high blue sky. So he peered between his feet through the chin bubble. It looked as if he'd make the top. Soon, if he didn't overshoot. He looked left; picked up the pole top. The Huey began to shudder, to fall through. He pulled power and shoved the cyclic forward to level the skids. Left pedal to counter torque. His vision slid down the pole. *Shitbird* came into view. And two figures began running, bent over low. More power.

He hit the ground with forward airspeed. He lowered pitch slightly. The skids bit into the stony top of Manere Mountain and squealed like nails drawn across a chalkboard.

He felt two thumps and saw two bodies sprawling in back. He pulled an armload of power—if the armed ants had held their fire till now, it would be because they were confused about the identity of the newly arrived helicopter. But now that PJ and Winston had piled in, there would be no question of friend or foe.

The Huey's tail lifted first as Mark held the cyclic forward and pulled pitch. The toes of the skids scraped again as the craft broke from its blocks, not gaining more than a foot in altitude. The skids dragged through the bushes, rising up from the north slope of the hill, and Mark dropped the nose and added power.

The Huey dived off the rim.

It followed the slope down at less than ten feet off the trees.

The maneuver put Manere Mountain between the Huey and most of the ants swarming over the hill. Those on the north side were so startled at the run that they flattened out and one astonished military policeman rolled thirty feet before coming to rest unceremoniously against a mesquite.

There may have been firing from behind, but Mark

couldn't tell. He was smiling broadly at the woman he loved as she climbed over the console and slumped into her seat. She strapped in and plugged her helmet into the intercom system.

"You were worried I wouldn't make it," said Mark as he swung the craft to the west to take them low level between the tops of the Ivy Mountains. He needed to circle wide again to escape detection by the helicopters that would soon be launched to follow him.

"I was scared to death. What happened to you?" She did not return his smile.

"You look awfully gray."

"I was almost killed. What happened to you?"

"Malfunction," he said. He looked into the rear but all he could see was a pair of boots with Nomex cuff flaps fluttering around the ankles. "How's my friend doing?"

She gave him a disgusted look. "The man scares me to death, Mark. I've never seen anybody so . . . he . . . never mind, I'll tell you later. He's plugging into the intercom."

For an instant, Mark's face registered surprise. Then he said, "How's it going, Paul?"

A clicking came across the intercom.

"Busted intercom switch. Cripes, what next?" said Mark. He looked back over his shoulder. From behind the seat wing he saw two hands on the helmet. The head wagged as the hands patted the helmet.

"Can you at least hear?"

The helmet and visor nodded.

"I've got less than two hours of fuel to make our

search for that beast in the impact area and get away. I expect we'll need at least an hour's head start to avoid getting picked up in the manhunt. So that leaves us about forty-five minutes for searching. We have to save some time for escape and calling our insurance numbers about this research logo."

He reached over and patted the console compartment that held Howell's book.

"After that, Paul," he said, looking back over his shoulder, "I'm depending on you to keep us from being shot on sight, buddy."

The helmet and visor nodded.

PJ looked incredulously at Mark.

He caught her expression and thought she turned even paler. He had to admit to himself that he didn't feel so confident either.

7

She ran screaming from the motel room.

Her name was Millie, and she'd seen many things in her years as a maid at these cheap places with the hourly rates. The pay per room wasn't any better than any other motel, but she got to clean them more often as the clientele slipped in and out, getting tips hourly for the most part.

The clientele had changed a lot in recent years. Like the two men, drunken and staggering in to spend the night, one practically carrying the other. Such exorbitant rates for an all-nighter. They had to know this was not a normal place. So they had to be less than normal. Unless queer was normal nowadays.

It took a long time for the police to come. They were all out busy on other matters, said the clerk. Bad for business to have a murder on the premises. The longer it took, the worse the night looked. People just didn't rent rooms, especially hourly rooms, when flashing lights lingered outside one of the rooms— even if it was an ambulance.

"Looks like a lovers' quarrel," said the hardened ambulance driver about the long, nude corpse lying on the bed, seeping blood from two holes in the back of his head and two more in the front.

"That's whut I sayed," said Millie. Fully recovered from her initial shock and more interested in collecting some gruesome details to share with her neighbors, she clucked in disgust at the body of Paul Winston—though less in disgust of him than at the ruined bed covers she'd have to replace.

It took Mark less than fifteen minutes to cover the twenty-six miles on his circuit back to the impact area. It would take about another five minutes to start his orbits from Cold Springs Road. That would leave less than half an hour for searching. No way. He knew they hadn't a prayer of finding that beast.

"Where are you going to start looking?" asked PJ.

"Good question. Why not go where all the police action is out on Cold Springs Road." He had been cruising along the Cowhouse for more than five minutes, sometimes just above treetops where it narrowed, and sometimes just above the grass where the valley opened out. In those places, the herds of cattle scattered at the approach of the Huey.

"Might as well put up range-control frequency on FM. If they've shut down all the ranges, we'll know we've been spotted."

He stayed above the Cowhouse north of Smith Mountain. There the creek ran muddy at times during firing or when rain carried the shrapnel-loosened silt down to the banks. Hundreds of white parachutes dotted the moonscape.

"I guess we should buzz the cops and sweep back—"

"There," said PJ, pointing out between her feet.

"What?" said Mark, hauling the craft around to the left, already knowing by the alarm what she meant.

"It can't be . . . not so easily."

Their eyes met. Confirmed.

"It's the beast," she said.

He saw it.

It was in the open near a pitted concrete bunker that served as one of the targets for forward observers all along the ridgeline to the east. It hovered over a torn carcass of a cow, alternately tearing at the flesh and rearing up to thrash at the sky.

"It looks like a . . . werewolf," she said.

"Take the controls."

She met his eyes. Her hands gripped her thighs.

"I'm not setting it down," she said. "Not again."

"I wouldn't ask you to. You can't anyway, with all the duds. I'm going to lie down in the back with Paul. You hover near and we'll shoot the somebitch."

She took the controls, reluctantly.

"I promise," he said. "This will be like shooting fish in a barrel. I can't believe it's going to be so easy."

Mark unbuckled, unplugged, and clambered into the cabin. He pulled his pistol and motioned for the other man to join him.

Mark stretched out on the cabin floor, his armpits at the edge. He held his .38 out so he could dampen the vibrations of the helicopter when he aimed. Five. He remembered the number five. That's how many rounds he had. There wouldn't be any more instances of forgetting as with that other beast. The hands of Winston were out alongside his, the Nomex flaps fastened at the wrists with Velcro tabs, a 9mm automatic extended.

PJ hovered down slowly to about ten feet above the ground. Mark wished she'd get lower. She moved sideways, closing the range.

At thirty feet the beast crouched protectively over its meal. At twenty feet it reared up, standing on its rear legs. Good God, it *did* look like a half wolf, half man. She edged closer.

Mark drew a bead. He opened fire, squeezing off three quick shots. The automatic spat at least that many rounds. Little puffs of dust blossomed from the black fur of the beast before the rotor wash dissipated them. Most of the rounds missed, but there were at least two or three hits.

The beast toppled forward and scratched its death throes into the craters and dust formed by the periodic artillery showers. Mark could see several pointed metal tubes lying in the area.

The automatic beside his hands flinched twice more. Two more dust puffs rose and were swept away from the fur. The beast lay still.

Mark let his hands drop over the side.

So easy.

The other pair of hands withdrew into the cabin. One hand pulled the cuff down over the wrist.

How could it be so easy after all he'd been through? What a letdown—a pleasant letdown, he had to admit. He knew his blackout could come and he'd be all right. The beast was dead. He had PJ. He had the insurance policy of the research log. He had Paul Winston to call off the dogs. But something was wrong—*the flight suit*. It didn't fit Winston. He couldn't pull the cuffs down when he tried the flight suit on. He hadn't shrunk overnight. It wasn't Winston in the cabin with him.

Mark rolled hard right, ending on his back, throwing a knee, bringing his .38 around. The automatic spat in his face. His cheek tingled, and he knew he'd been hit. It might have been in the neck if he hadn't rolled. And it might have been in the mouth if his knee hadn't caught the man in the ribs.

He brought the pistol to bear on the visor, but a hand clamped on his wrist. His own left hand found a wrist as well.

But all he could do was hold on. His shoulders lay stretched out of the cabin, and he could get no purchase as the edge of the floor bit into his shoulder blades.

A man drove a knee into Mark's groin.

It brought him instantly to the verge of vomiting. He turned his head and found the other's hand, the thumb pointing at him. The knee backed off. It would come again, a pile driver that might incapacitate him this time.

His mouth was already open wide from the unheard cry he'd already uttered. All that was left to do was close his teeth on the thumb that went into his mouth.

No fair.

No fair biting. It simply could not be a fair fight if

you bit or used sticks or kicked in the groin—or pulled hair or grabbed the other guy's nuts. Those were the rules of fighting when he was growing up.

But Mark's teeth went unfairly through the skin. He nearly gagged on the warm, coppery flow into the back of his throat. His canines were on the joint next to the web joining the thumb to the hand. He remembered how he cut up chickens for frying. Through the joint. The knife would pass through the joint. Maybe the teeth would as well.

The knee hit him again in the groin.

It simply forced him to clench his teeth all the harder—until upper and lower canines meshed and the thumb came loose in his mouth. He felt it twitching, still scratching at his soft palate.

The gun went off in his face and jumped out of the man's hand. The hand pulled away, trailing strings of sinew from Mark's mouth.

Mark gagged at the pulsations against his tongue. He spat the thumb out. He knew he'd won this one, fairly or unfairly.

He knew he'd won until the knee drew back again. Mark twisted, desperately throwing his hip up. The knee caught him in the thigh and slid him toward the door. Now he was trying to wrench the .38 away. Mark pulled the trigger.

The man's head jerked away and blood spurted from an unzipped wound that started under the chin, drew a slit alongside the cheek, and disappeared under the visor.

Now it was over. . . . At last. . . . Over.

The man's chin drained blood like a crankcase

drains oil. He coughed, spewing a spray of it and squirting a renewed flow from the hole in the crank-case.

Over and done. Mark waited for him to weaken and fall.

The knee drew back again. The nine fingers tried to better their slimy grip on the pistol.

Mark tried to fling the pistol away. It fell beside him on the cabin floor.

The knee came.

His center of gravity fell out of the Huey, driven by the blow.

He grabbed the cabin floor. A bleeding, thumbless fist smashed down on the backs of his hands. The blood did more damage than the blows. It lubricated his fingers, and he lost his grip.

Mark hit the skid with his chest and lost his breath. He held on but felt the black edges closing in on his consciousness. He knew it was truly about over now. When he was down PJ would be at that guy's mercy.

The thought chased away the fuzziness. He held on, trying to throw a leg up on the skid. He thought of love and caring and worth and everything that was important to him. And, he decided, she had become his everything in these past months, especially these past days he had to endure without her. *She* was his everything, and he never wanted to be without her again. And he wanted to become everything to her. As he vowed to do it, the thumbless man started stomping on his head.

* * *

PJ caught only the last part of the desperate battle going on behind her seat. She saw the beast fall. She saw the finishing shots hit the dead carcass. She held the Huey at a hover, waiting for Mark to climb back into his seat and give directions.

But the Huey began bucking gently as the weight shifted in the cabin. She tried to look back, but the wings of her seat made it very hard for someone her size. Finally she was able to see the man who called himself Paul Winston standing, stomping on something over the edge of the cargo floor. She strained to look out and saw a pair of legs flailing. The man was stomping on Mark.

She did the only thing that occurred to her. She swept the cyclic to the right and dropped the collective.

Mark was bracing for another heel to the helmet—he couldn't think of anything else to do—when he felt the right skid drop.

He saw that the man's weight was on one foot and that foot was lifted off the cargo floor, suspended for a second of weightlessness—like a cartoon character that had walked off the edge of a cliff. When gravity caught up to the man, he fell as the Huey was rising again. His back caught the edge of the cabin floor, and Mark thought he heard a cry. The figure slid over the edge and was gone.

No. He clung to the skid beside Mark.

They hung together for a second. Mark looked at the face below the visor. He expected to see pain, supplication, regret, compassion, confession—anything but what he saw expressed in those sneering, bloody lips. He saw hatred—pure, inviolate malice. He remembered his father finding a muskrat in a soggy woodpile on the land. His father had battered the animal with a shovel. Yet even as the man leaned on the shovel, forcing the blade against the neck, an enormous set of incisors bit into the metal, leaving a shiny scratch in the rust. Even when the head had been severed with an ax, the muskrat held its grip and had to be scraped off with a two by four.

There was the look of the muskrat barely a foot away. There was the expression that personified the horror Mark had felt when Winston—the real Winston—had described The Corporation—capital T, capital C. This was the man who had killed Winston. He or somebody like him had killed Beth and Britton and Spellers and Dodson. This was the professional killer who would now kill him and PJ if he had the chance. This was a part of the organization that would create monsters to kill others. This was the corporation—little t, little c—that was a monster without equal, above the Constitution, above the laws of God and man.

Those genetic nightmares were not the monsters. This man and men like him were the monsters. The smoldering hatred erupted inside Mark like an inferno. This man was the enemy. This man was a beast. Those in the corporation were the beasts.

And Mark saw this beast mustering himself for another blow. For an instant, he was filled with hatred himself. The hatred gave him strength to twist in the air, bringing his knee up hard, driving it into the other's groin, determined to follow through to the Adam's apple if necessary.

The man coughed blood. The blow lifted him up on the skid. When he fell, he lost his grip on the Huey. Still, he somehow found the strength to cling to Mark. And the look of the muskrat was still there. Mark tried to figure how he might throw an elbow into those lips. But it was all he could do to hang on with their combined weights tearing his arms from their sockets. He felt an extra tug.

He braced himself for one quick blow. It wasn't necessary. The look of the muskrat vanished. In its place was etched a contorted mask of horror. The man's mouth was begging as he slid away, down Mark's body and . . . into the jaws and claws of the reincarnated beast that had already begun shredding his legs and buttocks, tearing away Holt's crotch even as he fell.

With the extra weight gone, Mark was certain he could climb aboard the Huey, at least throw a leg over the skid so PJ could fly away to a safer spot.

But he couldn't catch the skid with his leg.

His shoulders screamed in pain.

He looked up, begging PJ to fly away.

The .38 vibrated into view, sliding out of the cabin. It would hit him in the face when it fell.

He was slipping.

He tried to duck the pistol. It hit his lip. He grabbed for it but missed and lost his grip. He went down, falling ten feet onto his back. He was stunned, breathless from the fall. He was on the ground.

He and the beast saw each other at once.

It lurched away from the corpse that was already unrecognizable as a man. It fell and scrabbled along in the dirt. Mark struggled to his feet. If he could find the legs to run, maybe the thing would die before it could catch him.

But he stumbled because his groin ached and would not allow the legs to work properly. Lying on his belly, he knew he was gone. He screamed his good-byes to PJ, who he knew would never hear.

He spun and saw the beast rising for another charge. The pistol lay by his side. One round. That's all he had. He knew. He'd counted this time, by God. For all the good it would do him.

One round that had to go to a vital spot, someplace that the other rounds had not been able to inflict terminal damage.

He looked up and saw the helmet and visor of PJ, the lips forming a scream, forming his name. He wished the visor were up so he could see those green eyes one last time. He waved her away.

She shook her head and started a turn. The maneuver took her to a level spot twenty yards away. She set the Huey down.

Mark looked for the monster.

The beast rose and staggered toward him, all claws and fangs.

Still breathless, he knew he could never cover the twenty measly yards to the Huey—not with the beast midway on his path.

Mark aimed. There came from the beast a triumphant, gurgling roar. His arm fell and he fired between the monster's legs. . . .

8

The silvered aristocrat had had it. He had decided to offer up his resignation. If the Spec-two committee wanted to meddle in this business, they could have the whole bill of fare.

Imagine. Calling him in at this hour to raise hell, to demand a situation briefing. In his own office. He'd been briefing them on the Texas situation day and night for the last seventy-two hours. Nothing was new. He'd have known.

This was it. He was going to quit. Right after he reduced that hulking obesity—or was it obscenity?—to nothing. First he'd fire the man, destroy his career, run him out of D.C. so he couldn't get any job—let alone take over The Corporation. This was time to retire. Even if under a cloud.

He let himself into his office, tugged the heavy door shut and hit the lights.

"What the hell . . . ?"

A pockmarked granite face smirked at him.

"I'm going to have to get that combination changed first thing. You never know what the hell is going to come crawling in."

"You scum. Who the hell do you think you are? Get out of my chair."

"Whose chair?" The hulk sat erect.

It dawned on the aristocrat all at once. His blood drained to a heavy pool in his stomach.

"I have insurance," he said weakly.

"Doesn't everybody?"

"I'll retire. I'm tired of it all. I want out. You can have the chairmanship."

"I already have it. Don't you see where I'm sitting?"

"Okay. I'm going, bowing out gracefully."

The granite head shook slowly. The dirty complexion darkened.

"I have"—the aristocrat choked on the words—"I have my insurance."

The hulk pushed a file across the massive desktop. "You mean this?"

The aristocrat turned and started punching the combination to his lock.

An angry pop sounded behind him.

The aristocrat's head smashed into the doorjamb, leaving a red splash on the splinters.

Moments later, the hulk stood over the body, watching the dark stain spread out from beneath the jellied skull.

"Fuck it," he growled. "Never liked green carpet anyways."

Mark lay dreaming again.

The beast was attacking for the hundredth time. He shot his last slug into the fuze of the artillery round. What was it, 155 millimeter? Eight-inch? He didn't know. All he knew was that he was grateful he had been lying flat when the explosion erupted from the earth.

Then came the rain of dirt. Hot metal. Gore. Then came sleep.

Then came dream number one hundred one.

But this time it came with a frightful question: *What had happened to the Huey? Where was PJ?* He struggled, trying to drag himself up out of the dream. A pair of hands held him down. He fought. A pair of lips soothed him. And he was awake.

"PJ. Thank God you're all right."

"I thank God for you."

He sat up, feeling dizzy, his right ear still ringing and throbbing.

"Where are we?"

"Marble Falls. Doctor Matt Junker. You gave me his name and said I could trust him. You were right."

"What happened?"

She told him about feeling the explosion as she dismounted the Huey, about seeing nothing for minutes, about finding his body and loading him half-consciously into the cabin, about flying away to a hidden spot along the Colorado River, about dropping him off, about taking off again, about leaving the Huey where it might be found but far enough from him so he would be safe, about taking the research log and making the phone calls according to the instructions inside.

"What about the army?" he asked. He shifted his

body and groaned. "My ear. My head. My cheek. My
. . . groin."

"You're going to recover and make beautiful ba-
bies."

He smiled. "But what about the army?"

"We're retired. Honorable discharges. A little 'dis-
ability' pension offered. Nothing, really. I refused it
—for both of us. I thought you wouldn't want anything to do with them, particularly their thirty pieces
of silver." He nodded and she continued. "We're on
our own without restriction of any kind as long as
our insurance policy doesn't fall into the wrong
hands, as long as the copies of it are safeguarded, as
long as letters don't have to be sent and phone calls
made—though we have been asked not to return to
Killeen or Fort Hood."

"No need to ask," said Mark. "Nothing, but nothing could take me back. I've left my memory deep in
the heart of Texas."

"And your identity."

"Huh?"

"We're new people."

"Oh. How will our friends get in touch? Poole?
Maggie?"

"We'll have to leave them behind. Also the Camaro.
It's been reduced to a pile of blistered, bullet-riddled
junk anyhow."

He smirked. "How much later is it?"

"Two days."

"It's over?"

"It's over."

"We don't have our friends. Our identities. All we
have is—"

"All we have is each other."

"That's enough," he said.

"That's everything," she answered as she came to
him.

In the scrub near Riggs Ford—west of Smith
Mountain and in the valley of the Cowhouse—Dodson's she-wolf dragged her battered body toward the
stream for a drink. Her wounds would heal exter-
nally. But she felt a deep pain inside—almost as if
some kind of angry life were stirring in her uterus.

The end . . .
begins again.